# *Eating Wasps*

**Anita Nair** is the author of several novels, including *The Better Man*, *Mistress*, *Idris: Keeper of the Light* and *Alphabet Soup for Lovers*. She has also authored a crime series featuring Inspector Gowda.

Anita's other books include *Malabar Mind*, a collection of poems; *Goodnight & God Bless*, a collection of essays; and six books for children. She has written two plays and the screenplay for the movie adaptation of her novel *Lessons in Forgetting*, which was part of the Indian Panorama at IFFI 2012 and won the National Film Award in 2013. Her books have been translated into thirty-one languages around the world. She is a High Profile Supporter for the UNHCR and the founder of the creative writing and mentorship programme, Anita's Attic.

## Praise for *Eating Wasps*

'*Eating Wasps* is a beautiful, unsettling read.'

—Twinkle Khanna, Actor and author

'Nair's prose is breathtaking and showcases with great clarity the emotional as well as physical landscapes these women traverse.'

—*Firstpost*

'Nair's grasp of the art of telling stories in parts, a format we are familiar with from her previous books, takes the readers through the lives of her characters without any disconnect. … the women in *Eating Wasps* find themselves battling both internal and external demons in spite of the freedoms available to them.'

—*The Hindu*

'Anita Nair is probably India's most popular and prolific writer. She spins stories with dazzling speed and intensity. *Eating Wasps* is vintage Nair, who excels in writing passionately and sensitively about women.'

—*The Week*

'Nair has perfected the craft of writing her female characters. They come across as next-door characters and look as if they emerged effortlessly from the author's pen, but mind you, these are no stereotypes. … The characters stay with you long after the novel is over and you wonder how life would have shaped up for them if they had chosen different paths.'

—*Financial Express*

'Perhaps a book like this, which gives an unvarnished glimpse into the lives we lead, will force us to listen, to be kinder, and to treat ourselves better. Highly readable and visceral, the novel reminds you that you are not alone, and that your feelings are not invalid.'

—*Scroll.in*

'Set in Kerala, the stories of Nair's heroines span multiple castes, classes and religions as if to underscore the point that women of all hues and from all backgrounds are confronted with problems which are more or less universal.'

—*Outlook India*

'Nair's poetic prose set alongside unvarnished truths of the everyday lives of women makes *Eating Wasps* a satisfying and disturbing read all at once.'

—*Hindustan Times*

'It's a book where the characters could be your girlfriends—you sit down with them after a long day and curl up with their stories of pain and longing. You listen to them and you know: you are not alone.'

—*DNA*

# Anita Nair

# Eating Wasps

cntxt

First published in hardback by Context, an imprint of Westland Publications Private Limited, in 2018

First published in paperback by Context, an imprint of Westland Publications Private Limited, in 2020

Published by Context, an imprint of Westland Books, a division of Nasadiya Technologies Private Limited, in 2023

No. 269/2B, First Floor, 'Irai Arul', Vimalraj Street, Nethaji Nagar, Alapakkam Main Road, Maduravoyal, Chennai 600095



ISBN: 9789357761840

10 9 8 7 6 5 4 3 2

This is a work of fiction. Names, characters, organisations, places, events and incidents are either products of the author's imagination or used fictitiously.



Typeset in Berling LT Std by Jojy Philip, New Delhi
Printed at Nutech Print Services Pvt. Ltd

For Leela Kalyanaraman,

whose courage and spirit I can only marvel at.

'Draw your chair up close to the edge of the precipice and I'll tell you a story –'

Scott Fitzgerald

# PROLOGUE

On the day I killed myself, it was clear and bright. It was a Monday. A working day.

25 October 1965. A day just like every other day, except I was dead and the world ground to an abrupt halt as the news spread.

People everywhere, in homes and alleys, in tea shops and at the railway station, the court and the college hostel, Swami's printing press and the King George market, those who knew me and those who didn't, all looked at each other and then looked away. She is dead, they said. She killed herself. Is that true? There isn't a suicide note. Was it a murder made to look like a suicide?

They tried to explain my death: She had an incurable disease. She was in love with a married man. She was in love with a man who dumped her. She was pregnant. She was depressed. Something humiliating happened at the college which led to this.

The speculation was as dense as the grief.

An ordinary woman had become a legend, a tragic heroine, and it was the nature of my death that had turned me into someone extraordinary in their eyes. I was Kerala's Virginia Woolf. We even had the same bristling, brooding gaze, a well-known artist claimed. Everyone, even those who didn't know me, added to the legend of Sreelakshmi. Except him. Markose didn't mention me, ever.

Instead, he came in the dead of night to the cremation ground.

The dead do not clock time. He came on silent feet and with a ravaged face. He poked through the embers with a twig. Please don't, I wanted to scream. Please don't do what I think you are about to do. My love for you devoured most of me. What's left, let death feast upon.

Markose took away the bone of my index finger from my right hand. He took my soul with him. He wrapped me in a red silk cloth and then, with the desperation and furtive stealth that had characterised our relationship, he placed me against his lips.

He had liked to see me write. He once said that I held the pen like no one else he had seen. 'Do you realise your index finger has no role to play in it?'

It's my guiding finger, I said, smiling and leaning forward. He wrapped his fingers around my index finger like he would never let go.

'The *Weekly* has asked me to write a new novel. What should I write about?'

His embrace tightened. As long as it's about me, I thought it said.

He stroked my index finger with his thumb. I imagined touching his beard and running my fingers through its length, tugging at the knots and untangling them one by one. Who else would I write about? I wanted to ask. All of me is yours.

As it had been when I was alive, Markose kept me out of sight. He placed me in the mustard-yellow velvet pen-case I had gifted him when we last met. He would use the pen every day, he had said. Where the pen once lay, the bone of my guiding finger was given a resting place. I had not just killed myself, I had dug my own grave, I realised, as he embarked on an elaborate subterfuge.

There was a beautiful wooden almirah in his room with two opaque glass panels in the top half and a porcelain knob. He kept his collection of deeds and certificates, files and important papers there. He had the carpenter remove the shelves and fix a wooden pole beneath the line of pigeonholes. He was going to hang his vestments in it, he told his wife. They needed a sacred place of their own.

The carpenter fashioned a false back for the almirah. He did it all the time for important people. They had to be careful with aspects of their life that had to be kept secret. Markose sent the carpenter out on some pretext and took me out of the case one last time. He stroked my remains as he had once stroked me and then put me back in the velvet-lined case. When the carpenter returned, he had the pen-case crucified on the back of the cupboard. The false back was fixed and I was well and truly staked alive. As long as a part of me lay trapped in the physical world, there would be no escape.

The atheist and scientist in me baulked at the thought of an afterlife, but the writer in me wanted to know. Only, there was nothing the writer could do except wait in the forgotten vault.

The years passed. Not once did he take me out of the secret compartment in his almirah, or his heart. Soon, he stopped gazing at the almirah, as he used to each morning when he woke up. In those first few days, he would touch the satiny side of the cupboard as though he were running a finger down my thigh. He would open the doors and press a kiss on the false back, murmuring my name.

His wife didn't like the old-fashioned almirah with its door that stuck, the creaking hinge and air of mustiness. Let's get a steel cupboard, I heard her say. Steel is clean and efficient. Steel is the future.

When the steel cupboard appeared, the almirah was moved downstairs to a room filled with odds and ends, broken chairs and bronze vessels green with verdigris.

Time passed. The almirah was moved to another place, some distance away from his home. I stayed in the pen-case in the secret compartment but I had no way of knowing where I was.

All I did was brood on the last few days I had been alive. Would I have done it differently if I had the chance to relive it?

Love fades. Love does, no matter what we believe.

All that's left are the what-ifs.

Once, I had a name: Sreelakshmi. Once, I was a woman. Once, I was a writer whose stories evoked love as much as disgust, inciting anger as often as they offered solace, a writer whose words sawed their way through the conventional. Once, I had withstood the sting of wasps.

But when I died, I was reduced to a forgotten bone, a ghost of her former self, and I may have stayed thus for the rest of eternity, locked in that pen-case and buried in that secret compartment, but for a child.

# 1

# URVASHI

Even before she opened her eyes, Urvashi felt a curl of trepidation, the sourness of fear at the thought of what awaited her.

She picked up her phone.

*Where are you darling?*

*Baby, miss you…*

*Hey, heyyy, heyyyy*

*Hi, hello, hello, hello*

*What did I do?*

*Why are you doing this to me?*

It had already begun.

There was a time when she would wake up breathless with anticipation: What would the day be like? In that ringlet of space between sleep and wakefulness, everything seemed possible.

But now she stayed in bed, buried under her snowballing thoughts, until the fullness of her bladder nudged her to kick the light quilt off. She would trudge to the bathroom, feeling just as exhausted as she was when she crept into bed the night before.

She turned her face just a little to peer at the man lying beside her. An arm was sprawled over his forehead. Every few seconds, a snore escaped his mouth. Most days, she wanted to straighten the arm and stuff his mouth with a wad of tissues. Most days, she wondered if she could bring up the subject of twin beds or even separate bedrooms. But this morning, she pulled the quilt to his chin and slid out of bed.

Her eyes darted to the clock on the bureau. A quarter past six. She hummed under her breath as she brushed her teeth, then stood under the shower, letting the jets of water tingle every pore of her body, sending little butterfly shivers down her toes. There was a curious stillness beneath all that sensory overload. A mind-numbing stillness that lingered even as she smoothed cream into her skin, her fingers travelling to those otherwise forgotten islands between the toes and the knobbly bits of the elbows, and the back of her knees. When there was no more of her skin to lose herself in, she pulled on a fresh caftan and went downstairs to be the perfect wife.

She switched on the music system in the living room. The speakers hissed. The night before, Mahesh had put on an Edith Piaf CD to go with the wine they were drinking. They had sat in the balcony overlooking the church grounds next door. All their friends envied them the view, as they did this perfect marriage Urvashi and Mahesh seemed to have fashioned over eighteen years.

They had both pretended to listen to the music. It was easier than acknowledging that they had nothing left to say to each other. She had wondered if she should tell him what was going on. But Mahesh had been lost in the myriad joys his mobile phone offered and she hadn't known where to begin. So she had let the moment, and the thought, slide.

She changed the settings to the FM station she liked to listen to in the morning. An effervescent radio jockey who sounded like she had just swallowed orange juice spiked with steroids garbled: Good morning, Bangalore!

Most days, Urvashi imagined taking a cast-iron skillet and smashing it down on the RJ's head. Try saying good morning now! This morning, the false cheeriness merely grated on her nerves. She picked up her phone and checked the app for a cab. It wasn't time to call one yet. But she was reassured by the notion that a cab was just seven minutes away. In a strange way, the recent demonetisation of the rupee had changed her life, made her feel less like a middle-aged nobody. Who would have thought Prime Minister Modi would emerge as a champion of urban women's empowerment?

In the days after the demonetisation was announced and the ATMs stood silent and empty, Mahesh had suggested she use the phone to go cashless. Now it seemed her phone held her life together. E-wallets that allowed her to transact without any cash. Cabs, lunches, drinks at the bar, the kurta she didn't need, the books and geegaws, and none of it on the credit card statement that her husband checked, peering through his glasses at the laptop screen. No questions asked. No prevarications. My money. My life.

The doorbell rang. Urvashi breathed a sigh of relief. The maid was here. Most days, they greeted each other with a grunt and a wrenching of the mouth that was meant to be a smile. But this morning, Lakshmi wore a face washed with curdled milk into which someone had thrown a large mug of cat pee.

Urvashi narrowed her eyes and asked, 'What happened?'

Lakshmi grimaced. 'You wouldn't understand.' She gestured with a sweep of her arm to suggest, you who have everything, what would you know of suffering or the human condition?

Urvashi pretended not to see it. She wasn't going to compete with her maid over whose existence was more fraught. She said carefully, 'Make yourself a cup of tea. You look like you need one.'

Lakshmi snorted and walked into the kitchen.

Mahesh came down the staircase, two steps at a time. He was in his gym clothes, with a towel strung around his neck. The shock of silver-grey hair that marked him with a silver-fox sexiness contrasted with the youthful face – a kindly god's generosity – which he enhanced with the occasional use of coloured lenses. The well-toned body completed the picture that had his female colleagues refer to him as Mahesh Clooney.

Urvashi would watch as the women creamed, panties and soul. A gentle ooze of delicious desire for this man who would drop to the floor and sit cross-legged when the party spilt over the chairs, couches and onto window perches. Nursing a drink. Rationing his smoke. His hazel-coloured lenses twinkling with wry humour. She would watch as a queen might, surveying her subject with a curious concern and little else. Seeing the casual touching of elbows as he talked to a woman. Nothing could be misconstrued. Would you accuse a feather of sexual energy? Tell that to the Marquis de Sade. A feather is a feather till the right one comes along to turn it into a quill, an ear-tickler, a conduit to buried hunger, or a decorative piece stuck in a vase.

She looked at Mahesh, ornamental plume, husband of many years, and smiled.

'What time is your flight?' he asked, filling his gym bottle with water.

'11.10,' she said.

'Shouldn't you be getting ready to leave?' he frowned.

'Yes. In about ten minutes.'

'What about breakfast?' he asked.

'I'll get something at the airport,' she said, knowing what would come next.

'Overpriced, oily rubbish… why don't you take a sandwich instead?' he said. He went to her and stuck his cheek out for her to kiss it. 'You have a good flight and a good retreat. Although why you can't stay home and maintain silence is beyond me.'

Urvashi leaned forward and pressed her lips against his cheek. He smelt like the inside of a thermos flask. Once she had loved this man with a passion that had frightened her. He had been her north and east, south and west.

'Bye, take care,' she said in response.

On her way out, she paid Lakshmi her salary and told her to take the next week off.

'What about Sir?' Lakshmi frowned, not bothering to hide the censure in her eyes: What are you thinking of, going away and leaving Sir on his own? You aren't going home to your parents, or on work, or to visit an ailing relative, or attend a wedding. You are just going away. Who does that? Men, as everyone knows, are helpless creatures who don't know how to serve themselves even when rice and curry are placed before them. They are incapable of washing their underwear or scouring the grease off a pan till it gleams. Ask a man to sharpen a knife, he will. But ask him to dice an onion, he will weep as he chops it into fat clunky slices.

'He is going away too,' Urvashi said, and clicked the door shut behind her.

Later in the day, she would call Mahesh and tell him that Lakshmi wouldn't be coming by for a week. He would move to his sister's till she returned, she knew. Clooney wasn't going to cook, clean and keep house on his own. The thought of the empty house filled her with a sense of relief. There would be no one here if he chose to make a surprise visit.

*Who are you with?*

*Why are you avoiding me?*

*Who are you fucking, you bitch?*

*Tell me*

*Tell me Tell me*

The resort driver was at Arrivals, a wide grin on his face. 'Have you been waiting long?' Urvashi asked, as he moved forward to take her little case from her. She gave it to him without the token protest. The heat and humidity pressed down on her. It was like being smothered by wet blankets on a hot day. All she could think of was getting into the air-conditioned car he would bring to her – sooner, if she let go of the bag.

'Not very long,' Jaimon said as he led her to the pickup point. 'How was your flight?'

'Nice,' Urvashi smiled. Jaimon didn't speak much English. They conversed in a lingo that was made of two parts Malayalam (his), two parts Tamil (hers), and one part English.

'Two minutes,' Jaimon said, heading to the parking lot.

Urvashi put on her sunglasses. She lifted her hair from the nape of her neck and wound it into a knot.

Jaimon pulled up alongside her. She slithered into the car. The air conditioner was on full blast but the car had been baking in the morning sun. 'Two minutes,' Jaimon said, spotting the sweat bead up on her upper lip.

'Has it been raining?' Urvashi asked.

'Every night,' Jaimon said. 'There's even water in the river, I don't know after how many years. If the rain goes on like this, the river will come into the resort.'

Urvashi smiled and retreated into silence.

'Shall I play some music?' Jaimon asked, fiddling with the knobs.

'Yes, but play this. I suppose you have a USB port,' Urvashi said, rummaging in her bag and handing over a pen drive to him.

She saw Jaimon's features still into surprise coupled with annoyance. His passengers either asked him to shut the music off or endured it. They didn't expect him to listen to their playlists.

Urvashi pretended not to see his expression.

But Jaimon seemed to approve of her playlist. 'Can I copy the songs and give it back to you?' he asked when they stopped at the toll gate.

Urvashi smiled. 'Of course.' She closed her eyes and lay back against the seat. She didn't want to talk, just let the music seep into her. The words of the song made her eyes smart. A sense of loss filled her. What or who was she grieving for?

Jaimon sighed. She had been different the last time. Less assertive. More interested. And more inclined to chat. He wondered if he had done something to offend her. This silent treatment was what his mother and sister meted out to him when he irked them. Oh well, he thought, she won't be able to hold the grudge for long, she'll come around eventually. She couldn't know that he met all sorts of people as a cab driver and a morose one wasn't going to throw him.

Urvashi opened her eyes and looked out. From within the air-conditioned car, it truly was God's own country, she thought. The rains had left a patina of green on everything: field and roadside; cement steps and trees.

'Would you like to stop for coffee or tea?' Jaimon asked. A slow drizzle had begun.

Urvashi shrugged. 'Do you want to?'

Jaimon shook his head.

'In which case, let's not. I just want to get to the resort as soon as I can,' Urvashi said. She had asked for a room overlooking the river.

As they turned into the lane leading to the resort, they passed two women huddled under an umbrella. Jaimon stopped alongside. 'Any problem?' he asked in Malayalam.

The younger woman smiled. 'No, everything is fine.'

Jaimon smiled and tilted his head at a slight angle to suggest, in which case...

'My sister's neighbours. They are here to see a doctor at the Ayurveda college and I am letting them stay the night in my room. The other woman is blind. Very sad story!'

Urvashi knew he was waiting for her to ask what their story was. But that was the Urvashi she had left behind on the flight, along with her magazine. This one wasn't remotely interested in anyone else's stories, only the resolution of her own.

She switched on the data on her phone to let Mahesh know she had landed and was on her way to the resort. The messages spewed out with muted vigour:

*Forgive me baby. I didn't mean it*

*Hey, how are you?*

*How is your day?*

*Guess what… I just picked you a little something… you are going to love it*

*Say something*

*Hey*

*Hey*

*Bitch… whore… cunt*

As they turned into the driveway with the golden lions atop the pillars, she felt safe. The driveway was long and on either side was a dense canopy of trees. Alongside were shrubs of hibiscus, pagoda, pinwheel and ixora, interspersed with beds of lilies and canna. As if all that fecundity wasn't enough, there were pots with anthuriums and desert roses. Everything was in full bloom and the central lawn was green and lush. She felt a rush of relief. 'Beautiful! I feel like I've escaped into a secret garden.'

Jaimon smiled. Almost on cue, a peacock strutted across the lawn and the driveway before disappearing into the wooded area beyond. Jaimon slowed down.

'This is new,' Urvashi said.

Jaimon shook his head. 'They come down from the hills. Climate change, you know. Some of the nearby villages beyond Shoranur have had leopards too. And near Palakkad, wild elephants are coming into the town.'

'Where is Padmanabhan?' Urvashi asked, scanning the grounds for the elephant that was usually tethered to the giant teak tree.

Jaimon wondered if he should say that Padmanabhan had gone for his morning walk. But this one wasn't a tourist he could amuse with such nonsense. 'I don't know,' he said. 'Probably taken for a temple festival somewhere.'

'So even elephants have a day job?' She laughed.

Jaimon twirled the end of his moustache and curled it upwards. Heroes in Malayalam cinema seemed to do that routinely before making an important statement. 'In Kerala, if you don't work, you don't eat. That's our…' he groped for a phrase to explain, '… rule.'

The doorman, tall and impressive, with a handlebar moustache, rushed to open the door. His name was Sebastian, Urvashi remembered. She smiled at him. It felt as if she was learning to smile again. And having learnt how to, she couldn't stop.

Unni was supposed to have been waiting for her at the front office. That was what Radha had said when they spoke last night. 'Just get here and Unni will take care of you.'

'Won't you be there?' she had asked.

'Both Shyam and I have to go to Chennai on some urgent work. We'll be back in two days.'

Urvashi had hoped to spend time with Radha. But again, it was probably for the best, she thought.

The reception area was empty and silent except for the whirring of four fans. Then she heard loud voices from the verandah on the right.

'Are you sure you checked everywhere?' The man's voice sounded strained. 'What about the cottage with the parrot?'

'She went there yesterday evening. She was fascinated by the parrot. There is a man there. An autistic man. What if he…' The woman's voice broke.

'Madam, please… Naveen is a gentle soul. And he is our owner's relative,' a subdued voice tried to placate the couple.

'Mr Unni, that doesn't mean he can't be dangerous,' the man shouted.

Urvashi heard Unni exhale. 'Shall we go there and look for ourselves?'

Radha had told her that Unni, the resort manager, was a prince minus a kingdom, a privy purse, or even a job. Shyam had rescued him from penury and given him Near the Nila to rule. The resort's main building and its grounds had once been the summer palace of the royal family. Shyam bought the palace and the prince, Radha had said with a sarcastic laugh some fifteen years ago, when Urvashi and she met at a college reunion.

Urvashi wondered, yet again, what had happened to change Radha. It wasn't just about mellowing with middle age. The old anger and brittleness were gone, replaced by the calm maturity of someone back home from the wars. Suddenly, Urvashi knew that if she survived the present, she too would never be the same again.

She sank into one of the chairs in the reception area. The room had a high-vaulted ceiling and wooden fans with five leaves moved the air, keeping it cool. On a wall painted mustard-yellow was a cluster of black-and-white photographs. Against the walls were potted palms in brass containers. Water lilies floated in a huge verdigris-muted bronze uruli. A Lakshmi lamp hung in a corner, with flowers instead of wicks. In the evening, they would be replaced with wicks in oil and lit to cast a warm glow in the dingy corner. Near it was a planter's chair with foldable leg rests.

A good-looking couple walked into the reception area. The woman dropped into a chair while the man stood at the counter, tapping his fingers on the wooden top impatiently. The woman looked at her and smiled. Urvashi smiled back, taking in the perfect hair, the manicured nails, the fine linen clothes, the Rolex watch, the diamonds in the ears and the Louis Vuitton bag. A Twitter troll would term her one of the Page Three lot, she thought wrily.

'Rupa, why don't you go back to the cottage?' the man asked, walking towards them. 'I'll instruct the manager about the car before I leave.'

'Are you leaving already, Keshav?' the woman asked, unable to keep the petulance out of her voice.

'Well, I did tell Mini I would be home by four. A few of our relatives are coming by…' The words trailed away. The man ran his fingers through his hair. 'I told you they were coming, didn't I?'

Urvashi saw the woman's mouth tighten into a line of

displeasure. If there were going to be words between them, she didn't want to hear it. She stood up and went to look at the photographs on the walls. There were men in turbans and women with stone-studded brooches on their saris. In the centre was a largish photograph of an imperious looking man seated on a straight-backed chair with a dog sitting on the floor beside him. Shyam had picked these up from an old photo studio in Bombay, she knew.

Beyond was an arched doorway into which a glass door was fitted. Urvashi stepped into it and saw that it led into a long, dark corridor that seemed to end in an open verandah overlooking the river.

She walked along the corridor calling out, 'Hello, hello, anyone here?'

# Sreelakshmi

The little girl had come seeking a hiding place a little after daybreak. She flung open the door and jumped inside, her body thudding against the false back. The wood of the secret compartment in the almirah gave and fell apart in splinters and wood dust. The pen-case slipped out and popped open. I fell out. The child took me in her hands and held me as if she were clinging to a straw while the river currents sucked her in.

I clung to her as she did to me. I had known nothing but tulip-shaped shadows and reined-in breath but now, with one heave and a push, I was born again.

A memory separated itself from another lifetime.

I was four years old. In my mother's tharavad at Karakkad, there was a glass jar in a cupboard in the vadakeara. The storeroom was filled with mud pots of sun-dried tamarind. From the ceiling hung ripening bananas and giant cucumbers and yams. The cupboard held dried ginger and pepper and each time it was opened, a rush of spicy sweetness would run up my nostrils. But it was the glass bottle my eyes fixed on. It was always three-quarters full of honey.

My grandmother used honey as a salve for burns and as a sweetener for the various foul-smelling medicines she seemed to take several times a day. She mixed honey with warm water for us to drink when we had a cough and it was also added to bananas and beaten rice to make prasadam. She never let us have honey as honey.

I would trail her each time she went to the storeroom to fill a small bowl with honey for her daily dose of medication. When she had finished spooning it in, she would let me lick the spoon. I hoped one day she would offer me the bowl of honey and tell me: It's all yours.

'Where does honey come from?' I asked her.

'The hive,' she said, pushing the glass lid back firmly in place.

'Who makes the honey?' I asked, wondering if it was stirred in a pot.

'Countless honey bees sit in there making honey.'

'Do honey bees eat honey?'

'I suppose,' she said, filling a vessel with handfuls of sun-dried tamarind.

'So honey bees are full of honey?' I asked.

'You could say that,' she laughed.

Later that day, as I wandered in the garden, I saw a hive. This then was the source of my grandmother's bottle of honey. I thought again of how sometimes the spoon yielded no more than a lick-worth of honey, a drop that was sweeter than sweetness itself. My grandmother had a whole hive filling her bottle, but she wouldn't give me more than a leftover drop. And I was too proud to ask her, even though I saw that she offered it to my sisters and cousins if they asked for it.

One of the first things you learn as a child in a joint family is to cry loudly while holding your breath till you go blue in the face. That is guaranteed to get you attention and whatever you yearn for. I was a strange child, everyone said. I wouldn't ask. I wouldn't demand. Instead, I waited for whatever I wanted to come to me. Or I found a way to fulfil my desires on my own. So it was with the honey.

I watched the hive. I observed that the bees in it were much bigger than any I had seen before. I wasn't surprised. My grandmother was as imposing as an elephant; she had two jackfruits growing on her chest and her middle was as fleshy and soft as the mattress we rolled up every morning. Her bees would be like her, I thought.

The plump bees worked tirelessly for my grandmother, making honey just as Nayadi and Janu, Karuppan and Cheeru worked in the fields to make the paddy that filled the granary. Only, the rice bees were like stick insects and didn't hum. Mostly they looked like they had never had a day's rest. My grandmother must like her honey bees better, I decided. Just as she liked my elder sisters better than she liked me.

'Don't go near the hive,' my mother said one day.

I pretended not to hear her. All she talked to me about was what I couldn't do. She told me not to go near the bathing pond or the river, near the mango tree or the snake shrine. The bathing pond held a crocodile, the river had a whirlpool and an octopus, the mango tree was home to red ants and a ghoul and the shrine – she called it pambum kavu – was where snakes lived. Apart from the red ants, I was yet to meet any of the others.

One morning, as I stood near the hive, one of the bees came straight at me with a loud angry sound. As it came closer, I opened my mouth. The bee flew straight in and I bit down on it, my entire being in readiness to receive the honey I knew it was filled with.

I had never tasted anything so foul and acrid. Some of it went down my throat, but most of it I spat out. My oldest sister, standing some distance away, had watched me astounded. She rushed screaming to summon my mother. 'Amma, hurry, Sreelakshmi ate an insect…'

My mother and two elder sisters stood around the spat-out remnants of the bee. 'Are you mad, child?' Amma asked. 'Why were you trying to eat a wasp?'

'I thought it was a honey bee,' I said, between sips of water as she made me rinse my mouth out again and again.

'No, that isn't a honey bee. It's a wasp with a sting that is very painful,' my eldest sister snorted.

'Weren't you scared?' my second sister asked, looking at me as if I had sprouted two horns and a tail.

'No,' I said. 'I thought it would taste of honey.'

My grandmother took me away then, to give me a purge and make me vomit whatever had gone in.

Only my father, who was home that day, laughed aloud. 'Kadugu-mani has imagination and a lot of spirit,' he announced, guffawing again. He called me his Kadugu-mani; I was small and spluttery like a mustard seed, he said. I didn't know what imagination or spirit was, but I presumed they were desirable because he pulled my cheeks and laughed again.

My grandmother, who was preparing betel leaves for herself, looked at him. 'Who would think of eating a wasp?'

My father frowned. 'I think the Chinese do. They say a deep-fried wasp is crunchy and nice.'

My mother snorted. 'Anything deep-fried tastes decent enough.'

'That is true,' my father said. 'How else can anyone eat your payar kondatam?'

Both my father and I hated the string beans that were a staple in our home. When the harvest was particularly bountiful, my mother chopped the beans into two-inch pieces and sun-dried them with salt. When deep-fried, they turned into little brown sticks with a salty crunch that everyone but my father and I relished. I preferred to stick one in the corner of my mouth and strut around saying, 'Look. I am smoking a beedi.'

The next day, my grandmother took me into the storeroom and brought down the glass jar of honey. 'Here, have a teaspoonful. Actually, have as much as you want. And the next time, just ask me. Don't go eating a wasp,' she said, trying not to laugh.

I dipped the spoon into the honey jar and took out a brimming spoonful. I brought it to my mouth, glistening and viscous, and sucked the honey off in one greedy move. It was sweet and heavy, and coated my tongue with the taste of the wasp. I thought I would gag and throw up, but I forced myself to swallow it.

I never ate honey again.

The story of my eating the wasp became both family joke and legend. If I did something silly, they laughed, 'What can you expect from the girl who ate a wasp?'

The wasp held me in good stead when I opted for science, specifically zoology. 'Why not study Malayalam? Or history? Or mathematics?' my brothers-in-law asked.

One of them worked in the railways, as my father had. The other was a man of means. None of us knew what he did but his family had enough money, a few buses that plied certain lucrative routes, vast tracts of paddy fields and an Upper Primary school. He was the one who added, 'We can always take you on at the school once you finish your graduation.'

But my father drawled from his armchair, 'She knows what she is doing.'

He had been an absentee father, entirely absorbed in his work at the railways, first for the British and later for the Indian government. 'I am a railway man' is how he began most conversations. almost as if he were sentenced for life to be one. He travelled across India and referred to distant places with an easy familiarity. If it wasn't for him, I would have been married off at sixteen like my sisters and girl cousins. But he recognised my hunger for learning and wanted me to study in a good institution that would shape my mind in readiness for the new India, he said. So he managed to get me admitted to Madras University for my graduation and if I topped the class, he promised, I could go on to Banaras Hindu University for a postgraduate degree.

The man of means wasn't going to give up so easily. 'Zoology isn't an easy subject. It involves getting your hands messy. Dissection too.'

My father glared at him. 'She is perfectly suited for zoology. Don't question her ability to do it. Remember she ate a wasp. That requires some courage!'

Where did my courage disappear afterwards?

Only those who have been truly afraid can understand the crippling hold it can have on you. In the days before I killed myself, I walked a desolate land, barren and brown. I inhaled fear; it crawled on my skin with spider legs. It darted like black floaters in the periphery of my vision. Even the water I drank tasted of fear.

Which is why I knew immediately that this wasn't a mere game of hide-and-seek. The child's heartbeat was loud and frantic, as if she had escaped a demon with a blood-red tongue and glistening yellow fangs. This child shouldn't have been here. Someone should have been holding her, comforting her, making her feel that her world could be right again.

I was startled by a whimper. A tiny exhalation of anguish that was stifled even as it emerged. The child's face crumpled and tears gushed down her cheeks. Her body heaved but she wept without making a sound, rubbing her eyes with her fists. In that dark confined space, the child and I sat. I felt the warmth of her fingers, the fear and quiet desperation oozing from every pore.

Ghosts and writers are more alike than you think. We can be what you want us to be. We can hear your thoughts even if you don't tell us. We can read the silences and shape your stories as if they happened to us. And I was both: a ghost and a writer.

# Age of Fear

All through the summer vacation, her mother's reproach dogged her every step. A constant shadow that grew long and short, darted to the front, hovered at the back. It seemed to Megha that she could do nothing right. Life was a series of mistakes; something always occurred between what she had set out to do and what she eventually did. She broke an expensive glass dish; she brought a stray kitten home; she ate too many green mangoes; she climbed a tree… Her mother's censorious gaze shifted focus only when her brother Suraj appeared.

Then the sun shone and her mother was so filled with love for her firstborn that she rinsed the reproof from her mouth and her lips shaped themselves around words of praise, cooing sounds of endearment as she caressed his arm, pulled at his cheek or patted his hair down. Her little boy scout. He knew how to make knots and smash a cockroach to bits. He did a good deed every day and smiled his radiance at the world. Not Megha, who chewed her nails and whose brooding sullenness seldom expanded into a smile.

The moment the spotlight shifted from her to Suraj, Megha, all of six years, lit up from deep inside. The silence, the absence of scrutiny, the withdrawal of attention, all of it brought a skip to her step. Megha was free. Megha wasn't afraid. Megha was Megha. And soon school would begin and Megha would have little to fear.

On the first day of school, she woke up as soon as her mother called her name softly. All morning, she was the perfect girl her mother expected her to be. But breakfast defeated her. It was the same every day. Usually she had the time to camouflage her fear. But that morning, with everyone's eyes on her, she saw the food come alive, each item on the plate lurking, threatening to undo her perfect beginning as a Class 1 student.

The fried egg stared at her with its yellow globular eye, daring her to poke it and make it weep; the toast, brittle brown at the edges, lay waiting to be crunched up like bones in her mouth; the plantain was asleep in its green skin, a baby in its cradle. Only the milk in its tall glass stayed resolutely fluid. Megha took a tentative sip.

'Mummy, Megha isn't eating,' Suraj mumbled through a mouthful of bread and eggs, crumbs spraying onto his plate.

'Why aren't you eating?' Mummy frowned.

'What if the egg cries in pain?' Megha asked.

Suraj thrust his fork into the yellow orb of her fried egg, screeching, 'Eeeeee... Is that how your egg cries?'

As the runny yolk spread across the plate, Megha felt vomit rush up her throat. She retched as she fled to the bathroom. For once, Mummy was livid with Suraj. Papa glared at him. When Megha came back to the table, she heard Papa say in a voice that made her insides curl, 'Don't push me, Suraj. I will not tolerate bullies.'

Mummy and Papa had wanted to go with her to the truck stop. But she had insisted that she would go alone. It was just down the road. She set forth with her new school bag, her stomach churning in that place just below her belly button.

The green army truck waited near the jamun tree. A little metal ladder was attached to the rear and a man stood by the ladder, assisting the children. Megha's heart beat faster as the line went up the steps.

As her place in the line drew closer to the cunning little ladder that would take her into the army truck with its olive-green metal sides and hard top, Megha closed her eyes and thought of the picture of the covered wagon in her favourite storybook. Her cousin Nisha had brought it with her when she came visiting from Am-er-ica.

The story was about a family travelling through the Wild West in America, Nisha had explained. Megha had looked at the ballooning sides of the wagon and thought of the army truck she would be taking to school once the holidays came to an end. When Nisha wasn't looking, she tore the picture out and stuffed it in the front of her dress.

She had thought hard about what to do with the torn page. Leaving it beneath her pillow or tucked into her drawer of vests and panties would incur Mummy's wrath if she found it. Mummy would know she had torn it from Nisha's book.

Her aunt Priya, Nisha's mother, complained about the maid's son, who had ruined her daughter's storybook. 'The one we brought from the States!' she sniffed.

Mummy tried to mollify her. 'I have told Kamala that her son will have to stay in the servant's quarters and not wander through the house any more. We have too many precious things lying around to take a chance. Especially with servants.'

At first Priya Aunty had wanted Krishna to be part of the games Nisha and she played. Mummy hadn't approved but she had agreed.

Mummy often said that Priya was full of egalite nonsense from her years in JNU. Megha had wondered what this place JNU was, and about this thing called egalite. Did you eat it or drink it? Or was it something you drew up your nostrils, like steam?

America had strengthened Priya's silliness. She gave her maid and driver the run of her house as though they were guests and not servants, Megha heard Mummy tell Papa. And then Mummy mimicked Priya Aunty and said, 'Not servants, Akka, we call them staff!' Mummy laughed, saying she thought that phase too was now over.

Megha felt her throat dry up when she heard little Krishna had been banished. She liked playing with him. He didn't mind her dressing him up or painting his face. Mummy had given her a make-up box of her own. It consisted of discarded lipsticks, a stub of eyeliner and a blush with a large hole so the metallic bottom of the box was visible. Krishna and she often made strings of rustly cellophane sweet-wrappers which she wound around his wrists and the crown of his head.

But Megha didn't dare confess that she had been the one to tear the page out. Mummy would be angry. Papa would be disappointed. That was his favourite phrase. 'I am disappointed in you,' he would say, shaking his head while his blazing eyes drilled a hole through her flesh. Mostly, the disappointment ended in a spanking. Mostly, it was Suraj who disappointed him. Not Megha.

As for Suraj, there was no knowing how he would react. He might tease her or pinch her. Or just ignore her. Sometimes, when Mummy was hard on her, Suraj would offer her a blue kingfisher feather or a round white pebble to cheer her up. Or he would play big brother and repeat everything Mummy had said, prefacing it with the words, 'I am disappointed in you.'

So Megha had stuffed the torn picture into the front of her uniform shirt that morning. The waistband of the blue skirt would keep it safe.

'Who is this?' the man by the ladder said as she drew closer to it.

'Megha Naidu,' she said above the loud hammering of her heart. He looked just like the man who stood by the covered wagon in the picture. He had the same round face with a button nose and a wide smile. His belly stuck out like a little pot and his head was like a snooker ball. Bald and shiny.

'Lieutenant Colonel Naidu's daughter,' the driver said. 'She's the last one. The rest will have to wait till we return.'

Prem Uncle. That's what you can call me, the man said as he slammed the little metal gate after him. The benches were packed and a few older children stood clinging to the metal barricade. Like monkeys in a cage, Suraj said with utter disdain, now that he cycled to school.

'Here, sit by my side,' Prem Uncle said, clearing a place for her on the edge of the bench he stood by. Megha felt a spurt of happiness as she sat down. The surface was hard and the truck smelt not altogether pleasant. Talcum powder and hair oil, soap and shoe polish, heated metal and the reek of old tarpaulin. But Megha was too excited to care.

When the last bell rang through the school, Megha rushed to the pickup point at the school gate. In her bag was the new school diary. Every day her teacher would make a note of the homework and she would show it to Mummy. She would never make mistakes again; she would never forget what she was meant to do. Megha skipped as she walked. And there it was, the green army truck and its keeper, Prem Uncle.

'Look who is here!' he said, smiling down at her. 'What were you doing? Waiting by the door?' He tugged the flesh of her cheeks. 'Chubby chubby cheeks, curly curly hair… such a pretty girl!' Megha grinned at him. She felt the corners of her grin loop over her ears like the tapes of false beard Suraj had worn for a fancy-dress competition. No one had called her pretty until now.

'Wait by my side,' he said as the rest of the children fell into line. Megha stood beside him, wearing the aura of the chosen one. That self-righteous smug expression she saw habitually on Suraj's face when Daddy gave him a spanner to hold while he tinkered with his bike engine. Or Mummy let him make tea for everyone on a Sunday afternoon. Only now, it was her turn finally. Just then, she saw Suraj cycle past. He braked to a halt. 'Has my sister been naughty, Uncle?' he called out, frowning.

'Naughty? No, she is such a bommakutty!' Prem Uncle called back. 'I don't want her getting crushed in the hustle and bustle. I don't want your father getting upset that his princess wasn't looked after. That's all!'

Suraj nodded and cycled away. And Megha slipped her hand into Prem Uncle's palm. No one had called her a doll, ever. I am a bommakutty, she sang under her breath. Megha is a bommakutty, la lala…

This time Prem Uncle seated her on his lap and as the wind blew tendrils of hair into her face, he tucked them behind her ears with a careful attentiveness.

When they reached the jamun tree, he reached out and plucked a handful of plump jamuns. She saw the other children dart her envious looks as she popped one into her mouth. The sweet, acrid flesh coated her tongue with the taste of ashes and stained her mouth purple. 'Look Prem Uncle, I am a monster,' she said, sticking her tongue out at him, crossing her eyes and growling. He pretended to be afraid. Megha giggled.

Prem Uncle pinched her cheeks again. 'You cannot be a monster. You are a princess. Princess Megha.'

That evening, Megha asked Mummy to show her how the word princess was written. Then, on the first page of her diary, she carefully copied out her name: Princess Megha.

Megha's reign as princess of the green army truck lasted a whole week. The fall from grace occurred the day her mother came to school. Megha's class teacher handed over her textbooks and notebooks. 'I hope Megha is no trouble,' Chaya said.

'She is a sweet child. No trouble at all. If we can work on curbing her imagination, she would be top of my class.'

Chaya sighed when Mrs George showed her the first page of the diary.

'What's with this princess nonsense?' Mummy asked as they drove back home.

'You should see her. She sits on the truck orderly's lap and bosses over everyone as if she's a princess,' Suraj said, turning to look at Megha as she sat sullenly on the back seat. She hadn't wanted to come home in the car.

Mummy frowned. That evening, Megha saw Mummy and Papa huddled in a conversation of whispers and crinkled foreheads. 'It's too far for her to walk on her own and she's too young to cycle,' Mummy said. 'I guess I'll have to drive her to and fro every day.'

Megha's heart sank. Why couldn't she go in the green army truck?

Papa shook his head. 'No need. I said I'll sort it out.' He picked up the TV remote and switched channels. End of discussion.

Megha prayed fervently that night. Surely God would make sure that she went only by the truck every day? But which one of the gods in the puja cupboard should she pray to? Venkatachalapathi, with his black face and torso smothered in gold; Shiva, who stood with the moon in his hair and a snake around his neck; the tubby elephant-faced Ganesha; or the smiling Lakshmi on a lotus? In the end, she decided to pray to all of them and hoped one of them would explain to Papa why it was best for her to go to school in the truck.

Next morning, Papa walked with her to the pickup point.

Bharat Naidu had dwelt on it late into the night. Chaya was overreacting, he thought. She hadn't been happy about Megha taking the truck to school. 'Sometime in her life she has to learn that there is a world outside the pretty environment you have created for her. She has to know and learn how to deal with people who are not as privileged as she is. Let her travel by the truck, fight for her space, be jostled around a bit. It will build her character,' he had told her.

He didn't want his daughter growing up afraid. He didn't want to taint her mind with suspicion about people or their intentions. Besides, he couldn't go around accusing a man just like that. Especially in these sensitive times. One didn't have to be afraid but one certainly had to be careful.

'Good morning, Saabji.' Prem Uncle sprang to attention when they walked into the periphery of his vision. 'Good morning, beta,' he added, smiling at Megha. Her heart turned a somersault. No one smiled at her like Prem Uncle did.

Then she heard Papa say, quite needlessly, 'Good morning. This is my daughter.'

'I know, Saabji,' Prem Uncle said.

'Good. You will take good care of her,' Papa began. Then, in a tone that she couldn't decipher, he said, 'I don't want her sitting at the edge. Make sure she sits on one of the benches well inside the truck. She's asthmatic... allergic to dust.'

There, that was sorted out. Chaya's fears dealt with, and no risk of offending the man. Like Brigadier Menon said, 'If one knows how to, you can separate the leaf from the thorn without inflicting injury on either party. That's the hallmark of a good strategic thinker.'

'Up you go,' Prem Uncle said to Megha, gesturing to the metal ladder.

Megha climbed the rungs and went to sit on one of the benches. Mummy had said that was where she was to sit. Not on the bench by the edge and certainly not on Prem Uncle's lap. 'You don't sit on strangers' laps. You don't take sweets or gifts from people you don't know. Do you hear me?' Mummy had said sternly as she brushed Megha's hair.

'Why?' Megha asked mutinously.

Mummy paused. She looked at the brush meaningfully. Don't push me girl, or I'll spank you, she seemed to say with that look. Then she said, 'Because I am your mother and I say so.'

Megha felt as though everyone was staring at her, snickering at her plight. If only Prem Uncle would smile at her. Instead, he avoided her gaze and when she tried to catch his eye, he looked through her. Megha wanted to bury her head in her lap and bawl. What did I do? What did I do wrong, Prem Uncle?

The day passed in a haze. In the English class, when they played her favourite word-building game, Megha stood with her mouth open like a goldfish, unable to make a sound or form a word or pitch in eagerly, as she usually did, to get it right before anyone else did. She got all her sums wrong and the flower she drew looked like a turd. 'Scooby doo Doggy do,' Benjamin laughed. He sat next to her in class. With a great show of sympathy, he added that he would show her his bum if she showed him hers.

'What's wrong?' Mrs George asked, seeing Megha sitting on her own instead of joining the class in a game of hide-and-seek.

'It hurts. Here,' Megha said, pointing to her chest and then to her belly. It hurt inside her head too. Mrs George frowned. Colic, she thought. 'Would you like to go home?'

'No, no.' Megha's voice emerged in a mewl. Mrs George smiled. Strange little girl, she thought. Usually they were happy to go home in the middle of a school day. Children loved the drama of it – a parent or a sibling coming in, the halting of a class as the child packed her books, lunch box and water bottle into her bag, the envious glances of the other children. But Megha seemed to want none of it.

Megha looked at Prem Uncle's face from her place in the line. But he seemed to not see her, though he had a joke, a comment or a laugh for everyone else. She bit her lip, willing the tears to not appear.

The next day and the next, Megha grew more and more miserable. She had never known such grief. 'What's wrong?' Mummy asked, feeling her forehead on the third morning.

'Nothing,' Megha said.

'She's looking pale,' Papa frowned.

'She hardly eats. Look at her plate,' Mummy said. Everyone stared at the almost untouched breakfast on her plate.

'You have to eat, baby girl,' Papa said gently.

Megha shook her head. 'I'm not hungry.'

When Megha reached the pickup point, only a few children were waiting. A bug was making the rounds, Mummy had said. For a moment, Megha wished the flu bug had bitten her too. What did it look like? The lady bug was red with black spots. The flu bug would be the colour of snot with green dots perhaps. That way, she wouldn't have to see Prem Uncle and feel the bite of his indifference.

When the truck started, she crept towards him. 'Go sit on your bench,' he said, frowning at her.

Megha crept back, but in the evening, as the truck reached the drop-off point, she sat resolutely on her bench. The truck stopped and the driver stepped out. 'Prem, I've taken permission to leave early. Aziz will be here in fifteen minutes for the next pick up,' he said.

The children trickled out one by one. The truck was empty now. A dense silence hung in the air. Megha continued to sit on the bench, digging her heels into the metal floor of the truck, her eyes glued to Prem Uncle's face. 'Don't you want to go home?' Prem Uncle asked finally.

'Sorry, Uncle,' she said in a small voice.

She saw his eyes search her face. She saw him purse his lips. Then he came up the ladder and sat on the bench at her side.

'Really?' he asked.

She nodded. 'Really. God promise.' Megha didn't know what she was sorry for. She didn't know what her crime was, or what had made Prem Uncle cast her aside. But she knew sorry almost always worked. She said it again. 'Sorry!' She placed her hand on his arm, imploring him to take her back into the circle of light he had drawn around her.

'Give me a kiss then,' he said quietly.

She leaned forward to peck his cheek.

'No, no,' he whispered. 'Here.' He pointed to his lips.

She leaned forward and pressed her lips fleetingly against his. They felt dry and papery. Coarse, like a dog's dry nose when it was ill. She had noticed that when Mac, their neighbour's dog, developed a stomach infection a few days ago.

'Hmm… that doesn't feel like you really mean you're sorry,' Prem Uncle said, pulling her roughly into his lap. 'Open your mouth,' he growled.

She opened her mouth obediently. His tongue felt like a snake. A fat, wet snake that probed her mouth and arced around her tongue. Megha closed her eyes. She didn't know what she felt. His mouth smelt of cigarettes and stale food. His saliva was like globs of snot. A sense of shame climbed from the pit of her stomach into her mouth. Just when she thought she was going to retch, he pulled away.

'Open your eyes, Princess,' he said, lifting her off his lap.

He smiled at her. It was the sunshine smile she had yearned for. Only now, something about the radiance seemed to have shirred at its edges.

'You understand, this is our secret,' he said, leading her carefully towards the ladder. 'No one must know. Just you and I. Promise?'

She looked at him helplessly.

'What?' he demanded.

'Yes, Uncle,' she said quietly. It felt as though she had been pushed off a high swing on its way down.

'Tomorrow, my princess, Uncle will show you a few other ways in which you can make him happy.'

Megha said nothing. As she clambered down the ladder, the corrosive taste of iron filled her mouth. A dirty taste. She would rinse her mouth out with Listerine. Daddy had a giant bottle in their bathroom so he could rinse away the smell of cigarettes.

'See how fresh I smell,' he would say, blowing into Mummy's face if she ever complained of his stale breath.

When Megha woke up, it was with a helpless rage simmering within her. That morning, she stabbed the eye of the egg with a viciousness that made Suraj stare. She crumbled the toast, chopped the banana baby into bits and, on her way to the pickup point, she threw a pebble at Mac, who lay in the garden next door.

Ahead of her was the green army truck and Prem Uncle wearing his brilliant sunshine smile. But all she felt was that same sour-tasting anger she had woken up with. 'You can ride with me in the front of the truck, one of these days.'

'Only me?' she asked. Maybe everything would be all right again. Maybe being a princess wasn't so bad after all.

'Only you, Princess! It's not a place for everyone. But you'll have to give me many many kisses.'

'Oh,' she said, suddenly deflated.

'Don't worry about it now. I'll tell you when the time is right.' He smiled that sunshine smile again.

All day, in school, Megha felt a hollow in the pit of her belly. All day she could think of nothing but his fat tongue in her mouth. It made her heave. When it was time to ride the truck home, she dragged her feet so she would be flanked by the other girls and boys. Perhaps Prem Uncle would fail to spot her if she cowered behind the others. If she could inch past him to one of the benches on the side, she knew she would be able to escape his clutches.

The side-benchers got into the truck first.

An arm snaked out and grabbed her wrist. 'Where are you running off to, Princess?' his voice asked.

She thought of the patch of oil Suraj had pointed out to her on the road a few days ago. A rainbow of colours, but put your foot into it and you could slip and fall, he was explaining as they watched a bike skid. The biker had escaped with a few bruises but Megha remembered the sensation of abject fear as she heard the screech of the bike and watched the biker's helmet fly across the road. She felt it now, that horrific fear and helplessness.

He looked at her face and she knew he knew. 'Why is my princess not meeting my eye?' He smiled his oil-slick rainbow smile.

She tried to slide her wrist out of the fingers which encircled it like a bracelet. But his grip only tightened as he called out to this child and that, the smile never leaving his face.

He propped her on his lap. She wriggled to get off. 'Papa said I mustn't sit by the edge.'

'All right then, we'll sit inside the truck,' he whispered, holding her fast to him.

'Mummy said I mustn't sit on a stranger's lap,' Megha said.

'But I'm hardly a stranger, am I?' He smiled, drawing her closer to him. She wriggled, but the hand around her waist drew her back into his soft fleshy belly.

'Are you a girl or a fish?' he said. He turned to the other children around them and asked, 'What do you think?'

The children tittered. One girl giggled, 'She's a kitten!'

'That's right. Not a fish but a kitten! Meow....' He grinned.

The truck gathered speed.

Megha's chin drooped onto her chest. Something nudged her. She turned around. He caught her gaze but didn't speak. There it was, a fist nudging her bum. But his hands were around the two children sitting on either side. His fingers were playing with the ribbons in the girl's hair. She felt foolish and angry, just like the time when Suraj had walked into the bathroom without knocking and found her sitting on the pot with her pants around her ankles.

When the truck finally stopped, her chest hurt with the effort to not breathe, not move. She had figured that the more she moved, the more the fist nudged her.

He lifted her off his lap and sat her on the bench. 'Stay there,' he said. Like Sunil Uncle next door spoke to Mac. Stay there.

He walked to the front of the truck and opened the metal gate with its attached ladder. 'No pushing, no jumping,' he ordered as the children tumbled out.

Megha stood up. She slid the strap of her bag over her shoulder and marched resolutely to the ladder. When she stepped down, he grabbed her wrist. 'Where are you going, Princess?' he asked with a smile that spliced his face.

Megha sank her teeth into his hand. She bit down as she had seen Mac do. Hanging onto his hand with her teeth. He yelled and tried to pull his hand away from her mouth. There was a moment's horrified silence and then a sudden flurry of sound, as though someone had flung a stone into a tree where crows nested. Raucous cries and flapping wings.

Megha fled. She tasted blood in her mouth but she didn't stop. When she was at the end of the street where they lived, she pulled out her water bottle and rinsed her mouth. Again and again. But the taste of blood, of what she had done, wouldn't go away. She retched. A thin watery fluid filled her mouth. She spat it out. The taste of vomit was better than the taste of blood.

Mummy darted worried looks at her as Megha sat at the dining table toying with her aloo pakoda. 'I thought it was your favourite,' she said in an affronted voice.

Megha hid the pakoda in the front of her dress. Mac would wolf it down. It would make him happy and Mummy would be pleased that she had finished it.

She went next door and offered the pakoda to Mac. 'Sorry, Mac,' she said. 'I am sorry for throwing a stone at you.' She watched Mac eat the pakoda in two swift gulps. Then she went to the room she shared with Suraj and lay on the lower tier of the bunk bed. She pulled a sheet to her chin, turned to the wall and huddled there miserably. What would Mummy and Papa say when they heard? There would be scoldings and punishment.

Perhaps they wouldn't hear about it. Please God, she prayed, make it go away!

Dusk came and the lights were switched on. She heard the TV come on. There were voices in the living room. Mummy, Papa and Suraj. She exhaled. No one had come to complain about her. She continued to lie there, her eyes shut and her thumb stuck firmly in her mouth. Please God, make it go away!

A little later, she heard someone open the door. The footsteps went back. Then came two sets of footsteps. Mummy pulled the sheet away and cried, 'So this is where you are hiding, bad girl!' She sounded relieved for some reason. Suraj stood at her side, grinning down at her.

Megha sat up, her heart thudding.

'Come, eat your dinner,' Mummy said.

Megha looked at the faces around the table. Nobody said anything much at first. Then Mummy said, 'What happened in the truck?'

Papa propped his chin on his palm. 'We heard you got into a fight.'

'And when the man in the truck tried to stop you, you bit him,' Suraj finished triumphantly.

Megha's head drooped. 'I am sorry,' she said. A teardrop fell on her plate.

'Mummy and I have decided that you won't be taking the school truck any more,' Papa said. 'I am disappointed in you.'

Megha felt the crow that had been sitting on her chest rise up and fly away.

'But tomorrow you must take the truck one more time.'

'I don't want to travel by the truck,' Megha said in a small voice. 'Please.'

'No.' Papa's voice was stern. 'Mummy will pick up and drop you, once we are back from our holiday in Kerala. But tomorrow you will travel by the truck. I want you to apologise to the girl you fought with, and to Prem. He needed three stitches, I hear.

When I called him, he was gracious enough to say, "She's a little girl. Don't be hard on her. And tell her that she is still Prem Uncle's bommakutty."'

'Do you know that a human bite is more dangerous than a dog's?' Suraj asked. 'I think I am going to call you Megha-Mac from now on.'

'Suraj,' Papa said, warning him to shut up.

Megha gave her father a watery smile.

In the morning, Suraj went with her as far as the truck. 'Don't bite anyone, Megha-Mac,' he said as he rode away.

Prem Uncle ignored her. And she him. She went to sit on one of the benches at the rear of the truck. Perhaps he would ignore her in the evening too, and then it would be over. But there was the matter of the apology. She would whisper a sorry and flee.

In the evening, Suraj came to the truck, wheeling his bicycle. 'Have you said sorry yet?' he asked. She shook her head.

'Are you scared?' he asked.

She nodded.

'Remember what Papa said. Just look him in the eye and say sorry. How hard is that?' he said. 'Do you want me to stay with you?'

She shook her head. And then she wished she had said yes, as she watched him ride away.

She tried to catch Prem Uncle's eye. But he looked away each time, and pretended not to notice when she went near him. She sat on the bench in the rear of the truck. She would wait till everyone left, say sorry, and run. She would never have to see him again.

The truck ground to a halt. The children tumbled out, even more boisterous than usual; it was the beginning of a long weekend.

Megha crept towards the metal gate. Prem Uncle saw her and jumped back in. 'You are still here,' he said.

'I am sorry, Uncle,' she said.

'What was that?' he asked.

'I am sorry, Uncle,' she said, looking him in the eye.

'You aren't, are you?' he said softly, almost to himself.

She didn't say anything. Most of the children had dispersed. The driver of the truck had shut off the engine. She wondered where he was. She could see the last stragglers leave.

'Are you really sorry?' he asked.

She bit her lip. 'Yes,' she lied.

'Then show me you are sorry,' he said, pulling her to the back of the truck. With his other hand, he pulled down the tarpaulin flap rolled up to the roof of the truck. As it came down with a flat thud, Megha heard the wings of a hundred crows flap around her. Beaks, claws and hungry caws as countless birds descended. She stood still, knowing there was no escape.

# 2

# URVASHI

The corridor was long and narrow, with a low wooden ceiling, and wreathed in shadows. At the farther end was an arched doorway, leading to the river. A curtain of rain fell steadily. Urvashi inched her way through the corridor until a creak startled her. The long moan of a wooden door, stiff with age and disuse, opening. Urvashi felt the hair on her neck prickle. At the end of the corridor was an alcove in which an old almirah was placed. Urvashi felt her heart stop. What was in there? The door creaked as it opened a fraction.

Involuntarily, her hand went to her mouth. She took a deep breath and clenched her fists, as if to steady herself. The door she had shut behind her had caused this one to open. Or perhaps the draught.

She flung open the doors of the cupboard and gasped. Inside sat a little child with eyes that seemed frozen in fright, her thumb in her mouth. Her face was pale and she sat crouched with her knees to her chin. Seeing Urvashi, she shrunk even further. 'No, no… Uncle…' she whimpered.

Urvashi reached out and scooped the child into her arms. 'Oh baby, what happened to you?'

The child clung to her, hiding her face in her shoulder. Something prodded Urvashi's neck. It was a twig of some sort that the child held in her fist. Urvashi eased it from her fingers and thrust it into the pocket of her kurta.

'Sweetie, why are you hiding here?' Urvashi whispered. But the child wouldn't speak.

'Don't be afraid. Everything will be fine,' Urvashi continued to murmur into the child's ears even as her arms tightened around her.

She went back to the reception area where a very worried looking Unni stood talking to a couple. A teenaged boy stood beside them.

The couple rushed to take the child from her, calling out in voices shaking with fear, worry and relief, 'Megha!'

Unni's voice rang out. 'Thank God, madam, you found her. She has been missing since the morning.'

'Baby,' the mother said, taking the child into her arms. The trembling white-faced child hid her face in the curve of her mother's neck.

The father's face was a study in despair and helplessness. He put his arm around his wife and child. The boy, their son, stood unable to comprehend anything except that his sister was frightened.

'Where was she?' Unni asked.

'Where did you find her?' the father said, turning to her. 'We looked everywhere. I even checked the pool floor. We were out of our minds with worry.'

'Inside the cupboard in the corridor,' Urvashi said, looking at the child as she buried herself deeper in her mother's embrace.

'Something has frightened her very badly,' she said softly, stroking the little girl's hair. 'She kept saying, No, no, Uncle. Who is this Uncle?'

The mother's eyes met the father's. Urvashi saw the consternation on their faces. And on the little boy's...

Urvashi leaned back in her chair and sipped the tender coconut water. The family had been effusive in their thanks and Unni had set about making her comfortable, all the while apologising for making her wait.

A young woman dressed in a cream-and-gold Kerala sari checked her in, constantly darting anxious looks at her. Urvashi felt fatigue crowd her like ants on a piece of sugarcane, gnawing at her and draining her of everything sweet and fluid. She wanted to get to her room and lie down.

A big group of Europeans came in, dragging their bags behind them. Sunburnt, voluble, and full of the kind of feverish energy that most foreigners seemed to be infected with on their first day in India. A greed to see all, know all, absorb all.

Unni followed them in, looking anxious but also pleased. He took a key from the young woman at the reception and came towards Urvashi. 'So sorry to have kept you waiting, madam, but we've had a crisis-filled morning. First the child went missing, and now a group of foreigners who were meant to come tomorrow have turned up. There was a mix up of dates.'

'I hope there is no problem with my room,' Urvashi said. Radha had promised her a room, no matter how full up they were.

'Yes, yes, I mean no, no…' Unni said as he brought her the guest registration form. 'Madam, we have given you Radha madam's personal cottage. She wanted you to have it. They were getting it ready, which is why you had to wait.'

He looked at her with a worried expression. 'Any objections, madam?'

Urvashi rose from the cane sofa. 'No, I am honoured, in fact.'

Radha had built the cottage by the river after her uncle died. Koman had been alive when Urvashi visited Near the Nila the first time. She had spent a morning talking to him. She had been intrigued by the Kathakali dancer who had turned his back on the world but not his art. She had interviewed numerous artists before – musicians, painters, dancers, actors, and they seldom deviated from their set piece of platitudes: Art is my god. I am a worshipper at the feet of my deity. Art defines the world, etc. Koman, on the other hand, had told her, 'Art doesn't make anything happen except for the artist. It has no bearing on real life. To most people, it is a filler of time and space, a point of diversion and no more. It is to satiate this need that we artists slave.'

'You are lucky to have him in your life,' she had told Radha over lunch.

Radha nodded. 'I know. He has always been there for me.'

Unni went with Urvashi to the cottage, wheeling her bag. The rain had stopped and a watery sun had emerged, turning the water drops into diamonds.

'Is Najma here?' Urvashi asked.

'She is at the cottage, getting it ready for you. She had to go to the hospital earlier in the day. She had an appointment that couldn't be moved. If she had been here, you wouldn't have had to wait a moment.'

Urvashi remembered that Unni was a great one for chit-chat. 'Najma is so efficient and smart. It is tragic that she was in a fire, or that girl would have a fabulous job somewhere,' he continued.

Najma was waiting in the verandah. She smiled. 'Hello, madam, very good to have you back.'

Urvashi smiled back at her, trying not to flinch.

'How are you, Najma?' She smiled, taking the young woman's hand in hers.

'I am well, madam. Thanks to you.' Najma's eyes met hers. The gratitude in them made Urvashi want to hug her. Instead, she patted Najma's hand and let her show her into the cottage.

'They have made a few changes,' Najma said. She tugged at the blinds to reveal the picture window where there used to be a wall.

Jaimon had been speaking the truth. The monsoon had set in early this year and the river, which had turned into a few puddles over the summer, was now a broad strip of water. A kingfisher rose in the air, a streak of iridescent blue against the gentler blue of the sky. The flash of happiness in the here and now; the absolute freedom from fear. Urvashi touched the back of the wing chair placed near the window, as if to steady herself. Easy girl, easy. She took a deep breath.

'Are you all right, madam?' Najma's voice was gentle.

Urvashi smiled ruefully back at her. 'No, no, don't worry. I am fine!'

'You will let me know if you need anything.' Najma touched her elbow.

'I will, Najma. I am fine. Just a little light-headed with the relief of being here.'

Najma smiled. A plastic stretching of the mouth. 'I know that,' she said.

Their eyes met.

Through the open door of the cottage, the call of a crow pheasant filled the room.

'What are you going to do this evening?' Najma asked as she checked the mini fridge for water and juice.

'Nothing,' Urvashi said, sitting on the chair. She just wanted to curl up and sleep for as long as she could.

'It's already five. Maybe you could go for a swim. The pool has just been done up and looks beautiful,' Najma offered.

'Maybe I will,' Urvashi said.

'Do you have any laundry, madam?' Najma asked.

'Just what I am wearing.'

'Please put it in the hamper. I'll collect it later so it catches today's wash load,' Najma said, preparing to leave.

Urvashi stood looking at the river. Birds flocked near the steps that led into the water. On the bank across, two men were bathing. A perfect day. A perfect view. A perfect room.

?

??

????

*How can you do this to me?*

*I love you… I love you… I love you…*

*I will kill myself… I swear I will*

The beeps echoed through the room the moment she switched the data on. Hastily, she put the phone off.

She still didn't understand just how she had convinced herself that downloading the dating app on her phone was going to liven up her senses.

It had begun on her fifty-first birthday. 'Just who am I, Mahesh?' Urvashi asked as they sat in their balcony for their customary drink and catching-up-on-the-day chat. Mahesh frowned at his wife. 'What a strange question,' he said, sipping his whisky.

'You are you,' he added. 'Who else would you be?'

Urvashi peered into her glass of wine. 'What do you see when you see me?' she asked quietly.

Mahesh touched her shoulder and squeezed it gently. 'Why Urvashi, I see a beautiful woman; my wife and the mother of my children. I see a successful journalist; I see a woman who runs the marathon and can drink a man under the table.'

Urvashi wondered if this was how a person being buried alive felt as clods of earth fell on the coffin lid. Except that she was trapped for life.

'Why? How do you see yourself?' Mahesh asked, trying to read her expression in the light of the street lamp.

Urvashi shook her head. I wish I knew, she thought. I wish I could define who I am. I wish I could say that what I do makes a difference in the world, in some way.

She knew how Mahesh would respond if she told him what she was thinking: Who have you been hanging out with? Those feminist spiritual types?

At least there would be no more of the 'Is it your chums?'

Only a man could have nicknamed menstrual cramps as chums. In the days when she still bought sanitary napkins, she would glare at the pile in the supermarket section and think, with chums like mine, I don't need enemies.

She took a deep draw of her Merlot and chirped with all the honesty of a clockwork cuckoo, 'Oh, Mahesh, I have to tell you what happened this afternoon...'

Thus a moment passed. Or was it buried?

A few weeks later, she had gone for a girl's night out; the kind she usually shied away from. She had drunk more than she should have. A sip in lieu of a syllable. The pub was festooned with shadows.

Urvashi thought of how pubs increasingly made her feel like she had stepped into a children's park. High-pitched laughter, shrieks and loud voices, bonhomie that accompanied the first day of a school vacation. She had felt Surya's eyes on her. She had tried to join the conversation but her friend wasn't fooled. 'You have as much life in you as a torn shoe,' Surya said.

Urvashi had smarted at that. She had glared at Surya; tall, svelte Surya, who looked like she chewed on jasmines and spat out nails. The arch of her neck and the line of her throat, the manicured nails, short hair and piercings. Surya had touched her hand as if to apologise. 'I hate to see what you have become,' she said softly.

'And what is that?' Urvashi muttered, glad that none of the others were listening.

There was a lull in the conversation. The music had quietened and, in the near silence, Surya's words rang out. A spoon on a crystal goblet.

'A fucking pillow,' she said. 'Nothing more than that! Dressed up with brocade and tassels. Do something to liven up, Urvashi.'

'Like what?' Leela asked.

It was Usha who came up with the idea of the dating app. 'Let's make you a fake profile. Let's have some fun.'

'Are you on it?' Urvashi asked, feeling a giggle grow in her.

'What do you think?' Usha raised an eyebrow.

And so she had a profile. She was the sassy older woman. A cougar on the prowl, Leela drawled.

In truth, Urvashi felt more like a cat that had been spayed and declawed and let loose in the alley.

'Would you have an affair?' Urvashi asked as she drove Surya home. It was close to midnight.

'I have relationships,' Surya said. 'Do you think I am celibate?'

She pulled up outside the block of flats on Primrose Road. 'Thanks,' Surya said. She leaned in to kiss her cheek and added, 'You don't need my permission or approval, you know. It's your life, Urvashi.'

Later in bed, Urvashi had opened the dating app and stared at it.

She didn't have a bad marriage. That would be unfair to Mahesh, she told herself. He had always done what a husband was meant to, and he had done it well. The mandatory kiss when he left for work, or if she left earlier. The occasional surprise gifts and the big tickets for birthdays and anniversaries. The holidays once a year to some place in India and once, outside. The usfie of them together on Facebook with his arm around her. Keeping track of her drink at parties. The routine compliment – babe, you look lovely! Doing the dishes and cleaning up after the monthly dinners at home for friends. The Sunday morning breakfasts. The Saturday night lovemaking, the steady strokes as he moved in her after she had first ridden him to her orgasm, the grunt of satisfaction at the post-coital cigarette because somehow, in the movies, it went so well with sweaty bodies and the radiance of a good fuck. Some days, Urvashi thought her life was so perfect, she could scream.

Suddenly she couldn't bear to be in the room. She unpacked her bag in a frenzy.

'Is that all?' Mahesh had asked, seeing the overnighter on the pouffe in their bedroom.

'Yes,' she said.

'For a whole week?' He stared at her.

'Are you really going away? Or checking into a hotel nearby?' he added with a grin, as though joking. But she knew he wasn't.

'I don't need more than this.' She lessened the snap of her words with a smile. She didn't blame him for thinking what he did. It felt strangely liberating to shed, to have so little to deal with.

She changed into a swimsuit. A single piece that revealed her arms and legs. The men would stare. Indian men did, no matter where they were.

In a hotel in Oslo, Mahesh had looked up from his phone and gaped at her when she emerged from the bathroom in a bikini. She had seen his eyes light up and his lips part ever so slightly. 'Whoa!' he said. Urvashi saw that his wife suddenly seemed like another woman to him.

Tummy fat, bat wings and cellulite notwithstanding, she was a goddess. A goddess who, as she stepped into the heated pool on the rooftop, felt the unmistakable singe of a gaze. She had wondered if it was Mahesh sitting on a lounge chair and peering at her over his bifocals.

It had been the pool attendant. She had felt his eyes rake her body as if she were a choice peach beneath a glass lid.

Mahesh had glared at the man till he slunk away, his ghost penis tucked between his legs. 'Bloody Indian!' he mumbled, loud enough to be heard. Urvashi had been grateful for his intervention. But later, in their hotel room, she had accused him of being prejudiced. 'You want to defend that man who was gawking at you?' Mahesh had laughed, a short bark of righteous disbelief.

'How do you know he was Indian?' she insisted.

'Oh well, bloody South Asian then,' he snapped.

Urvashi had wondered at herself. Was she angry or just feeling conflicted? Which woman doesn't want to be a goddess? And which goddess would be happy being a mere woman?

How long ago was that? Urvashi wondered as she tied a sarong around her waist. It was still light, but the sun would soon set and she would swim lazily in the pool till her limbs felt leaden. Till she was too tired to be tangled up by her thoughts.

As she stepped out of the door, she saw Najma talking to one of the housekeeping boys at the cottage. She went back in and collected the laundry bag and gave it to her. 'So I can save you a trip,' she said.

'Enjoy your swim,' Najma said.

It was her weekly day off but Najma had nothing much to do. She carried the bag to the housekeeping room where the clothes were sorted and listed. She took out the kurta and felt something in its pocket. She slid her fingers in and found a long, slender white object that looked like a piece of plastic. She wondered what it was. She slipped it into the pocket of the apron she wore. She would drop it off at the cottage so Urvashi would find it when she got back. Who knew how valuable it was, or what sentimental significance it held?

# Sreelakshmi

From the moment the woman rescued the child from within the almirah, and me with her, I knew something was about to change. Our destinies were meant to collide.

A ghost and a writer – there is little either can do to change things. And I was both. But I had wanted to make it better for Megha.

So, when I heard footsteps, I had exhaled. A ghostly sigh. Easy enough when you are drawing from fifty-two years of pent-up breath and deep regret. The heavy wooden doors of the almirah creaked open, wailing their protest. We held our breath, the child and I. The footsteps stopped outside the almirah. Megha shrank even further. 'No, no… Uncle…' she whimpered.

The woman held me for only a brief moment before she slid me into her pocket, but I was already intrigued. Urvashi. The celestial nymph who had turned men into putty and gods and demons into slobbering idiots. Was this Urvashi anything like her?

In my earlier life, I had never known what it was to dither over a decision or be stuck between two worlds. Each time a maggot-like doubt crept into my mind, I would remember my father saying, 'Don't forget she ate a wasp. She isn't afraid of taking on anything.'

So, when I topped the university and was given a gold medal, I told him I wanted to study further, and in Varanasi, as he had promised me once.

It was late in the evening. My father was sitting in his favourite armchair, staring into the leaves of a mango tree as if it held the secrets of the universe. He leaned back in the chair and said, 'Don't you want to get married?'

'No,' I smiled. 'Marriage can wait.'

He didn't speak for some time. Then he said, 'I will make the necessary arrangements.'

I touched his hand to convey my gratitude. He put his palm over mine. 'I am putting my reputation on the line by sending you away that far. You are nineteen years old already and your sisters were married when they were sixteen. No one is going to approve of this. You know that, don't you? So make me proud of you, Kadugu-mani,' he said. He hadn't used his nickname for me in a long time.

My grandmother wept that I was going to Kashi before she did. In her world, people went to Varanasi to die. My mother and sisters sulked about my father ruining my marriage prospects. My brothers-in-law grumbled that I was getting to be too headstrong and needed reining in. But I went about my preparations without letting any of their remonstrations dent my resolve.

During my years in Varanasi, I had a friend who was studying for a master's in Sanskrit. Narendran was from Thrissur. We may never have become friends otherwise. But as we came from neighbouring towns, we forged a connection. In that alien city, our yearning for the sounds, sights and tastes of home, and our language, drew us together into a complicity of disdain for everyone around us. Eventually it settled into a friendship of sorts.

Narendran was in love with a Bengali girl and neither of them had any hope that their union would be blessed by their families. He came from an ancient line of tantrics and Subhasini's family were progressive Marxists. I was the third in their outings so no eyebrows would be raised.

One Tuesday evening, we had gone to see the aarti on Dashashwamedh Ghat on the Ganga. I had been told it was a spectacular sight and had persuaded Narendran and Subhasini to go with me. Incense and the intensifying chants of devotees filled the air around them. The priests raised many-tiered lamps and as they offered their prayers to the river and sought her blessings, Subhasini said to Narendran, only half in jest, I thought, 'If you abandon me, I'll kill myself and come back as a bhuta to haunt you.'

Narendran crinkled his nose. 'Hush Subhasini, it's twilight. Don't say such things, you'll stir the malevolence of the dead!'

'Do you seriously mean that?' I laughed aloud.

'Of course not.' Narendran laughed and turning to Subhasini, he said, 'Bhuta are multi-coloured dwarfs with the face of a boar or a ram or a buffalo, though in your case you may get the deer face. Since blue is your favourite colour, would you want to be a blue dwarf with a deer face, my love?'

Subhasini giggled and I looked at him, surprised.

Later, when Narendran and I were on our own, I raised the subject again. 'You were not joking. Tell me, do you really believe in ghosts and other such nonsense?'

Narendran looked up from the text he was annotating. 'You know about my family, don't you? We are Namboodiri tantrics and the line goes back several centuries. When I go back home, if I go back, that will be my life too. While I am away, I can shrug it off as my overheated imagination but while I am there, I am forced to accept that there are truths beyond my comprehension. That another world exists, beyond the one we know. It makes no sense but I can't dismiss it. And in all honesty, I am convinced.'

'How can you, Naren?' I laughed. 'We are modern people. We know there is a scientific explanation for every natural phenomenon. How can you believe in rubbish like bhuta, preta, pisacha? That's what our grandmothers told us to keep us from getting into mischief.'

'That may be so, Sree, but don't dismiss the afterlife. There is much that we do not know. And it's best to leave it alone.'

I didn't like the sombre note in his voice. And yet, I couldn't leave the subject alone. 'So is there a distinction between the three, or are they all just synonyms for a ghost?'

Narendran shook his head. 'To you, this is all nonsense, but there is a very definite distinction. Bhuta are the elements around us – prithvi, vayu, apa, akasa and jyoti – though the *Natyashastra* also refers to them as dwarfs of many colours with the faces of animals.'

Narendran paused and took a deep breath. Then as if he were reading out a text to me, he recited, '*Kalatattvakosa*, the Sanskrit thesaurus, also calls bhuta, like all creatures in general, sentient, insentient, divine or malevolent. Preta are the souls of those trapped in the time before funeral rites are performed. They are said to have been corrupt or compulsive, deceitful or jealous or greedy people who, because of their karma, are afflicted with an insatiable hunger for something. This makes them try and prevent humans from fulfilling their desires. The pisacha are flesh-eating demons with bulging veins and red eyes. They feed on human energy and can alter thoughts and behaviour. None of them can be destroyed. They can be driven away or put under a restraining order.'

'You really believe in all this, Narendran?' I asked softly.

'You are a student of science. You believe in what you can prove. I am a student of language. What you probably don't understand is that there is a language in which to speak to the dead as well. It may not follow the cardinal rules of language as you understand it, but it exists, and I have communicated with creatures of the afterlife. How can I disregard what I know?'

'You are mad!' I laughed aloud.

'I must be,' Narendran said quietly. He shut his book, got up, and walked away from me.

If Narendran came my way now, I would tell him, Naren, you were right. There is an afterlife. At least, I do know that I am a ghost. And that ghosts are merely the dead in the wrong place.

But you were also wrong. It is possible to be all three: bhuta, preta and pisacha. Look at me: I am an insentient being. Forever hungry, wafting between the hell of my thoughts and the world I am in. Feeding on the memories of anyone who holds me long enough because it's easier to lose myself in other people's stories than dwell on my own.

So there I was in the staff quarters, on the western side of the resort, in a room inhabited by a young woman. She stood in front of the mirror in a bathroom that was aglow with evening shadows.

Like I had stood on the morning I killed myself. In my room, with its books and papers, a desk, an almirah, and the narrow spinster bed with its lone pillow. Looking into the mirror lit by the radiance of the morning sun. The meagreness of my life, the paucity of possessions, the absolute ordinariness of my existence crawled over my reflection like maggots in a wasp's nest. Forever hungry.

She stuck her hand into the pocket of the apron and took me in her hand. She rolled me around as if I were a round piece of marble. There was nothing fearful or despairing about the touch.

She turned her face to the gloaming light. I flinched. She didn't. How could anyone become indifferent to such horror, when it stared you in the face every day? But she continued to gaze, as if to remind herself that she was more than the image that looked back at her. And she continued to hold me in her hand.

# Najma

For as long as she lived, Najma would never forget that moment when she stepped into the Bangalore East station. One by one, the diamond-shaped facets of everything that went into the invention of a moment locked into place: her measured tread; her hesitant gaze; the fear jostling in her mouth with the taste of bile; a sense of triumph that she had taken that first step. In those uncertain days, when she hovered between sanity and a crippling numbness, she had told herself that if she ever made it back on to a railway platform, she would know what to do with her life.

She took a deep breath of all those familiar scents. The heat of the sun pressing down on metal, the whiff of sweat and urine and the exhalation of relief, the sun-baked baskets and cardboard cartons, the rapidly drying wet cloth draped over flowers and vegetables, and the salt of waiting.

She walked to the water faucet and pressed the nozzle. The tap was dry, as it had been that morning, thirty months and six days ago. She hadn't stepped into the Bangalore East station since that time and it seemed as if nothing had changed.

What had she expected? That it would have turned into the metro station on MG Road with its tiled floors, glistening chrome and art boulevard, and in one fell swoop all her memories of this place would be laid to rest?

She saw a ragpicker with a sack of rubbish. A young woman waited beside a carton tied with rope. An old man dressed in saffron robes and with a long white beard sat on a bench. Two dogs were sleeping with their heads resting on their paws and a group of boys huddled on the bridge that went over the railway line. At this quiet hour, the railway platform was home to lost souls and strays. And she was both.

At three in the afternoon, there were no long-distance trains passing this way and it was too early for the regular commuters. Which was why she had chosen this particular train. The Bangalore–Marikuppam passenger.

She sat on a bench with a polished granite top. This was a new addition to the station. The heat seared her skin through her clothes. It was a comforting heat, for though it was a hot April day, she felt cold and shivery. A lone mynah hopped along the platform. On their own, her fingers crossed to ward off any impending evil. One for sorrow. Two for joy. Three for a girl. Four for a boy. Five for silver… She had forgotten the rest of the childish rhyme.

She uncrossed her fingers. That child was gone. As was the woman in whom the child had lived. When the worst that can happen to anyone has happened to me already, what more sorrows will you cast my way? Najma asked the bird silently. The mynah cocked its head and flew away.

The train was empty when it arrived. She got into the compartment nearest to her and found a window seat. Seven stations, 51.9 km, one hour and five minutes before she reached Tyakal station. Time enough to compose her thoughts and prepare for what she was going to do.

Baiyappanahalli. Krishnarajapuram. Whitefield. Devagonthi. Malur. Byatrayanhalli. As the train stopped and started, she ticked the names off in her head. During that year, when she rode this line six days a week, every morning and evening, she had seldom even glanced outside. Some days she would be lost in her thoughts, happy thoughts. She was twenty-four and all of life was waiting for her.

Other days she would either read a book or eavesdrop while pretending to read. There were regular commuters who travelled with her both ways and she had just begun to get familiar with them. There was an old man in a skull cap, with the callus of prayer on his forehead. There were two teachers who whispered to each other all the time and a pot-bellied man with a briefcase who slept through the journey. There were others too.

Later, she would tell Ammi all that she had seen and heard. Ammi wanted to know every detail. What was the colour of the tall teacher's sari? Did the fat teacher have plastic flowers in her hair? What about the old man? Did he squabble with the vendors? What was it about? Did the briefcase man toss out his lunch that day as well? Did you manage to see what was in his lunch box? They would giggle together with schoolgirlish glee. Her journey provided Ammi with as much entertainment as the TV serials she watched every evening.

Najma glanced at her watch as the train left the station. It was running late, but she had given herself enough time to catch the Arakkonam–Bangalore passenger, which had been her regular evening train.

She got off at Tyakal. There was nothing much to be said about the place. And even if there was, her mind was too churned up to dwell on it.

There were a few people on the platform. No one even looked her way. Once upon a time, she used to wonder what perverse mind had created the burkha; its hideousness appalled her. Besides, her Ammi used to say that there was no need for her to hide herself as if she were a shameful creature.

'I don't want you to be like me,' Ammi had said. 'I don't know how to stride; I don't know how to make my way unless I am wearing a burkha.'

'Do you mean that for real? Or is it some convoluted metaphor?' Najma frowned.

'What is a metaphor?' Ammi asked, peering deep into her eyes as if by doing so, she could read Najma's mind.

'Using something to explain something else,' Najma said slowly, choosing her words with care.

'What do you think?' Ammi shrugged.

Ammi was an unusual woman. She had named Najma for a star because she believed her daughter was destined for great things. She was uneducated herself, but she made sure Najma went to school and college. She wanted her to be a teacher and so Najma became one. If ever she had any second thoughts, all she had to do was look at her Ammi – the rough, chapped skin of her palms, the stoop of her shoulders and her swollen knees – and she knew what it was that Ammi wanted her to escape.

Ammi worked as a kitchen help for a catering company that specialised in Hyderabadi cuisine. She was a fine cook, but all she did there was clean and chop; prepare the garlic and pound the spices. She looked old and spent, but her spirit was like a beacon. And they survived because of that.

Ammi found Najma the job at the school in Bangarpet. The owner of the catering company was related to someone on the school board. Besides, it was a school run by a Muslim charity and they were happy to employ Najma.

Ammi and she made plans. Once her job was made permanent, Najma would rent a house in Bangarpet and they would live there. Until then, she would commute by train. The Bangalore East station was close to Tannery Road where they lived and everything seemed to fall so well into place.

After the interview, Ammi and Najma had gone shopping. 'You need new clothes,' Ammi said.

Ammi had borrowed the money from a friend. The owner of the catering company had already advanced her enough, she said.

'How will you pay it back?' Najma had asked.

'You will. Not me,' Ammi grinned. Ammi had the widest smile

Najma had ever seen. Najma grinned back. She was going to be a woman of means. She had forgotten.

'In which case, we are both going shopping,' Najma said, grabbing her elbow and leading her into Mumtaz Emporium.

Ammi pulled back. 'No, no, I don't need any clothes.'

But Najma wouldn't budge. Finally, Ammi bought a pale pink kurta with elaborate blue and silver embroidery at the throat and around the elbow-length sleeves. It had a blue salwar and a gauzy dupatta in pale pink with silver tassels. Ammi held the sheer dupatta between her thumb and forefinger. There was a childlike gleam in her eyes as she rubbed the fabric between her fingers. When was the last time Ammi had bought herself something nice, Najma wondered. When had she ever allowed herself to want something? Desire is a luxury, she always said. Not that desire was evil or wrong, but it could cause heartbreak.

As for herself, Najma chose what she thought a schoolteacher ought to wear. Churidar kurtas in pastel shades and tiny prints. And dupattas, because the school insisted that all lady teachers cover their heads.

'Should I get a burkha?' Najma asked Ammi.

She frowned. 'Why would you need one?'

Najma laughed. She felt relieved, and blessed. Her Ammi couldn't even sign her name, but she was more progressive than some of those women who came to talk to them about female empowerment. Her Ammi made her feel that she had every right to be who she was.

Ammi was twelve when she was married to Najma's Abba. Ammi's own father had been a drunk, who sold his daughter for five hundred rupees to a man twenty-three years older than her. At first, Abba found her wanting as a wife. And then, when she was fourteen, he couldn't stop wanting her. He resented anyone or anything that made a demand on her affections. He kicked her pet kittens to death and growled at the neighbour's child. He accused her of sleeping with the neighbour and the samosa vendor; the postman and the fruit-seller. When she became pregnant, Ammi said, all she prayed for was that he would leave her. He died when Najma was a year old. By then, Ammi had had enough of being a wife.

'Why didn't you marry again?' Najma had asked. Ammi was only seventeen when she became a widow. 'I loved being a mother. But I never wanted to be another man's slave and whore in one body,' she replied.

Najma didn't know if she missed having a father. How could she miss something she had never known? Besides, as Ammi pointed out to her, a father may have had her in a burkha by the time she was eleven and married off by fourteen. 'Is that what you would have wanted?'

Najma had looked up from the design of the peacock feather she was creating with henna on Ammi's palm. Both Ammi and she knew that the henna would fade in a day or two but it was Ammi's birthday today. And she had wanted henna on her hands and a masala dosa for lunch.

At first she thought Ammi was being ironic, but then she realised Ammi really wanted to know.

'I know women who don't want to be responsible for their lives. They are happy too. Would you have wanted that?' Ammi asked.

Najma shook her head. There was nothing she valued more than what Ammi had given her: the freedom to choose.

But today, Najma was thankful for the burkha. Behind it, she was safe and free.

Najma didn't know who he was. She had seen him in the morning train for almost a fortnight. Once or twice, she had found him loitering by her seat, his surma-lined eyes trying to catch her gaze. But she didn't think much of it. Until, one evening, she noticed the young man was waiting outside the school gates and tailing her as she walked to the station. She was annoyed but not afraid. She wasn't going to let him intimidate her. She wondered if she should tell Ammi about the boy. But she was reluctant to worry her about something that probably was nothing. These days, Ammi was looking less careworn. All she talked about was moving into the house in Bangarpet. 'I'll watch TV all day and we won't allow a single grain of biryani into the house,' Ammi joked.

Najma would laugh and say, 'But what about me? I like biryani, you know!'

'Sorry, you'll need to eat it elsewhere.' Ammi sounded like a sassy fourteen-year-old. It was as if the years had fallen off her.

Every detail of that evening was clearly etched in her memory. She'd had a headache, so she stopped for a cup of tea at the railway station. The Bangarpet station tea was famous. There was a long line of people, but the tea-stall attendant knew her by sight and he bypassed them all to serve her.

When the Arakkonam–Bangalore Passenger she went back home on every day arrived, Najma found her usual window seat. He came and sat across from her once the train left Devagonthi station.

For the first time, she wondered who he was. He had a familiar odour that she knew from her Ammi. The smell of basmati rice cooking, and of spices and fat. It stayed on Ammi's skin even though she scrubbed herself every evening with a loofah. 'Promise me, when I am dead, you will drench me in attar. I don't want to go to jannat smelling of biryani and kebab,' Ammi would laugh, but only half in jest.

The young man must work for a biryani caterer, Najma

thought and pulled out a book. When the train began to move, she felt his eyes on her. She glared at him, but he wouldn't stop. The train wasn't full, so Najma rose and took the window seat across the aisle. He followed her there and persuaded the man sitting opposite her to move. Najma heard him say that he was her fiancé.

'What?' Najma demanded, rising to her feet.

'Sit down,' he said.

She saw the curious looks. She wondered if she should appeal for help, pull the emergency chain. But then she saw the intensity in his eyes and it unnerved her.

'Who are you?' Najma asked in Urdu.

'Imtiaz. The man you should marry.'

'It's for my Ammi to decide that,' she said.

'Yes. Like a good Muslim, I did the right thing. I asked your mother and she laughed in my face,' he snarled.

Najma was told later that, in Urdu, his name Imtiaz meant a 'mark of honour'. He worked in the same catering company as Ammi did. He had seen Najma; he had fallen in love with her. Madly, he said. He would die if he couldn't marry her. But Ammi had laughed in his face. He was a helper like her. 'My daughter deserves better. She is a teacher. Why would she marry a lowly kitchen help like you?' she asked.

She may as well have slapped him. The friends to whom Imtiaz confided his humiliation and rage told him that no man would let such a slur go unpunished.

Najma could see that he was furious. No, it was beyond that. She thought of the fifteen-year-old boys she had taught as a temp teacher at a government school. She had seen this look in their eyes sometimes. A manic gleam of rage that made them break benches and smash the blackboard.

'There is no need for you to be so frightened,' Shirin Begum, one of the more experienced teachers, had said, seeing Najma pale and shaken in the staffroom. 'The male hormone is an unruly beast and these boys have a hundred wild animals running amok in them. There is no point in being confrontational either. Just take a step back and don't raise your voice. They will back off if you speak to them calmly. They do it to get a reaction from you. That's all.'

Najma had put on her most benign face and tried to pacify him. Boys will be boys, she told herself. If you know how to handle them, they back off. Unless they are in a group. Then they turn into malevolent feral dogs.

Najma wasn't afraid. They were in a public place and there were people around.

'Ammi doesn't mean to be unkind. She is just so overworked,' she began.

'Your Ammi is an arrogant bitch. Like you are. The two of you think you are above all of us,' he said.

'What?' Her voice rose at the profanity.

'She thinks you are too good for me. Does she know that you are no better than a two-bit whore? Do you think I haven't seen you? Flaunting your face for the world to see. Using your beauty to have your way with men. From the tea-stall boy to every man on this train… How many men do you want, you whore?'

The other passengers, the teachers and the briefcase man, began moving away. Najma didn't know how many of them understood Urdu, but the venom in his voice was unmistakable. Nobody wanted to get involved.

The old man in the skull cap murmured, 'Education doesn't mean you disdain the Koran. What kind of Muslim woman steps out without a hijab?'

'Tell her, Mamu,' he said. 'Tell my aaras that she is shameless.'

'Aaras? I am not your fiancée,' Najma said firmly and huddled into her corner. She was frightened, but what could he do to her in a train full of people? In five or six minutes, they would reach her station. How could she know that in those five or six minutes, the axis of her world would shift?

The old man got up and went towards the door. The skies were dark with thunderclouds. She hoped it wouldn't rain till she reached home. 'Please leave me alone,' she said.

He leaned forward and stared at her. 'I won't let you become anyone else's wife,' he said. And then he took out the bottle of acid he had brought with him and flung it in her face.

Do you know what it feels like to have acid on your skin? Do you know what it does to you as your skin melts and your nerve ends scream? Do you know what it's like to hear the screams and not know if it is you who is screaming or someone else? Do you know what it is to lie hovering between life and death and all you can sense is someone weeping at your side? Do you know what it is to shriek and cry when your Ammi comes to your side and the smell of biryani takes you back to that man, that moment? Do you know what it feels like to see the shock and horror in the eyes of everyone who walks past you? Do you know what it's like to look at yourself in the mirror with one eye and know you will never be you again? Do you know what it feels like to discover that everyone who was in the train compartment that day denied having seen anything? Do you know what it's like to live knowing your life is destroyed and the man who did it walks free?

The police came to the hospital. But Ammi was too distraught to make sense. They made an attempt to talk to various people in the compartment and the station. 'We may as well have spoken to a wall of hollow bricks,' a constable told Ammi.

There was nothing to be done. 'Time will heal everything. It's like watching grass grow,' Ammi said. 'You think you can't see any difference, but one day you will see that the grass has indeed grown.'

Najma hated her mother then.

The days passed. Najma wept. Or stared at the wall, wondering what she could have done differently.

'I know the name of the man who did this to me,' Najma said one day, unable to bear the thought that he was out there and free.

Ammi looked up from what she was doing: shredding leaves for the poultice for her face. Ammi was still trying to heal what was left of her face and neck.

'Imtiaz,' Najma said. 'He said he asked you if he could marry me.'

Amma stared at her. Her mouth opened and parted with words that wouldn't form. Najma could hear Ammi's heartbeat, or was it hers? A vegetable vendor's call floated in through the window: tomato-beans-carrot-beetroot; iruli-bellulli-aaloo…

'He did this?' Ammi asked. Her face was suddenly bleached of all colour and expression. 'Why didn't you tell me?'

'He said if he couldn't marry me, no one else would.' Najma couldn't help the words, they burst out. 'Why did you, Ammi? Why?'

Ammi crumpled into a heap. 'What should I have done? Say yes to him… he was nothing. A loafer like your Abba. Is that who you wanted?'

Najma turned away and looked at the wall. She knew she was being unfair.

Ammi had done precisely what Najma expected of her. But she needed to lash out at someone. Inflict hurt, just as she was hurting. And who else was there but Ammi?

Ammi went looking for him. She went to the catering company. Imtiaz was no longer there. No one knew where he was, or if they did, they wouldn't say. She went to the mosque to speak to the elders there. They listened gravely, nodded solemnly and told her to keep faith in Allah, for Allah would help them. She went to the police station. She told the constable who had visited them a few times what Najma had said. He said he would do his best to trace Imtiaz; his boss said the same. It was a serious offence and they would like to see him in jail for the rest of his life. 'No, no, don't. Just let me know when you find him. I need to resolve this myself,' Ammi told them.

The constable cleared his throat and said, 'Ammi, you can't take the law into your hands. I understand your feelings, but the law is the law.'

Ammi shook her head. 'Who said that I would hurt him, sir? I just want to speak to him once.'

Najma listened as Ammi told her what had happened at the police station. 'You are wasting your time. What will you do when you find him?' she asked.

Ammi stared at her unseeingly. Then she slumped to the floor.

Najma tried to rouse Ammi. Eventually she pulled on Ammi's burkha and stepped out of the house on her own for the first time. She hurried to their neighbour's house to summon help. The doctor at the government hospital said Ammi had suffered a stroke and that she would never move or talk again.

They lived on the little savings they had. Najma knew she must look for work, but who would give her a job? Who would hire a teacher who looked like something from a horror movie?

Besides, she was afraid.

A college friend suggested that Najma go for counselling. She told Ammi what she was going to do. She didn't know if Ammi understood but she saw a gleam of something in her eyes.

Ammi had been a fighter. She would be happy that Najma was trying to gain a toehold in life again.

The counsellor had a friend who said she might have a job for Najma. She would train her in her new line of work. But you need to shed your burkha, she said. Listening to her, Najma felt an ice cube slither down her spine.

She told Ammi what the counsellor had said. Ammi's eyes spoke the same truth: you cannot hide from yourself.

But Najma wasn't ready. She didn't think she would ever be. The counsellor had told her about plastic surgery; the monster face she had could be tamed into something that wouldn't give children nightmares.

Ammi died. Their savings were over. Najma knew that she had to do something. She could either kill herself or think of what to do next.

She thought of Ammi, of what she had slaved for. Of how she had denied her own needs. Had anyone even called Ammi by her name recently? Did she even remember that her name was Nazariya?

Something in Najma hardened. A little fist clenched. Was it resolve? Was it the will to live?

Najma saw the train approaching in the distance. Her heart began to hammer as it pulled into the station. She found the compartment, the one she knew they would all be in. She got in and sat down. Through the eyeholes of her burkha, she saw them. The old man with the skull cap. The two teachers. The man with the briefcase.

When the train began to move and everyone had settled down, she pulled the top part of the burkha away from her face. She heard the collective gasp of horror. Her melted face, the stretched-out skin of her neck, were not easy to look at.

'I am Najma,' she said. The words emerged in her tinny new voice. The acid had damaged her larynx as well. 'I am the girl you never saw. I want you to take a good look at what that man did to me. If you didn't see me then, I hope you will now.' She looked at them, one after the other. 'Tell me, do you ever wonder what happened to me after someone took me to a hospital that evening?'

There was silence. One of the teachers began sniffling.

She looked out of the window. Ammi, she told her mother, who sat drenched in attar in a jannat free of hope and fear – for isn't that what heaven is like? I did it. I did what you asked of me. I faced the world. I will never hide behind a burkha again.

The breeze blew into her face and she felt the wheels of the train gather momentum.

I am Najma.

3

# URVASHI

The old bathing pond had always been part of the palace grounds. But it was only in the last few years, as the water in the river dried to an absurd and embarrassing trickle, that Shyam began mentioning the possibility of converting it into a swimming pool. He had seen something similar in a hotel in Galle, where Radha and he had gone for a holiday. 'He woke up one morning while we there and said – I need a swimming pool. Just like that! So we now have a pool at the resort,' Radha had told Urvashi with a bemused expression. That was a couple of years ago, when Urvashi last visited.

The old bathing pond had sides made of weathered laterite blocks. At the far end was a high moss-tipped wall and, beyond it, an areca-nut garden. On either side of the pool were old trees – mango and jackfruit, jamun and tamarind, red silk cotton and satinwood. A hammock was strung up between two sturdy kokko trees. A rose-apple tree laden with waxy pink bell-shaped fruit grew in one corner. Urvashi reached up to pluck a fruit and nibbled at it.

The pool area was, as Najma had said, all prettied up. Even if you couldn't swim, you would want to stay near it as long as you could.

The thought of Najma squeezed her with a deep sadness. She seemed happy here. But who knew what was going on in her head when she was on her own? Did she look over her shoulder at every step? Did she flinch if a man came close to her? How did she live with what had happened to her? Where did she find the strength to not lose courage each time she saw herself in the mirror?

Urvashi thought of how she had felt when she found her first grey pubic hair. As if her legs had been chopped off at the knees. There had been moments like that earlier too. A pencil that suddenly seemed at home, snug and happy under the curve of her breast, from where it had once dropped. The crow's feet at the corners of her eyes that appeared easily when she smiled. She had stood in front of the mirror and stretched the lines between two fingers, wanting to see her face shorn of the years that had piled up so stealthily. But a greying pubis? There was no going back. Her tenure as a desirable woman was drawing to an end.

How could it be that her body was marching ahead of her mind, which seemed as young and hungry for life as it had always been? More importantly, what was she going to do? Did you dye your pubic hair? Or did you shave it off? Did you hide your nudity from the light or did you turn to your husband, grateful that he still sought your body once in a while, even if it was only a matter of routine? At least, during that cursory copulation, you still felt young, beautiful and untainted by time.

Later that same week, she had met Najma for a story she was doing on acid attack victims.

As Najma talked to her of her plans for the future, Urvashi had watched the girl's seeing eye sparkle in her ravaged face and felt repulsed by her own vanity. Would she have had the strength to pick herself up if she were in Najma's place?

Najma wanted to study further, but meanwhile she needed a job, she said. Urvashi had gone to Radha only after several others who had promised to help had reneged on their word. The truth was that no one wanted a girl with a wrecked face. 'Perhaps if she would wear a burkha... Don't they do that anyway? Though a burkha is bad for business too. You know how touchy parents are about religion these days,' someone on a school board had said to her half-heartedly.

Najma had been vehement in her refusal. 'I don't mind if it isn't a teaching job. I am not going to wear a burkha. I will not hide my face.'

'She's an acid attack victim and it isn't easy for her to find a job, although she is a trained teacher,' Urvashi had told Radha, like she told everyone else. 'There is one other thing. She doesn't want anyone to know that she is an acid attack victim. The pity and the speculation are just as devastating as what happened to her. If someone asks, say that she was in a fire. A gas cylinder burst or some such thing.'

Sometimes Urvashi wondered if Radha had created a job for Najma. She had called back in two days. 'It isn't much, but we provide rent-free accommodation and food, so she can save up. And it's a new place, so she can almost start afresh,' Radha said.

'What about Shyam?' Urvashi asked, knowing how particular he was about the aesthetic values of his resort.

'Shyam will not object,' Radha said firmly.

Urvashi wondered what she would do if she had to make a fresh start for some reason. Where would she go? For now, to the pool, she thought.

The European group had discovered the pool as well, she realised as she saw them going in and out of the water. She found a lounger and sank into its padded embrace.

On the lounger next to hers, a middle-aged woman in a brightly patterned blue-and-yellow swimsuit lay on her face while her husband drizzled the back of her legs with oil. She shifted onto her side and offered him some of the flesh of her thigh to anoint as well. The man leaned forward and dropped a kiss between her shoulder blades. She turned her head and smiled at him. Then she kissed the tips of her fingers and laid them on his lips.

Urvashi felt the breath snag in her throat. In that moment, the two of them, with their middle-aged spread, chubby limbs, sagging, blotched skin and scanty hair had the luminescence of young lovers whose gaze never falters from the other. Young love that does not distinguish between the hunger of the body and the spirit. One feeds off the other with a natural ease and an insatiable appetite. But as the years go by, the intimacy unravels bit by bit, until everything you do together leaves a residue of dissatisfaction, coating words and kisses.

Until you reach the point that she was at now, Urvashi thought, trying not to be overwhelmed by the sense of irreconcilable loss she felt each time she dwelt on her life. How could one bad decision snowball into another bad decision, into the next? What was that first bad decision?

Later, Urvashi would ask herself if there had been an exact turning point in her history of disappointment. And she would narrow it down to two episodes of dissolution. The first took place one afternoon at Lake Chilka.

The boatman had cut the engine and let it float to a tongue of land a few minutes after they had set off. A row of decrepit huts clung to the lake's edge. A woman sat at the door of one, washing an aluminium vessel with the murky brown waters of the salt-water lake.

A young man leapt into the boat with a bucket of clams. Urvashi had looked at the boatman and raised her eyebrows.

The boatman leaned closer. 'He's my friend,' he said.

The young man seated himself on a bench opposite her. He tapped the edge of the bucket. 'Real pearl,' he shrugged. 'If you are lucky…'

He prised open the first clam and shook his head as he tossed it back into the bucket. He chose a second one and threw it back in disgust. The third time, because fairy tales and folklore teach you that the third time is lucky, the clam yielded a pearl.

'Madam, you are lucky, very lucky… a real pearl!' The young man's excitement rang through as he wiped the perfectly formed pearl on a rag.

'Yours for just five hundred rupees,' he offered. He pointed to the horizon. 'It's late, so last pearl of the day…'

Urvashi took it from his proffered hand. A cheap pearl made in a Chinese sweat shop somewhere, stuck with gum within a clam and the clam shell glued together. She held it up and peered at it. 'Beautiful. I'll take it but I'll pay only two hundred,' she said firmly.

'No, no…' The young man shook his head.

They haggled for a while and eventually, after Urvashi affected a sulk and looked into the distance and the young man mopped his brow with a rag in capitulation, they settled on Rs 300. The young man took his bucket of clams and leapt off the boat in one fluid move.

'A pearl from a clam.' Mahesh shook his head in disgust.'So how much was it really worth?'

'About twenty rupees,' Urvashi said, holding the pearl up against the blue sky again.

'You are a fool,' he said. 'You knew he was cheating you and you let him.'

Urvashi brushed a strand of hair from her eyes.

'Look around us. He is doing what he needs to, to survive. There is more dignity in this than in begging.'

'Really? You think there is dignity in cheating?'

In the distance, the sky and sea met over a narrow strip of land. An overriding smell of fish filled the air. A tiny shoal rose from the waves, flew through the air and landed in the sea again. A lone fish fell on the deck.

Urvashi saw it leap into the air and flop back on the deck as it tried to find its way back into the water. She waited for Mahesh to rescue it. He didn't. She leaned forward, gritting her teeth, gathered it in her cupped palms, and tossed it into the sea.

'Our Lady of the High Seas,' Mahesh said. 'And before you start, I didn't want my hands smelling of fish. And I cannot condone daylight burglary, for that's what it was, and you are a fool for letting him get away with it. You might want to slot it as charity. But there is no charity without consequences. Next time, he is going to be even more devious...'

The wind ate some of his words and her love for him. She saw a man she didn't recognise. Someone without empathy for either man or fish. Had he always been like this?

The end of the holiday and the unravelling of her marriage could be traced back to that precise moment, she thought.

The next time, the strands fell apart even further. They were driving home from a play at the Chowdiah. As the traffic clogged at the traffic light with a particular tenacity known only to Bangalore, Mahesh hit the steering wheel with the flat of his palm and muttered, 'I should have offered that idiot Rohit a lift.'

The unspoken plea for a lift that Mahesh had chosen to ignore. He didn't like fraternising with junior colleagues.

'I could have asked him to drive. This is a fucking nightmare!'

'Is that how you think of people?' Urvashi snapped. 'How useful they are to you...'

Ahead, the traffic light finally changed and the traffic began to stream.

Mahesh changed gears as he spoke. 'That's who I am. I use people.'

Urvashi turned to look at him. 'Are you saying that to rile me?'

'What do you think?'

Urvashi didn't know what to think. Their marriage was a contractual obligation determined by their mutual usefulness. Had she been chosen to be his wife eighteen years ago because of his two kids? She had loved the children and nurtured them just as if she had birthed them. But where did she fit in, now that their son and daughter had left home to study in Pune and Stanford? Her mouth went dry.

Who was this man? How could she share roof and bed with him, let her undies tumble with his in the washing machine, split a biryani and do all those countless mundane but intimate things one does with a husband and yet not know him?

Urvashi leaned back in the lounger and closed her eyes. Death and divorce were meant to herald the end of a marriage. Not an unspecified, yet overwhelming disappointment in the other person.

Her phone beeped with a flurry of messages. Once again, it was a new number. Each time she blocked his number, he appeared in a new guise, her stalker, her very own ten-headed Ravana. You couldn't chop off one head and hope he would be dead and gone. He would surface again and again.

She switched the phone off and put it away. She closed her eyes.

Around her, the evening turned to twilight. She listened to the bird calls, her beating heart, and the slowly building resolve.

'You are lost in thought,' a voice butted into her thoughts.

Urvashi looked up to see a young woman in a T-shirt and track pants. She had a bottle of water in her hand and her face was flushed from the heat and exercise.

Urvashi smiled. The young woman dropped into a lounger next to hers. 'I was a little concerned. You hadn't moved for a bit,' she said, taking a sip from her water bottle.

'I'm fine. I was just thinking random thoughts. Are you here on holiday?' Urvashi fidgeted, wondering what the girl had seen on her face that made her pause.

The girl tilted her head and took a sip of water again. 'I think so. I've never been on a holiday before.'

Urvashi felt her smile freeze. She didn't want to know. Why did everyone think she was ready and available to lend an ear? Hear their troubles, put an arm around their shoulders and help them deal with their messy lives?

'How long are you here for?' the young woman asked.

Urvashi smiled, relieved. The girl had no intention of confiding in her, whatever it was she was battling. 'A week. And you?'

'Three days, and then we head to Kochi, Alapuzha, Thekkady, Munnar, etc.' She took another sip of water. 'Bye then,' she said, walking away.

Urvashi wondered why the girl seemed so familiar. By the time it fell into place, she was gone.

# Sreelakshmi

I wondered where Urvashi was. Was she sitting by the pool, or swimming perhaps? Or was she watching the twilight skies? Was she waiting for someone to find her? Even during our brief encounter, I had sensed an underlying tension in her. Like a wound-up coil waiting to give.

And then I thought of Megha and Najma. What would happen to the two girls? Would they carry forever the scars of their violation? Would it ever get better?

Back at Banaras Hindu University, my friend Narendran, in an effort to shrug off his tantric lineage, had found a haven in politics. He had always been part of the All India Students Committee, but when the AISC was disbanded after Independence, he joined the National Union of Students.

'I was at the first meeting of the NUS that Pandit Nehru addressed. I wanted to be part of the nation-building process. I saw myself contributing to the student movement and going on to become someone who would have a definite role to play in it. Instead of which, increasingly, they wanted us to turn into little lackeys. Respect the national flag and the Constitution, avoid foul language, and safeguard public property.' He paused, then added with a bitter laugh, 'And help the government to stop people from travelling on trains without tickets.'

I understood his frustration but I was glad that he wasn't going to be actively involved in politics. I murmured appropriate words to pacify him and suggested we go for a film. 'That new film, *Ziddi*, should be interesting,' I said.

'*Ziddi*? Are you mocking me, Sree? Do you know what it means?'

'Stubborn,' I said, trying not to grin. Now that he had put it that way.

'Let me ask Subhasini. If she says yes, we can go,' he said.

Perhaps Subhasini influenced all his decisions. It had always amused me to see the two of them argue about their politics. In its own way, it held them in check, prevented them from turning into zealots of some sort. A disenchanted and demoralised Narendran veered straight towards the Progressive Students Union, of which Subhasini was already a member. I chose to remain apolitical. Politics didn't interest me. And so we began drifting apart. Or was it that I couldn't bear to be the fire ant in their garden of Eden any more?

I was surprised therefore when, two months later, Narendran came looking for me. 'You have been avoiding me. Did I do something to offend you?' he demanded.

I shook my head, amused at his ploy. Making it my fault so I wouldn't castigate him for slipping out of sight. I took the middle ground. 'I have been busy and so have you… that's all.'

Soon we were walking together, across the campus. We talked about home and what was going on in Kerala. We talked about the thulavarsham and steamed bananas. We talked about the million shades of green that only Kerala has. We talked about the strikes against escalating school and college fees. As usual, when we were on our own, we slipped into Malayalam. It was only a little later that I realised that he had sought me out because he was lonely. Subhasini had gone home for the puja celebrations and he was on his own for two weeks. I was the stand-in.

I let him grumble awhile about Subhasini. 'For all her talk about progressive thinking and her worship of Bena Das, she is just a middle-class girl at heart.'

'Who is Bena Das? What did she write?' I asked, wondering how I had missed reading her. I had read Bankim Chandra, Sarat

Chandra Chatterjee, even Tagore, in Malayalam and attempted reading Premchand in Hindi, but was still looking for the Indian equivalent of Rebecca West. I wanted to read someone who rose above the romanticism of most women writers. I wanted robust prose; I wanted muscle and sinew, even if it was a love story.

Narendran shook his head, in disgust almost. 'Don't you see what is going on in our country? Do you realise there is a world beyond books and biology?'

'So tell me…' I tried to placate him.

'She was a student at the Diocesan College who tried to kill the Bengal governor, Sir Stanley Jackson, in 1932. She shot at him five times in the convocation hall but didn't succeed, and was sent to jail for nine years. Subhasini talks of her with reverence, but the silly girl still wants to dress up and be with her cousins and sisters for the puja…'

'She is a woman too, Naren, not just a political being.'

Narendran snorted but changed the subject.

The next few days, we met every evening, and what was once a nebulous friendship became something more. He stopped referring to Subhasini in every sentence. He seemed to want to spend more time with me. Given time, who knows what it would have turned into?

But the last time we met, it didn't end well. He said he was going to join the protest against the government's treatment of refugees coming in from East Bengal.

'How does it concern us?' I asked. 'The refugee problem is not a student problem. Especially not for a student from Kerala.'

I put my hand on his arm. It felt comforting to touch another human being. He glanced at my hand as if it were a furry caterpillar on his arm. I thought I saw horrified fascination in his eyes. And just a glint of desire before he flicked it away and stepped on it.

I took my hand away hastily. To ease his discomfiture, I asked, 'Are you going to answer me or what?'

Subhasini returned the next day and he no longer needed me. When I went looking for him, he was evasive about when we would meet next.

Later, I heard through an acquaintance that Subhasini didn't approve of the amount of time he and I had spent together while she was away. Narendran had tried to mollify her by saying that he felt sorry for me. That I had no friends and he was just being kind. He called me 'damaged goods' – or so I was told.

When the police came looking for him in February, I pleaded ignorance. I didn't know his whereabouts. I hadn't seen him in months, I said.

'So you don't know that he was at the protest organised on the Calcutta University lawns?' one of the policemen asked.

'No.'

'Do you know that six students were killed?' the second policeman asked.

'I read about it,' I said. 'But what does Narendran have to do with it?'

'He was one of the student leaders who turned the protest into a violent one. Six innocent people died that evening because of him. And God knows how many were injured in the stampede.'

I thought of how he had stopped meeting me once Subhasini returned. I meant nothing to him. For all his claim of empathy, he hadn't even realised the extent of hurt he had caused me. I thought of how he had looked at my hand on his arm. I thought of what he had called me – damaged goods. Why then should I bear the burden of his guilt?

'You should ask Subhasini,' I said. 'She would know. They were together all the time. I was just the third wheel really…'

That was all it took. A wide-eyed gaze, a casual insertion of a name, and they whisked Subhasini away. Narendran emerged to rescue her. I don't know if, when he came out of jail, they married and lived happily ever after. I had left Varanasi by then.

I never saw them or heard from them again. Neither did I want to.

There is a place for everything and everyone, I used to be told. But what was my place in this world? How long would I lie here, on a table in Najma's room? What would become of me?

It is only in stories and films that female ghosts wear white saris and glide along in the dead of night with flowing hair, singing deeply mournful dirges to unrequited desires. I was not a purple dwarf with a boar face, nor was I a shrunken creature with a narrow neck or distended belly, or charcoal-like, with bulging veins and red eyes. I was a piece of bone, bleached, calcified and brittle. At best, I looked like a piece of chalk. A teacher's chalk that could write but not on its own. A sliver of energy in quest of that moment when I could finally dissipate into nothingness.

The door was flung open with some force. A middle-aged woman with a troubled face and streaks of grey in her hair stepped into the room. She walked with a faltering step and sat down heavily on the chair by the table. As she placed her elbows on the table, her fingers brushed against me, then picked me up. I could hear her muttering under her breath. 'I wish she were dead. I wish she would die and free me of this torment. She said she was going to take me to confession and that was some hours ago.'

The malice in her voice pulled me out of the morass of my own misery. I wanted to know who she wished dead and why. And just like that, I became what I had always been: a seeker of stories.

They say that ghosts are afraid of sanctified spots. They tell you to enter a holy place to escape a ghost. They say ghosts will hover and wait at the entrance, unable to cross the threshold where divinity reigns. I knew I would feel no such qualms when I accompanied my carrier into the church. Nor would I be felled by a divine blow. A long time ago, I had realised that a seeker of stories finds entry into places where no one else believes it is possible to go.

When I was alive, I had never entered a church. I had always wondered at the sacramental rituals: the Eucharist, the liturgy and the confession. What did it do for the soul in distress? 'You don't even go to a temple. So why would you want to go to a church?' Markose had scoffed when I once asked to go with him.

I had smiled to deflect the stab of pain. If only he had said, I will take you one day. So I can show you a part of my life you know nothing about.

When the door opened, the woman who held me stiffened and sat up straight. 'Who is it?' she called, her voice a wobble. She gathered the end of her sari around her body to still the trembling.

'Hush, hush, Chechi, it's me,' a woman said from the doorway, not bothering to hide the irritation she felt. 'Don't make a fuss. Who else could it be?'

I could see that she had long exhausted any residue of patience when it came to her sister. 'You were not in our room. Why did you leave?'

The older woman raised her chin and snorted. 'I got tired of waiting for you. I went for a walk and entered this room by mistake. Is that a sin now?'

She rose, still holding me in her hand, and walked me into their lives and their secrets.

# Half a Sin

'Are you all right, Chechi?' Molly said gently, wanting to make amends for her surliness. She tucked an errant curl behind her ear.

Water can wear out stone, that's what Anto used to tell her when she confessed to snapping at her sister. Anto, who saw everything but said little. Anto, who cradled her head in the crook of his neck and said, 'Your sister would try the patience of even Job.'

Molly would giggle into the skin of his neck. And drink deep of his Anto fragrance – fat and eggs, vanilla and nutmeg and Cuticura talc.

'There was no need for you to use that tone,' Theresa growled. 'We are two women in a hotel room!'

'And so?' Molly said. In an effort to still the anger that crouched at the tip of her tongue, ready to hurl out like a rabid dog, she set about rearranging the plastic jug and steel tumblers on the table. The jug had faded from a brilliant blue to a subdued grey, its dullness echoing everything else about the room. The splotchy walls and the grim curtains at the window. The cheap wooden bedstead and the faded sheet stretched across it.

'This is a hotel room. Who knows what kind of people stay here?' Theresa snapped.

'We are two middle-aged women in a hotel room. Who is going to want to do anything to us?' Molly laughed.

'Men can't be trusted. All men are the same, Thomasina.'

When Molly refused to respond, Theresa called out petulantly, 'Thomasina, are you there?'

Molly glared at her sister. Once, Theresa had been a fine-looking woman with chiselled features and curly black hair. Her skin was the colour of the cream from a Jersey cow, people said. Some pointed out that her face and demeanour bore a distinct resemblance to the Virgin Mary. Such a well-behaved girl, with her downcast eyes and quiet ways. Whatever happened to you, Chechi? Molly asked silently, taking in the blotchy skin, the spots and lines, the pinched nostrils, and the scanty hair twisted into a knot at the nape of her scrawny neck.

'I am here,' Molly said quietly. In all these years, not once had her sister called her Molly.

'Then listen to me. I'm not talking about rape, you fool! There are other reasons to hurt us. You, with your six-inch zari borders and all those enormous gold ornaments on display. Tell me, how many bangles do you wear on each wrist? Six? Eight? Why do you dress as if you are a bride? That's the problem. We may be middle-aged women, but they'll want all that gold even if they don't want us!' Theresa's voice rang through the room with the triumphant note of a church bell. Hear ye, hear ye...

In the mirror, Molly saw herself reflected. Molly will never be as beautiful as Theresa, everyone said, including their parents. But Molly is smart and she has lovely eyes. Molly hated it when they said that. Those devastating words of faint praise; the ignominy of the consolation prize; the 'beauty is only skin-deep' aphorisms.

So she took to avoiding mirrors. I am who I am. I don't need a mirror to tell me that, she told herself, watching twenty-two-year-old Theresa carefully pluck her eyebrows or examine a whitehead. Molly was sixteen and resigned to being second best.

So the Molly in the mirror always surprised her. Who was this woman? When did she become her? The cheap cotton sari. Her bare wrists and the black thread round her neck, on which was strung a tiny gold cross. She looked what she was. A tired middle-aged woman with grey dusting her curly hair, who expended all her energy trying to make ends meet. Everything about her was striated with despair, she thought. Which man would want her? Not even a thief would look at her and sense an opportunity.

Molly didn't speak. After a while, you get used to the ringing of even the loudest of church bells. After a while, it becomes just white noise.

She went to stand by the window. The staff quarters of the hotel were at the end of the street and she could see people walking up and turning the corner. The church was on that road. Soon they would go in as well.

She opened and shut the window with a snap.

'What's that noise?' Theresa was querulous.

'It's the TV,' Molly said, looking at the blank wall. 'One of those new wall-mounted TVs. But there's a problem. It isn't working. I'll have one of the housekeeping people look at it.' An image of the sweeper woman with her bucket and broom swam into her mind.

Some days she yearned to lay her head on her sister's lap and weep. 'I don't like having to do this to you. Deceive you the way I do. But you leave me with no option, Chechi!'

For how could she give in and confess? If Theresa didn't have her resentment to cling to, she would turn into a pathetic, unseeing heap. This way, her sister was bristling but alive.

Molly wondered if Tito had had his breakfast yet. She had left him with a neighbour, who would look after him until they got home the next morning.

'Shall we eat before we go to church?' she asked.

She undid the parcel of dosas she had bought from a small tea shop adjacent to the church.

Theresa sniffed. 'I am not hungry,' she said.

Molly didn't say anything. She watched her sister tear into the dosa with greed as much as hunger. She licked and chomped, flecks of chutney clinging to her chin, her fingers oily and glistening, her eyes set in an unflinching stare, as always.

Molly poured coffee from the flask into a glass. 'Some coffee?' she asked.

Theresa grunted. 'I hope the coffee is better than the dosa. It tasted like cardboard. These star hotels, all show and nothing.'

Say it, Molly urged her in her head. Say it, Chechi. 'Just like you.' Will it make you feel any better? If so, spit it out. It won't be the first time.

Theresa sat mutinously silent. An unfinished insult can wound more than a spoken one.

Father George Koshy tugged at his cassock as he walked into the confessional. His wife had starched it again, so it stood stiff and unyielding.

Eliamma didn't entirely approve of him. She thought he was too friendly and familiar with his parishioners. This was her way of making him keep the dignity of his office. Give him a cassock that felt like an armour. He sighed. Some days he thought he would never get anything right.

It was a weekday and the church was empty but for two women kneeling with their heads bent in prayer. He watched as one of them turned her head and glared at her companion, who was kneeling alongside. The other woman sat with her shoulders slumped, her face drawn. He had seen a similar expression on the faces of women standing in line outside the fair-price shop. Knowing that the rice would have run out before it was their turn. And yet they waited, hoping for a minor miracle to occur.

Father George Koshy gave himself a little mental shake. He knew he was given to being fanciful. They used to tell him that at the seminary, time and again. These were just two women praying and here he was, reading a subtext into the tilt of one's neck and the way the other held her shoulders.

He gave them one last look and knew for certain that he wasn't being fanciful. There was something odd about them. Then he remembered. He had seen them the evening before. One of them had been lighting a candle while the other seemed to be giving her instructions. They had looked familiar, but they were not from this parish. Then Jaimon, the driver at the resort, who had accompanied them to the church, stopped to speak to him. He said they were his sister's neighbours; Jaimon's sister lived just an hour and a half away. But what were they doing here this evening? It wasn't as if this was a church of any special significance.

Then he saw them speak to the kapiyar. The sexton came to him and said, 'They want to confess.'

He sighed. He knew of people who did this sort of thing. Go to another church and spew their sins out to a strange priest. That way, there was no awkwardness, no embarrassment, when they met their regular priest.

But what sins could these two have to confess? Stealing a neighbour's hen or mouthing some slander? Most often, the confessions were about acts of pettiness which called for two tight slaps rather than redemption. He took a deep breath and walked to the antechamber where his sacramental habit was placed.

There was something to be said for the Catholic confessional. You didn't have to meet the confessor's eye, for one. But here, in the Orthodox way of worship, they stood by the altar and sometimes, when he took their hands in his before they began, he felt like he was being dragged into the swamp of other people's lives.

He changed into the black cassock and draped the grey stole around his neck. He glanced at his watch, a heavy-duty Tissot, which his cousin Bessy who lived in Canada had brought him two months ago, and wondered if he should take it off. But it was all metal and wouldn't break the unwritten edict of having nothing at the altar that was made of leather. Then he pulled out the steel cross strung on a narrow black cord and adjusted his little cap. He looked at himself in the mirror and smoothened his beard. He was to be both teacher and judge – hopefully he looked the part.

He settled in his chair in front of the altar and cleared his throat, the customary sign for the confession to begin.

'In the name of the Father and of the Son and of the Holy Spirit, Amen.

'I am kneeling here and making the sign of the cross. I hope you saw that, Father? If you didn't hear me the first time, I am saying it again: In the name of the Father and of the Son and of the Holy Spirit, Amen.

'Father, I am ready to begin.'

George Koshy was startled. Where was the muted spirit and hushed voice that confessors usually brought to this act? Instead, the woman's voice rang through the church; strident, and demanding to be heard. An eagle screaming to the skies, he thought. Oblivious to who might hear what.

'What is that strange noise I hear? Are you gulping water? Or is that your response?

'Bless me, Father, for I have sinned. It has been a week since my last confession and these are my sins.

'Before I go on, I would like to make one thing clear. Just because I am here making a confession doesn't mean that I have really sinned. I know in my heart and soul that I have not sinned. I have committed neither a mortal sin nor a venial one. But I am a true Christian and I believe in the sacrament of reconciliation. All I want to do is let the Holy Spirit in on what goes on in my head. Every week.'

Why didn't she just speak aloud in her own home then?

George Koshy muttered in his head and then crossed himself, ashamed of his unkind thought.

'Besides, the priest in our church at home is a fool. He sees only what he wants to see and hears only what he wants to hear. Like everyone else, he too is taken in by her. He thinks I need help. He thinks he ought to counsel me.'

'Look,' Father George Koshy began, hoping to stop the woman's diatribe in mid-flow. 'It isn't right for you…'

'Of course I know it isn't right,' she said, cutting him off mid-sentence, as if she were talking to a difficult child. Her tone was placatory but with a hint of steel. 'But you should see him when he is with her. Like a dog in heat, sniffing around her. All right, I know I shouldn't have said that, so forgive me, Father, for I have sinned by uttering this profanity in God's hallowed home. Tonight I shall say ten Hail Marys as my penance. That should do.

'The truth is, I do not like her. No, the word "like" doesn't adequately convey the volcano of feelings that erupts in me each time she walks into the room. Her smell, her voice, why, every step is an affront to me. That's how I feel about her. The truth is, even as I kneel here in this church that I have always wanted to pray in, I know no peace. I feel no benediction descend upon me, I do not hear the song of angels or the presence of the Holy Spirit. All I know is a deep hatred for her, the woman who waits outside for me. My sister.'

The priest shook his head in amazement. He could see the sister seated on a bench at the end of the corridor. She must hear every single word that was being spoken. Unless she was stone deaf, which would explain the diffidence.

'I suggest,' he began, but before he could speak further, the woman snapped, 'Don't even bother saying it. I know exactly what you are going to say. I know how hard you will have to try to conceal the censure and disapproval in your voice when you ask, "But how can you hate your sister? You must know it is a sin? Whatever may have transpired between you, you have to find it in your heart to forgive her."

'You are not the first priest I am confessing to. So don't go down that road. Listen… that's all I ask of you.'

Theresa closed her eyes in an attempt to stop the angry tears from spilling out. She knew what most people thought of her. It had been a losing battle from day one. She thought a great deal about forgiveness. There was a certain impudence to it which rather charmed her. A switching on of serial lights festivity that made the forgiver and the forgiven feel a flare of relief disguised as happiness. Theresa knew how to switch on fairy lights. But some acts were beyond forgiveness.

'How can I forgive her when there is nothing to forgive? Do you forgive a yam for causing your skin to itch? Do you forgive cats for triggering an asthma attack? Do you forgive a tree for smashing your home to bits? There is no place for forgiveness.' Theresa's voice rose another decibel.

George Koshy felt his shoulders slump under the cassock. The weight of a confession ought not to sit heavily on him. He closed his eyes for a moment. He took a deep breath. 'In which case, what are you here for?'

Theresa snorted. It was just as she had expected.

'I am a true believer. So here I am.

'I hated her right from the beginning. But that's how it begins even in the Old Testament, doesn't it, Father?'

That was when George Koshy gave up. It was all very well being the universal solvent, but sometimes even water has to stay still.

'In the beginning, God created heaven and earth. And the earth was without form, and void; and darkness was upon the face of the deep. And the spirit of God moved upon the face of the waters. And God said, Let there be light: and there was light.

'And I was born. How much my parents loved me. I was the child they had yearned to have, for almost eight years.

'And God saw everything that he had made, and behold, it was very good.'

Until the day Theresa saw her mother toss a secret smile at her father. What were they keeping from her? Soon her mother's belly began swelling and she felt the stretching of the skin, the growing of the flesh, open an abyss between her and Ammachi. When she came home from school, Ammachi was no longer waiting at the gate. Instead, she lay on the bed with a strange expression. She was in some distant land where Theresa was not allowed to follow. She would snuggle into Ammachi's side and try to put an arm around her. 'Don't,' Ammachi said each time. 'You'll suffocate the baby.'

Theresa wanted to gouge out the baby's eyes. She knew that it had come between her and her parents the day Appa banished her from their bed.

'It's time you learnt to sleep alone,' her father said, rolling out a thin mattress for her in the next room. 'Your grandmother will be glad to have you with her,' he added.

Theresa wondered if the new baby had caused her father's brain to turn into scrambled eggs. Her grandmother hadn't moved or talked for the last two years.

And yet, somewhere in her, Theresa hoped everything would go back to the way it had been, once the new baby arrived. She hoped they wouldn't expect her to play with it or help feed and bathe it, or worse, clean its bum.

She had often accompanied her mother on visits to distant relatives with newborn babies. The baby was usually bathed and smothered in talc, its eyes outlined in kanmazhi and a black dot planted on its right cheek. But neither the talc nor the hastily lit incense sticks could camouflage the odour of urine and baby vomit. Theresa would feel her breakfast rush up her throat. Why did anyone want to have a baby? All they did was cry and shit.

She just didn't understand. And yet, she had been willing to give this usurper a chance. Perhaps, when it was born, she would learn to love it.

'Have you ever wondered what the devil looks like, Accho?' Theresa's whisper made Father George Koshy lean forward. What was she seeing in her head? He shuddered.

No one noticed Theresa slip into the room where her mother lay moaning and screaming. She blended into the shadowy room, keeping vigil for the moment when her mother would turn to her and say, 'Squash it for me!' Just like she did when a spider scuttled out of the kitchen. Then it happened. No one knew Theresa was in the room when the baby emerged from between her mother's legs with a howl and a scrunched-up face. Theresa had heard the Sunday school teacher describe the devil and so she was certain. This was the serpent.

'Kill it! Throw it away! Squash it,' Theresa had screamed and the midwife's eyes had turned on her in horror.

'What are you doing here?' she had roared, thrusting her out of the room and slamming the door in her face.

That baby is your sister, everyone said. You ought to be punished for talking about her the way you do. 'What an unnatural child you are,' an aunt said, pinching Theresa's arm.

'She is unnatural,' Theresa retorted. 'She is the devil! If only you had seen what she did to my mother,' she cried.

'You did the same. How do you think you were born?' Januamma, the midwife, laughed at Theresa, her betel-leaf-stained mouth widening into a toothless crackle. Theresa shuddered. For a moment, it reminded her of the redness between her mother's legs. She turned away in disgust. Nothing was going to make her change her mind. The baby was the devil. Always would be.

Theresa would look at the baby lying in the crook of her mother's elbow and wonder how something so small could be filled with so much evil. She could see that the creature was sucking her mother dry. Her father, too, looked gaunt and tired all day, as if the baby was gnawing on his liver with her tiny gummy jaws from across the room. Even her grandmother, who seemed mostly dead, sat up as if possessed and began walking. The next day, she was in the kitchen cooking something 'to fatten the mother and child'. The day after that, she was sweeping the yard. The devil moves in mysterious ways.

'They said the baby brought light into the house. Such is Lucifer, Accho. He knows how to masquerade as an angel of light. I wasn't taken in though.

'I hoped the baptism would change everything. And that the devil and its insidious spell on my parents and grandmother would wash itself out,' Theresa said.

On the evening after the baptism, Theresa waited for her mother to put the baby to bed on her grandmother's mattress. She moved the little pillow that was hers to her parents' bed.

Theresa saw her parents exchange glances. Her father kissed her forehead and said, 'That is so sweet of you, Theresa, but babies don't need pillows. At least, not what you use.'

Theresa said nothing and took her pillow back to her grandmother's room. She knew that she had lost her place. But she wasn't just going to stand there and let it happen. When the time was right, she would know what to do.

Then, one day, Theresa was asked to mind the baby while her mother was bathing. Her grandmother was taking a nap. The devil was in the cloth cradle strung from an old sari. 'You don't have to do anything,' Ammachi said. 'Just give the cradle an occasional tap so it rocks gently.'

Theresa gave the cradle a little push, just as she had been told. It moved slowly. She was rocking the devil asleep. She pushed again. The cradle moved. Through the cloth, she saw the limbs kick. The devil was asleep, but it still kicked. That's how devils are. Pretending to be asleep while worming their way into hearts.

Theresa gave the cradle a shove. It went almost as far as the wall and came back towards her. It swung a few times, back and forth, on its own and she knew what to do.

She shoved harder. The cradle swung towards the wall. She waited for the devil's head to smash against it. And that would be the end.

Ammachi walked in just at that moment and grabbed the cradle before it slammed into the wall. She drew the devil out of the cradle with trembling hands. Her face was pale. 'What was I thinking, asking you to watch the baby?' she said, pulling Theresa towards her in a hug. 'You are little more than a baby yourself.'

It was then Theresa realised that the devil was wily enough to triumph over death. It was then she gave up trying to exorcise her from her life.

'My mother named her Thomasina because she was born on Saint Thomas day. I was Theresa. And no one called me anything but Theresa. Not once was a *kutty* or a *mole* tagged to my name. But she? Thomasina is a mouthful of a name, my father said. And not so common. The children will tease her at school. So he took to calling her Molly.

'Darling daughter. Little precious Molly.' Theresa mimicked the terms of endearment.

Theresa would weep into her pillow, telling herself that her God-given name was enough. It was the devil who was known by several names. We know God only as God. But the devil, she was Abadon and Beelzebub; she was Lucifer and the old serpent; she was Satan and the tempter, a thief and a wicked one.

The devil was clever. After all, she had once disguised herself as the angel of light. She knew how to form sweet words and sway the world with a smile so gentle that you wanted her to never stop smiling. Only Theresa knew it was a disguise. Behind that innocent smile, all was black, all was evil. But who would believe her? As Theresa watched, she saw the devil trick her way into the hearts of everyone around them, everyone she loved. Her parents, her grandmother, her uncles, aunts, cousins and then, her husband.

'Father, I loved Anto. How I loved him. He would alleviate the loneliness in me, I thought. He was not rich. My father didn't want a rich man for me, he said. He wanted a man who would make his home with us. So Antony, who was a middle son, neither the oldest nor the youngest, was found. It's funny about middle sons, don't you think, Father? The eldest son inherits the father's business, the youngest son has all of his mother's love. The middle son has nothing. That's why I knew I would be everything for my Anto.' The woman's voice broke.

George Koshy felt his breath catch at the back of his throat. He knew what it was to be the middle child.

'Your husband?' he asked, unable to help himself.

'My father set up a bakery for him. Antony's family had owned a bakery too. All Antony had to do was run it, but he was so proud of his baking skills that he wanted to create the best cakes you could buy in Vadakanchery.

'My father was pleased. He will be able to manage the bakery better, he told everyone. No one will be able to cheat him.

'I heard my father tell Anto that I may be difficult to live with. But Anto, my kind husband, said, "She is like dough. Like dough for bread. She needs to be handled with care. That's all. Don't worry."

'I liked that, Father. I liked the idea of being the bread in his life. And soon there was a little bun.

'Did I embarrass you, Father?

'Never mind, I am sure you have heard worse. Where was I? My perfect little bun. They cut me open as if they were opening the oven, and drew out my Tito. There was no hysteria, no mess.

One perfect little bun – Tito, the Ti from Theresa and the To from Anto.

'Did I mention that Thomasina, also known as Molly, also known as Belial, was married off to Mathew? I was finally rid of her, I told myself.

'Then Mathew drove his jeep into a bulldozer and exploded like a watermelon flung on the ground. He was drunk, they said. Thomasina came home.

'"I don't like it," I told Anto when we were alone.

'"But why? Where else will she go? She's harmless, Theresa. Stop it now. You are not little girls any more, to be squabbling. Have some pity! She's a widow," he said, pulling his T-shirt over his head and cutting all further conversation off.

'How it rasped. The slither of the cloth over his chest hair. Or was it the slithering of the serpent? The sound of her straying into our Garden of Eden. Bitch. Whore. Devil's spawn.

'No, don't even think it, Father. If I was a suspicious woman, wouldn't I have accused my husband long before? Wouldn't I have doubted his fidelity and questioned his troth to me? Anto loved me, I knew. I was the golden loaf. The bread of his life.

'Do you know how I realised something had changed? I would wait for Anto to come home. I hovered around him, waiting for him to pull his T-shirt over his head. He wore a white half-sleeve collared T-shirt every day. And a full-sleeve white shirt to the church on Sundays. I liked to rest my cheek against his chest. I liked to sniff deep of his fragrance. There is nothing more heavenly than a baker's sweat: vanilla and cinnamon, the chalkiness of flour, the richness of eggs and fat, salt and sweet, eggs and candied fruit and, through it all, the sourness of yeast. One day, I couldn't stop myself from rubbing my nose in his chest hair. He sprang back at my touch and murmured, "What are you doing?"

She did nothing specific to catch his attention, Theresa thought. It had since occurred to her that this was the wiliest of feminine wiles. The best thing to do to intrigue a man was to be indifferent to him. She felt bile rush up to her mouth as she remembered the moment when she caught his eyes following Thomasina as she stood on a stool with a broom, trying to sweep away the cobwebs. As she stretched, the stool wobbled, and Anto rushed to steady it. She saw Thomasina and Anto exchange a secret smile even as their eyes met.

Theresa knew where she had seen that look before. In Tito's eyes, when the bakery had prepared a particularly fancy cake. A special order. The leap of greed, a hard-to-bear temptation, the despair of knowing it wasn't for him. The imagined taste, the sweetness, the richness, oh, for a bite, even just a bite would suffice if he couldn't have the whole thing.

That's when Theresa realised that if she was Anto's bread, Thomasina was his prize cake.

Theresa took a deep breath. The weighed down silence told her what the priest must be thinking.

'Father, do you feel sorry for me? No, don't, Father. I stopped loving him the moment I saw his eyes light up at the sight of her. When you don't love someone, how can they hurt you?

'Do you know what happens when you put a man and a cake together? Crumbs. That's what you get. Anto, master baker, silly fool, never understood that.

'"What are you talking about, Chechi?" She turned on me when I confronted her. "You are mad. You need help… do you realise what you are saying?"

'I saw her eyes dart away and turned to see who was there. I saw the look in my Anto's eyes as he stood there, listening to us. The disgust with which he might have looked at a mouldy loaf which was imperfect to begin with. How could I bear it? If he wanted her so much, he could keep her…

'So I shut my eyes that day, and all was blank and all was fine. I didn't need to see how, when Tito said something funny, it was Thomasina he looked at before they burst into laughter. I wouldn't have to see how, when he sat with the accounts, it was to her he turned for help. Molly, tally this up for me, will you? Molly, check these bills. I can't seem to get it right. Molly this. Molly that...

'If I could see, I would have had to witness the eighty-six thousand four hundred ways in which the two of them deceived me, day after day, right in front of my eyes.

'So I never allowed myself to see again. The doctors call it hysterical blindness. Do I seem like a hysterical woman to you, Father?

'I did not hate her any more than I did before. How can there be degrees to an emotion as absolute as hate?

'Father, he died a year ago. It was a heart attack.'

Theresa knew precisely what had happened.

Sometimes an order for a fancy cake would be cancelled and Anto would bring the cake home. Tito would cut himself a great big piece but soon his face would crumple with disappointment when he realised it was the same cake merely tarted up. But he would still eat most of it and then be ill the next day.

Anto was the same. Perhaps the experience of bedding her didn't live up to his expectations. Perhaps all that guilty pleasure clogged his arteries. Perhaps he just couldn't handle it. Who knows? Who cares?

Theresa felt a smile grow from the depth of her belly. A smile that pushed its way up like the magic bean in the fairy tale. Higher and higher, till it blossomed on her lips. Purple flowers of malice.

She cleared her throat.

'God moves in mysterious ways, Father. All my life she tormented me. Now I am her tormentor.

'Do you think it's torture only when you pluck someone's fingernails out or rub chilli powder into their orifices? There are a countless ways to torture someone without actually inflicting bodily harm. And I realised that I have quite a knack for it.

'Once, I left an unniappam under the pillow in her bed. The ants bit almost every part of her. Tito got walloped that day for eating in bed. It was time he got a good beating anyway. The boy has no manners. Besides, you know what our scriptures say: suffer ye little children so you may come unto me.

'Another time, I took her good sari, which was hanging on the washing line, and gave it away to a woman who came begging. When Thomasina raised a ruckus, I told her that one of those wandering beggars must have stolen it. They would have too, if they had seen it. Everyone knows they are thieves and will take anything they find.

'Once, after I helped myself to the kanji we have for dinner every night, I dropped half a bottle of salt into what was left in the vessel. I am a blind woman. Such accidents are bound to happen. I thought it was time she tasted some of the salt from all the tears she had made me shed.

'I could give you the entire list, but we may have to stay here all evening. So let me make it brief by telling you that since she chose to make her home with me, she's been chained to my side. And I measure out my torture to her so she never knows when it will strike or what she will be called upon to do next.

'Father, this month I decided that she has to take me to all the seven and a half churches that St Thomas put up here.

'Which is why I am here, in Tiruvithamkode. In the half church.

'So tell me, Father, have I sinned? I cannot possibly wait for God to punish her. Nor is it fair to God, He has so much else to do. So I spoke to Him about it every day, every night, and I knew He wanted me to do it. If I am doing it with God's concurrence, how can you term it a real sin? At the most, you can call it half a sin… right?'

George Koshy sat up. If the starch in the white cassock had chaffed his elbows and the insides of his arms earlier, it was nothing compared to the discomfort and the sweat running down his face and along his neck now. The woman was not just blind, she was also deranged. Why would she think she was in Tiruvithamkode in Tamil Nadu when they were right here in Shoranur? Thrissur was what, twenty-two kilometres from Shoranur? And how did one offer absolution to a confused woman?

He closed his eyes to steady the thoughts that were squawking and rushing around in his head like frightened hens. He cleared his throat again in preparation to speak.

But when he opened his eyes, he saw that she had already risen to her feet and was being led away by the younger woman. It seemed to him that she had merely needed to confess. The act of contrition meant nothing to her. The priest felt uneasy. What should he do in such circumstances?

Father George Koshy was about to return to the antechamber to take off his vestments when another voice, softer but firmer, spoke. It was the sister. Her eyes were closed and her face was rigid as a mask. It was the face of an adulteress, a shameless, brazen hussy, who had no qualms about stealing her sister's husband. A wave of dislike washed over him. Sometimes he wondered if confession allowed people to get away with committing sins. Confess. Atone. Sin again.

He mopped his brow with a starched handkerchief.

Molly knelt facing him. She seemed to be holding something in her hand.

Molly had long given up believing in a god who watched out for his children, but religion gave her a sense of belonging. It was the first law of survival. As long as she did what everyone else did, she wouldn't be conspicuous and the others wouldn't turn on her. And yet, something about this church made her want to rest her forehead against its walls and weep.

It had been a long time since she wept or leaned into someone who could offer her solace and support. Would her heart feel any less heavy, any less lonely, if she could speak her thoughts?

'Forgive me, Father, for I have sinned. It's been several months since I went to confession.

'Ever since my husband died, my life is not what it used to be. I am so busy trying to manage, trying to keep my head above water, that I cannot even remember what day of the week it is.'

George Koshy felt an ache creep up from the nape of his neck.

Molly paused and resumed again:

'I do not want to know the passage of time. Without Anto, every day seems the same. He was the kindest man on earth, I often thought. And so patient. Which other man would endure his wife's widowed sister, as he did? A sister who spewed venom all day. A sister who behaved as if he was her servant. Anto put up with a great deal... my poor Anto.'

Molly heard movements in front of her. She kept her eyes tightly shut. A befuddled voice demanded, the words tumbling out, 'Anto was your husband? Is that what you said?'

'Antony Ebenezer Marrikal was my husband,' Molly said. She sighed. 'He made me want to be good.'

There was a time when Molly thought she had exhausted all the goodness she had been born with. Theresa had ensured that. She had walked on eggshells around her sister for as long as she could remember. When Molly got the extra piece of cake, or came home from school with a prize for winning a quiz competition, or when a relative complimented her, or when she insisted on watching a film that Theresa didn't want to go to, her sister would have fainting spells. They came on when she was hurt, angry, vexed.

'Theresa is sensitive,' her father said. 'We have to be strong for her,' her mother added.

'What she needs is a tight slap,' her grandmother said. Molly was inclined to agree with her. But who listens to the old and the very young?

So Theresa tyrannised their lives with her fainting spells. When she recovered from a faint, it was like the hush after an October thunderstorm.

On the day after Theresa's wedding, Molly lay in bed, stretching her toes. She crossed her arms over her face and thought, I don't have to wear a mask any more. I can stop being afraid.

But she had grown into the mask. She was too used to tiptoeing through the corridors of life, containing all emotion so nothing would show. It had turned her into a withdrawn child and later, a quiet woman. She sought solace in the thought that with reticence there would be no pain, no voice in her head demanding, 'But what did I do wrong?'

Until Anto appeared in her life and ripped the mask off.

'Which is why, when Molly was widowed a few years after my marriage, I didn't protest about her coming to live with us. I wasn't very happy at the thought of sharing our home, but I felt I ought to live up to some of Anto's goodness at least. So I made her welcome.

'There was a woman in the car with Mathew when the accident occurred. She was his mistress, it was discovered. He drove into a parked bulldozer. He had been drunk. Any woman would be devastated to be widowed a mere six years after her marriage. Imagine her plight, on discovering that she had been betrayed as well.

'As long as our parents were alive, there was some semblance of normalcy, but when they died… my sister went blind. That was the beginning of the nightmare. Sometimes I wonder if I will ever escape it.

'Anto didn't protest or even raise an eyebrow at my sister coming to stay with us. He did his best to include her in everything we did. Eleven years is all my Anto and I got together. Eleven short years, Father, and not once did he utter a word of reproach at what my sister put him through.'

When Anto died, the bakery had to be sold. No one seemed to want the cakes and breads they made; children didn't flock to them any more for buns or puffs. They were too old-fashioned, the bakery goods too familiar.

Molly sold it for what she could get, which wasn't much. She asked around and a few homes started placing orders for the dishes she excelled at – palappam, vateappam and idiappam. Soon she was supplying her dishes to a few shops as well. It was this that fed them now.

'But my sister wouldn't accept that we no longer had even the little money we used to have.

'Every day she clamours for one thing or the other. I find it impossible to satisfy her. If I refuse any of her demands, she takes ill and has a fainting fit. When she recovers from that, there's the loud weeping. It frightens Tito to see her behave so. It frightens me too, I confess. So I give in. I always have.

'But I have to be resourceful to meet her demands.' Molly paused. This was a priest after all. What would he think? What would he say?

He didn't seem to have anything to say, so Molly continued, 'This month my sister demanded I take her to the seven and half churches. I knew I could take her to Maliankara and Palayoor, Kottakavu and Kokkamangalam, but I couldn't afford to take her all the way to the others, especially to Nagercoil in Tamil Nadu. So I took her around all day in the local transport buses, claiming we were on our way to Tiruvithamkode.

'My friend's brother works as a driver at the resort by the river. He is letting us use his room while we stay here. I don't want to disappoint her. She has already had so much to bear in life. The death of her husband. Her own blindness. All she has now is me.

'I wait for you, Father, to tell me what should be my act of contrition. A little voice inside me keeps saying: But is it really a sin when one deceives to only make someone happy? Or would that make it half a sin, Father?

'But does the church recognise sin by fractions? Or is it an absolute?'

George Koshy looked down into the face that was raised to his. He saw the eager eyes of a child who saw so much more in a rainbow than the mere refraction of light.

'Would you know, Father, would you?' the child asked.

# 4

# URVASHI

The first length had helped shut out all thought as she gauged the pool depth and sides, synchronizing the movement of her limbs and breath, but soon her mind had prised itself free and she chose to shepherd it towards Brinda Patil. She swam up and down the length of the pool as she dwelt on the girl. She had made news headlines but Brinda had never explained what led to her decision. The journalist in Urvashi saw the potential for an exclusive. When she began to tire, she stepped out of the pool and picked up the towel to dry herself, still wondering how to approach Brinda. When the phone rang, she answered it without glancing at the number.

'So you think you can run away and I won't find you?' The menace in his voice was unmistakable. 'You think I am just going to let you go?'

She held the phone to her ear, blindsided, frozen with fear. Unable to disconnect the call, unable to stop listening, as he took everything she had confided in him – past loves and present anxieties, childish fancies and adult fears, everything they had done together that had once lit up their days, and turned them into poisonous barbs. The heavy treacle voice that had once caused her entire body to turn into an erogenous zone now made her shrivel up with disgust.

'You slut... who are you fucking now?' he shouted as she cut the call and switched the phone off.

She stood under the shower, hoping the water would still the voice that continued to ring in her head. She opened the little bottle of shower gel and tipped some into her palm. The fragrance of aloe vera filled the bathroom. She soaped herself, gazing through the skylight, up at the sky dense with rain clouds. Neither the setting sun nor the rising moon would penetrate the grey. It would have to rain itself out. That was what she had told herself about him ever since she decided to end the affair. That he would tire of stalking her, hurling abuse at her, threatening her, making her life hell.

In a strange way, she understood what shaped his almost savage intensity. She knew what it was like to be twisted by sexual jealousy, racked by the need to possess. She knew what it felt like to be placed very firmly on the perimeter of a marriage, always looking in without knowing how to be a part of it.

A day short of her thirty-second birthday, she had stood outside Xavier's salon. Through the glass doors, she saw the corners of his mouth droop and his lips purse when he spotted her.

'Hello, hello...' she said, anxiety overriding her usual reticence. 'I know I don't have an appointment. I know you must be terribly busy, but can you fit me in somehow? It's an emergency.'

She hoped he saw the plea in her eyes. If she had been a less sophisticated woman, she would have wrung her hands and allowed a plaintive note to enter her voice. But Urvashi wasn't going to let him see her desperation.

For a while now, she had been haunted by the thought that Raghu was tiring of her. Perhaps it was all in her head; nonetheless, the feeling persisted. So, when he mailed her saying that he would drop in on his way home from the airport or first thing in the morning, on his way to work, to help celebrate her special day, she had wanted to make sure nothing could go wrong. She would be the Urvashi he wanted her to be. The one he seemed to have missed. It filled her with an indescribable happiness that he wanted to be with her to bring in her birthday.

Xavier stretched his lips in a parody of a smile. 'Yes, of course, Urvashi. Just give me a few minutes to sort things out and find you a place. What would you like us to do for you this afternoon?'

'Everything. Hair, nails, facial. Raghu's coming back this evening, you see. He has been away for three weeks in the US. And it's my birthday tomorrow. I want to look good. He's so particular…' Her words trailed off defiantly. She didn't care what Xavier thought, she just wanted to look her best when Raghu and she met that evening, or the next morning. That was the thing about being a mistress. Like a doctor or a firefighter or a Boy Scout, you had to always be prepared.

Xavier looked at her, twisting the meditation ring on his thumb. She didn't understand his consternation. Only later would she find out about Asha, who had walked in precisely half an hour earlier.

Asha usually had very little done. A hair trim and root touch-up once a month; an occasional manicure and pedicure; the golden glow facial every third week. And never at the same time. Xavier had once told Urvashi that he sometimes wondered if she came to Trespass because she was lonely. Sometimes he thought it was just so she could feel somebody else's fingers ply her skin with the intent to please. He had hoped today would be one of those times. Eyebrows and upper lip to be threaded, or a change of nail polish. In and out in thirty minutes.

But Asha had wanted everything: hair, nails, face. She wished to pretty herself because he was coming back this evening and you know… Her words had trailed away, almost as if she was ashamed of this need to doll herself up for a husband of many years.

Xavier settled Urvashi on a sofa that overlooked the door rather than the innards of Trespass, gave her a magazine in which Asha and Raghunath were featured in the party pages.

For the last four months, ever since Xavier learned about the affair, he had made sure that Urvashi and Asha never ran into each other. At least, not in the precincts of his salon.

Urvashi knew Asha existed. But Urvashi was merely a niggling blimp on Asha's radar. Either way, God knows what would transpire if the two women were to meet. Xavier whispered a quick Hail Mary under his breath at the very thought. And then his mobile rang. Xavier looked at the screen and smiled. He walked to the balcony at the further end of the salon and murmured, 'Gina darling, you won't believe this. But something really bizarre has happened.'

Most of his clients thought Xavier was gay. It was what they expected a hairstylist to be. And Xavier fed into that stereotype.

Urvashi and he often laughed about it. That slightly camp note he affected, his rings and bling, and his cunning sense of colour.

Urvashi had met Gina, his girlfriend, and heard many stories about their lives together. Xavier was – a tiger in bed, a rooster in the yard and a pussycat with his clients. It excited her, Gina said. Like being with three men at the same time. You never knew which part of him would emerge. As she prattled on, Xavier had touched her hand with an affectionate reproof to say, shut up.

Urvashi had noticed that despite how he felt about her, Xavier kept Gina a quiet part of his life. As he said, one does what one has to do to keep going, including pretending to be gay.

Urvashi looked up from the magazine to see Tina, the new girl, beaming at her. 'Please come, madam.'

She led Urvashi to the only vacant chair. It was adjacent to Asha's. Urvashi felt like she was coming down a rollercoaster. The earth swung up to meet her. Hot air whistled through her ears and the cereal she'd had for breakfast rose to her throat, threatening to spray out.

She had thought it through in her head several times over. What she would do if she ever ran into the wife. She had told herself that she would be calm and collected. She had done nothing to lure him. He had sought her out. And he wouldn't have if the wife made him happy. It was quite obvious that she cared nothing for him at all.

She questioned Raghu relentlessly about her in the first few days. 'Sometimes I wonder if you are more interested in her than in me,' Raghu jokingly complained after yet another third-degree.

'I want to make sure that I am nothing like her,' Urvashi said.

'That you aren't, baby… and never will be!' he said, cupping the curve of her buttocks and pulling her close to him. 'By the way, just don't go to that salon she goes to, wherever else you may go. Trespass. That's the name. That's where she goes.' He rolled his eyes at her.

Out of sheer perversity, she had, and very quickly become good friends with Xavier, Gina and the girls.

Urvashi shrunk into her chair, even though Asha had her eyes shut. She was getting an under-eye treatment.

'What's that perfume?'

Urvashi almost leapt out of her chair. Tina had just draped a towel around her. 'Let's start with a head massage,' Xavier said, rushing towards her. She could see he was wondering how to avert what seemed like a certain Titanic moment.

The voice said again, 'Hello, I am in the chair next to yours. The perfume you are wearing is lovely…'

Raghu had given it to her. But there was a condition. Urvashi was not to wear it when they were together.

'She has a nose like a bloodhound. She'd sniff it immediately.

Wear it when I am not with you.' And it will be like wearing me on your skin, his eyes implied as his fingers caressed her.

'Yes, bubba.' She smiled to show she bore no rancour over what was being asked of her. He reached across and touched the tip of her nose.

She, a young political journalist, who eviscerated her subjects with the beady eyes and predatory claws of a carrion bird became an obedient child, just like that.

She knew it would begin all over again that evening. Perhaps it was the thought of that conflagration of fierce lust, the appeasement of that insatiable hunger to hold and hold and never let go, that had her offer in a skittish voice, 'Classique by Jean Paul Gaultier.'

And then, because her eyes were pressed tight against the world and there was no face to that soft voice, she added belligerently, 'My lover gave it to me. I am to wear it only when he's away, he said. He doesn't want his wife smelling a new perfume on him.'

Who gasped? The owner of the voice, Xavier, or someone else at the salon? Urvashi didn't care.

'What is it like, to be a mistress?' the voice asked after a pause.

Xavier held his breath. His hands stilled as they massaged Asha's scalp. Would she take the cotton pads off to look at this brazen woman? Thank God he had lathered bleach on Urvashi's face and slapped cucumber slices on her eyes. And then it occurred to him that Raghu was a strange kettle of fish indeed. What man would choose a mistress who, in some ways, was a youthful version of his wife? He thought of his ex, Anu, ribs, nipples and hard edges, so different from Gina, who was all buns and bounce.

Urvashi didn't speak. In that brightly lit salon where the mirrors magnified every spot and line, there was no fleeing the truth.

She thought of all the terms and conditions he had laid down. No calling. No texting. A missed call was permissible in an emergency. She thought of how she had learnt to anoint her skin with baby oil, shower in tepid water and pat herself dry so she glowed without any giveaway scent. She thought of the diet and exercise regimen she followed so she was all muscle and shine. She thought of all the reading she did to be able to spice up their conversation hour…

'It's hard work,' she said quietly. 'You see, I have to be everything his wife is not. Sexy. Interesting. Reckless. Wanton. Tender. I have to work at what I wear, what I say, how I eat. I can't ever take my problems to him. He gets enough of that from his wife. There are days when I want to curl up in front of the TV in an old nightie with noodles in a cup and that's the evening he wants to come over. And I have to transform into sex kitten and seductress. I bet you think mistresses just paint their nails.'

'You sound tired,' the voice said. 'If you dislike it so much, why do you allow yourself to be in such a relationship? Let him go.'

Urvashi heard the wisdom in the words. But if he went, what then? She had never met anyone who got her the way he did. He made her feel it was all right to be who she was, with all her flaws. He seemed to understand what made her tick. Was this love? Then how could she let him go?

Asha adjusted her head to fit into the dip of the washbowl as Xavier ran the warm water. It seemed he had decided to do everything for her himself this afternoon.

She had enjoyed the head massage. It had settled her into a curious state where she feared nothing. She couldn't still believe what she had asked the woman in the next chair.

As Xavier worked the hair mask in, Asha asked, 'Why did you call your salon Trespass, Xavier?'

Urvashi bit her lip, wondering where this was headed.

Asha continued, without waiting for a response, 'About two years ago, my husband trespassed. I knew something was not right. There was a lilt to his voice and a lift to his step. I lived with that for a couple of months. Then I intercepted a text message. A couple we knew had dropped in without notice. Raghu had left his phone on the dining table when he went across to the bar counter to fix them a drink. The phone lit up with a message: Coast clear?

'It was from a woman I knew. They had even met a few times at our children's birthday parties.

'I was very adult like. I let Raghu see I was devastated. But I didn't ask him to leave or demand to dissolve the marriage into a discussion on who kept the Turkish carpet and who kept the children. Raghu didn't seem to want change either, for he was almost relieved that he had been discovered. He was effusive in his apologies and, in his efforts to make up, he made it a second honeymoon for us.

'I allowed myself to be wooed and cajoled into accepting his trespass for what it was – a momentary lapse of reason. A turning of the head by peculiar circumstances.'

Asha paused, then continued as though unable to stop herself, 'One drunken evening I flung at him, "How could you? She's older than me and looks like a wizened little monkey. What did she give you that I didn't?"

'He didn't answer at first. Then he said that he had known her from another time. "We didn't really mean to. She was unhappy in her marriage and I comforted her and something flared up between us," he told me. He said he liked that she needed him.

'"I'll never mention this again, but if there is ever another time, Raghu, we are over," I said.'

Urvashi closed her eyes. What perversity of fate had made this situation possible? It was the stuff of which sit-coms and comic skits were made. This wasn't how it happened in real life.

An affair with a married man could go two ways: he either left his wife for you or left you to go back to his wife. Was she to spend the rest of her life wondering which one it would be? And whether she would become a bitter, faded creature spitting toads at the mere mention of the word love. For, even if he left his wife for her, how could she know for sure that he wouldn't do unto her what he had done to his wife?

Asha wouldn't stop talking. 'I had to live with the phantom of the other woman in my life. Some days, the bloody unfairness of it made me want to weep. It seemed to me that Raghu and she had managed to get a grip on their lives and move on. Only I was still stuck in that landscape. I began to see myself as an outcrop of dangerous rocks – a coast that had to be skirted around and navigated with care.

'There was also that gnawing fear. Would he do it again? He would, of course, be twice as careful the next time.'

Urvashi blanched. Any moment now, Asha would turn to her and demand, 'Do you know what you could be doing to the wife? Did you ever think about how she'll feel when she finds out? For she will, you know.'

'Urvashi, where are you going? Tina is not done with washing your hair yet.' Xavier's reproof halted her.

'Sorry,' she said in a small voice. 'I thought she had finished.'

'Just a few more minutes,' Xavier said, his eyes darting anxiously around the salon.

Later, as she lay in her cubicle while a girl massaged her back, Urvashi felt the knots in her body expand and release one by one.

God knows who it was that said confession makes the heart lighter. She felt as if someone had been at her with a gutting knife. All the inner darkness lay before her, exposed.

Yet, the thought of life without Raghu made her feel bereft; desolate, even. She may only be his mistress but he gave her a framework; a structure to locate herself within.

She thought of the woman she had turned into. Putting her life on hold, waiting for him to call or come over to her flat. Planning holidays that never materialised for there was something happening at work or his wife needed him to be home. What every other couple took for granted would never be hers: a walk down the road, a meal at a favourite restaurant, a tub of popcorn shared at a movie, buying groceries, shopping together for their home… All that she had was intimacy and a whispered memorandum of understanding that would have no validity in any court of law. And she didn't aspire for more. She was afraid to. She didn't want to lose him by asking him for more than he was willing to offer. How could she value herself so little?

Then there was the other toll that was exacted from her. The relentless insecurity of wondering if one day she would be replaced, just as the other woman had been. The one his wife had mentioned. She had known right from the beginning that he'd had other women before her. He had been too practised in the terms of their engagement. But she had never perceived a threat until now.

Who had he been with in the last three weeks? Who was he with when he was not with her or his wife? She would never know, for he had made it amply clear that she was not to contact him even if her house was burning down. 'What if I am dying?' she had asked once. 'You can't die on a Sunday or public holidays,' he had laughed. She had laughed as well.

She almost doubled over in pain as a cramp seized her stomach. What had she allowed herself to become?

She raised her head and asked for some water. She took a few sips and lay back, feeling a lot calmer. 'Would you fetch my bag?' she asked the girl.

Urvashi groped within her bag. She felt the hard edge of a coin and the curve of a tube of lip balm. She found the perfume under a scarf that lay tangled with a hairband and old bills. She took out the bottle. 'Please take this perfume to the lady I was sitting next to. Her name is Asha,' she said, thrusting it into Tina's hands.

'Tell her that the woman who sat next to her wants her to have it because she liked it so much.'

The part of her that yearned for Raghu coiled into a hard little pangolin ball. She felt a laugh gather in her as she thought of Asha greeting Raghu smelling of her. Of Asha telling Raghu about meeting a woman called Urvashi, whose lover had given her the perfume. Of Raghu reeling with shock as much as fear, wondering if his wife suspected him of straying again. She knew how it would all end. But she didn't wait to find out.

That evening, she went to stay with a friend. The next day, she started looking for a job in Bangalore. It was time to start life anew.

She had dealt with ugliness of her own making before. She would have to do it again, Urvashi told herself, as she put on a caftan. She switched on the TV. It was a quarter to seven. She would call for room service and go to bed early. In the morning, she would figure out what to do.

As usual, when chaos reigned in her head, she switched her thoughts to work; to the exclusive she could wrangle if Brinda Patil would speak to her.

# Sreelakshmi

The sisters, with their concept of sin split into fractions, took me back with them. Theresa had thrust me into Molly's hand as she finished her confession.

'What is this?' Molly had asked. Theresa stared at her unseeingly.

'Where did you find it, Chechi?'

Theresa shrugged.

What would they do with me now? The women crossed the road and I with them. They walked towards the staff quarters by the gate.

I did not recognise this world I had come back to. The roads were bustling with people and vehicles – cars such as I had never seen, buses, trucks, and so many variations of the motorcycle. The bicycle seemed almost extinct. How did people live, breathing this air filled with fumes? What made them hasten this way and that? The roads were lined with shops. Mostly restaurants and bakeries – didn't people in Kerala cook at home any more? Had it become like ancient Rome, where it was forbidden to light a fire in your home?

That was the other thing. People. In the last five decades, had they done nothing but procreate? Did they have sex only to make babies?

So many people, and all of them talking to themselves. I saw an elderly man waiting to cross the road. He was talking to himself. I saw a young woman do the same. I looked at them, not knowing whether to marvel or be appalled. Were they so caught up in their lives that no one had the time to listen to another person? Until I realised that there was a device in their hands or in their pockets and that they were talking into it. A phone to carry around? When was it invented? What else had changed while I was away?

I watched a young man sitting on his motorcycle outside the gate. I saw him raise the device and look at it at an angle. I peered over his shoulder as he touched the screen and his image appeared on it. I gasped. The phone was also a camera. I watched the boy touch what looked like typewriter keys on the frame. Words appeared in Malayalam. Send me yours, it read. He was sending the photograph and words to someone.

This new world defied description. How would our lives, Markose's and mine, have turned out if we had met when there were such gadgets to bridge distances?

Molly placed me on the table and went away. I continued to sit there, dreaming of the past and what might lie ahead. Many hours later, when everyone had fallen asleep and only the garden lights gleamed like multiple moons, I drew every vestige of strength from that tiny piece of bone I was trapped in and wafted through the night, through the garden. I paused to drink in the scent of the blossoms. I perched on the branch of an old mango tree with a night jar and caressed its throat so the notes emerged in a shivery trail of calls. I weaved circles of neon with fireflies and held up knives for the cicadas to sharpen. I hovered over the river I had played in once and watched the breeze furrow ripples. I was as restless as a ghost can be.

The sisters had awakened thoughts of my own sisters, whose lives I had once scoffed at. I thought of them as fussy little housewives who had chosen to bury themselves even while they breathed.

Both my older sisters had been married at sixteen. They had wanted to be married. They wanted a husband, a pressure cooker, curtains in the windows and doors, Sunday outings, and two children each. But I had never been a domestic sort of person. I didn't want marriage or children, or a pressure cooker.

Over the years, I had scoffed at the marriage proposals brought by my relatives. At first I had used the excuse of my master's degree and how I couldn't think of anything until I was done with it. My father had helped by pointing out that he hadn't spent all this money sending me to a world-famous university to have me wash dirty dishes, even if it was a pressure cooker in a kitchen somewhere.

When my father died, and I started as a tutor at a college in Pandalam, where I boarded with a distant relative, I suggested they wait until my position was confirmed. I could see that my mother was already in despair, certain that I would turn into a long-in-the-tooth spinster. She continued to send me details of unsuitable men.

They came in all shapes and sizes; professions and degrees of wealth. But they were all Nairs and from respectable families. They were all moderately light-skinned, with thick black hair and thin pencil-line moustaches, and looked perfectly capable of bedding me and husbanding me through life. All I had to do was say yes to galvanise them into action. I would never again want for anything but air in my lungs.

I found a reason to say no to each one of them. Eventually the pleasant-looking, well-heeled young men were replaced by tired-looking men with receding hairlines, slack of jaw and the sure knowledge that life would pass them by if they didn't do something about it. Having gone past the sell-by date, there were no more young men available for me. Should I have said yes to the stationmaster who had waited for his younger sisters to be married off? Should I have taken the widowed lawyer for a husband? Should I have agreed to be a wife to the divorced middle-aged doctor? It would have at least made it easier for my mother to answer all the questions about her youngest daughter's womanly status: Married, fecund, and settled for life with a pressure cooker of her own.

Once I was awarded the Kerala Sahitya Akademi award, however, I became a literary figure and with that, the marriage proposals dried up for good. As for my mother, it was as if I had suddenly become an asexual being. My world would no longer include the pressure cooker she had bought and kept aside for me.

I wept as I drifted through the night, not knowing where I was going, until I came to the western wall that separated the land from the river. I perched upon it and asked myself again: what did I do wrong?

In the morning, Molly carried me to the room where the deranged older one had first picked me up. She knocked on the door that wasn't fully shut. She waited for a few minutes, then sneaked in and left me on the table.

A little later, Najma walked in. She came straight to the table, picked me up, and put me in the pocket of her apron.

As she stood on the porch outside Urvashi's cottage, a voice hailed her. 'Hey Najma!'

Najma turned. It was the girl from Cottage 6.

'Hello, madam. Have you seen the lady who is staying here?' Najma asked.

The girl shook her head. 'No, but I can look for her…'

Najma glanced at her wrist watch. They were running a little late with the housekeeping roster and she couldn't stay here any longer. 'Would you give this to her when you see her? She may be in the restaurant or the poolside. Just tell her that it was in the pocket of the kurta I took with me for the laundry service.'

'Cool. Will do!' The girl smiled.

'Are you sure you don't mind?' Najma said, wondering if asking a guest to do an errand would get her into trouble.

'Don't be silly,' the girl said, taking me from Najma's hand and thrusting me into the pocket of her shorts.

The girl walked through the restaurant and wandered to the poolside. She stood gazing at the pool for a while and then she slipped out of her shorts and T-shirt. She was wearing a swimsuit beneath it. Slowly she slid into the pool and swam towards a man and a buxom teenager – her father and sister, I presumed.

We watched them, the woman seated on a reclining chair and I on the table.

I didn't need to look any further than this tableaux to know that the world had indeed changed. Once, women went to the pool to bathe and frolic. Men stayed away, and no father would swim with his daughters.

The older girl splashed the younger one. She dived into the water and dunked her father. She turned somersaults like a young river dolphin for the sheer happiness of being alive.

Then she called out, 'Amma, please order some pakodas and cold coffee with two scoops of butterscotch ice cream for me. I am starving.'

She emerged from the pool and picked up a towel to rub herself dry. Her body was toned and muscular, like an athlete's. She collected her clothes and walked towards a hammock. She drew me out of the shorts pocket and held me in her hands. As she hoisted herself into the hammock, I caught the look in her eyes, the serenity of a much older person. Of someone who has come to terms with life and what it may or may not offer her. But there was also uncertainty. A child's doubt, the sort that makes her wonder, just for a moment, if the answer to 12 x 9 is the same as that to 9 x 12.

# The Killer Instinct

They are all there. They sit in the front row, her parents and her sister, Ankita. She likes them to be there in those precise seats at every important match.

When she plays an important match in India, she always asks for a prime seat for Roy Uncle, as she calls him. Her father's best friend and their neighbour. The one who started it all.

On the sidelines is her coach and trainer. Brinda meets his eyes for a moment. She gives him the briefest of nods in acknowledgement.

Someone in the green room had mentioned that it was a fine day. But Brinda doesn't like to waste energy thinking about what the day is like.

'Is it windy?' she had asked. A badminton court is an enclosed space and even a mild draught can make the ball swerve. In her more fanciful moments, she thinks of it as the breath of providence, a blessing for whoever is in favour with the court god at that point.

So here she is, on a fine afternoon in August, feeling the spring of the wooden floor beneath the green spread. Gradually the butterflies and rhinos jostling in the pit of her stomach settle into slumber. She takes a deep breath and exhales slowly. She is home again.

The first time Brinda stepped on the cement floor of the badminton court at the club house, it felt like this was where she belonged.

'Baby, go sit on the bench and wait for me,' her father said as he came onto the court, swinging his badminton racquet.

'Why can't I play?' Brinda asked in a voice that surprised even her. Rajesh stared at his six-year-old daughter standing with her hands on her hips, legs akimbo, all belligerence and determination, and heard the earworm for the first time. *Hello, Mr Patil, what do we have here?*

'Tomorrow,' he said carefully. 'I have to kit you out first.'

He had felt her study his face to see if he was bluffing. And the earworm sang: *I told you, I told you. Hey, Mr Patil, there's no going back now.*

She crouched on the sidelines and ran to pick up the shuttlecock as soon as it landed outside the court. 'You should get her a racquet if she's so keen,' his partner Roy said, watching Brinda dart about.

A tinge of envy coated his words. One hopes to see genius in one's child. It makes the thought of your own mediocrity bearable if you know your child will find fame and fortune. He wasn't greedy. A flash of brilliance would have sufficed. But his son didn't seem particularly interested in anything.

Rajesh shrugged. *You just don't want to accept that this is more than a passing fad for her,* the earworm yodelled.

The next day, he took her to the sports shop and they chose a pair of shoes and a racquet.

'What about this?' Rajesh teased, dangling a yellow headband.

'Don't be silly,' she said sternly, as if she was being offered a doll with a pink bow.

Rajesh ruffled Brinda's hair. 'I wasn't being silly. You don't want your hair covering your eyes. Everything can become a distraction on the court. And that becomes a point lost or an advantage not taken.'

Brinda adjusts the yellow hairband. Her hair is caught in a tight fishtail braid but she doesn't feel complete till she knows the constricting pressure of the yellow band across her temples. Forget everything else, she admonishes herself. Focus. Focus. Focus. There's just you and your shadow across from you.

The earworm, now resident in Brinda's middle ear, murmurs with the strident tone of her coach: *Play her like you would play yourself.*

Brinda wins the toss. She always does. Destiny, wearing little angel wings, flutters the air around the coin so it always falls the way Brinda calls. She smiles and chooses her preferred side. That way, if the game moves to three sets, she will have the court aiding her.

The Indonesian is seeded four in the world rankings and Brinda is at nine, but here they are. In the semi-finals of the world championship. Winning this one would automatically escalate Brinda's ranking to top five in the minds of her adversaries, if not in the BWF rankings.

The Indonesian serves. Brinda returns. A few gentle shots fly across the net. The Indonesian has a name. *But you will not think of her name or age, she is your enemy and the enemy must be destroyed*, the earworm hisses. Brinda remembers that Tasya Sinaga has a mean drop shot.

It was on the second day on the badminton court that six-year-old Brinda had her first communion with something that was beyond her understanding. All she knew was it felt right, gloriously right.

Her father was serving. Until then, he had been careful to pitch his serves appropriately – after all, Brinda had spent exactly an hour on a badminton court. Not too fast and not too low, and not anywhere near the net or the baseline. Close to the point where she stood, so the racquet and shuttlecock could make easy contact.

But the earworm had growled in his ear, *You really don't want to test it? You are afraid of the consequences.* Wanting to shut out the creature who seemed to have taken permanent residence in his middle ear, Rajesh served one of his best serves ever.

From the middle of the court, he released a cannoning low serve.

*Whoa!* the earworm said.

She would either miss it or, if she made contact, she would send it back to him. There was little even a grown-up could do against a serve like that. It was cruel of him. Even the earworm seemed to agree.

The strings of her racquet met the shuttlecock. Force and velocity and something else came together. The note rang in her head even as it travelled from the fingers clasping the racquet up her left arm to the point just behind and above the left ear. A mysterious force that told her how to lob and place.

Later, on the circuit, Brinda would learn a name for that moment. But for the rest of her sporting career, nothing would ever compare to the rush of that moment when the racquet made contact with the shuttlecock and she knew exactly what to do.

Brinda stepped backwards and watched the shuttlecock travel into her father's side of the court. Rajesh knew all he had to do was take one step back to connect with it. They watched, father and daughter, as the shuttlecock kissed the net and landed diagonally, about eight feet in front of him.

The court went silent. This was not a six-year-old's return. Rajesh looked stunned. Across the net, Brinda stood with a broad grin on her face. She had known exactly what she was doing. And she had gone ahead and done it without once thinking that her father would appear a sorry fool; a man who had taunted a little girl and been felled with a deceptive shot. A jhutka shot, as they called it.

'Killer shot,' Roy called out, unable to help himself. And the earworm asked Rajesh, *So, Daddy, what now?*

The first serve is unremarkable. Brinda takes it with ease. This is no better than a schoolgirls' game. As she swings her racquet to send the shuttlecock across to the farthest end, she sees the Indonesian leap into the air and intercept it with a smash that has the crowds cheering. The Indonesian has the first point and the next serve. It's not the point. It's the psychological advantage. Brinda feels an angry sob rise in her. Bitch! Bloody scheming bitch.

The earworm sighs. *An angry woman defeats herself in battle. Wipe her arse instead.*

Brinda looks across to the sidelines. Her coach's face reveals nothing. Birdie Rao has a whole range of expressionless expressions. This one says, 'Right. She got you this once, but there is no next time, remember.'

Brinda pulls in her core. I am going to get you, bitch, she mutters under her breath as she waits for her serve.

She feels a lone bead of sweat run down the nape of her neck and along her spine. She shivers. The coach blinks. He knows what is coming.

The serve turns into the jhutka, barely kissing the net, so the opponent thinks the shuttlecock will fall back into Brinda's side of the court. The Indonesian relaxes, chalking another point to herself. But then the shuttlecock kisses the net, hovers and falls neatly into the Indonesian's side. Such a simple but cunning shot, guaranteed to shake the bedrock of confidence on which any player builds her game and wins titles.

Brinda looks at Birdie Rao. He tilts his chin a fraction. The earworm drawls, *Now don't fuck this up. Decimate the bitch.*

They talked about it all evening, Rajesh and Sunita. They didn't want to turn her into one of those children who was driven by her parents into becoming a high achiever, only to burn out in her prime. They didn't want to be the sort of parents who lived vicariously through their children. But if she had the talent, they would give her all the encouragement and support she needed.

A coaching camp was found. This was Bangalore, the city that was home to Prakash Padukone, Ashwini Ponnappa and Arvind Bhat. Brinda took to it like a duck to water, Rajesh told his badminton group at the club house in the condo they lived in.

Roy felt a snag in his chest. All his son wanted to do was play make-believe games with his Action Man. But in the days to come, he was glad that he didn't have to be the father of a champion. The making of a champion isn't easy.

One night, after a round of beers, Roy asked Rajesh, 'How did you know what to do? How did you know that you had to nurture Brinda's talent?'

Rajesh shrugged. 'I don't know. It's like there's a voice in my head that tells me what to do.'

'Would you call it parental ambition?' Roy persisted.

Rajesh leaned back in his chair. 'Aren't we all ambitious for our children? But if Brinda ever says, "No, I don't want this", I am not going to push her into continuing.'

Roy drank his beer and said nothing.

Rajesh and Sunita took turns driving her to the camp three times a week. There was the rest of it too: the relentless cultivation of stamina and speed on the court, the wrist work, the honing of the killer instinct. Roy didn't think he would have been able to handle it. Nor his wife Rinku, who turned into a screaming monster any time her routine was disrupted.

Be the boy you are, Roy whispered a prayer, watching his son sleep in on a long weekend. From the balcony, he saw Rajesh getting out of his car with a sweaty and tired-looking Brinda. It was a few minutes short of seven on a Saturday morning.

Brinda didn't think too much about what was expected of her. The first day, at her very first coaching camp, the coach, a former state champion, had eyed her skinny frame warily. 'We usually give them a week of trials before we decide to include them. Children of this age don't have the stamina to keep at something day after day,' he explained.

Rajesh and Sunita bristled. Had he even seen their daughter play yet?

By the end of the second day of trials, the coach had decided she was the next best thing to have happened to badminton after someone hit on the perfect sixteen-feather equation for the shuttlecock. But there was still the matter of whether she would show as much interest after a week of early risings.

On the last day, the coach asked her what she thought of the week-long trials. 'It was fun,' Brinda grinned.

The coach grinned back. Everything was fun for Brinda – waking up at dawn, starting on a new diet that included more protein and no junk food at all, watching replays of old matches, building strength, the relentless scrutiny of her body and mind, and having to deal with school work amidst all that.

Rajesh and Sunita no longer recognised their little girl. She seemed older than her years. They had another baby and, in the secret recesses of their minds, they hoped this new child would remain a child, not become like the golden creature with wings on her heels and a swagger in her soul. They would never admit it to each other, but some days they didn't recognise this child of theirs, to whom the only thing that mattered was winning.

Brinda seemed unstoppable. She won the under-10 category at the district level. When she won the under-15 state championship, the coach suggested that they up her coaching. 'She is going to bring us an Olympic gold someday and I am not the right person to make her an Olympian,' he said, trying not to choke on the lump in his throat. Rajesh waited for the earworm to speak up. But all he could hear was a resolute silence.

The new coach, Birdie Rao, was a national champion who had won several international titles. His badminton academy had produced national champions three times running.

Brinda was one of the youngest, but her acumen on the court was that of a much older player. That she was going to be a pro was a given.

A few weeks later, Rajesh noticed his daughter cock her head while on court, as if she was listening to someone. He wondered if she had her headphones on and was talking to someone as she played. Birdie Rao wasn't going to approve.

'Who were you talking to?' Rajesh asked on the drive home.

'When?'

'While you were on the court. Do you have a boyfriend?'

Brinda flushed. 'Oh, Daddy, don't get creeped out. But there's a voice in my head, an earworm that keeps murmuring instructions to me.'

Rajesh didn't speak. He tapped the steering wheel with his fingers, feeling an abject sense of loss.

The twelfth minute of the first game. 10–8. Brinda gnaws at her lower lip as she wipes the sweat from her arms and neck with a logo-crested towel. The Indonesian is taking a sip of a drink she is endorsing. We may be goddesses on the court but we are slaves to the brands that sponsor us, Brinda thinks with disgust. She stuffs the towel back into the open mouth of her tote bag.

Brinda serves. Her low serve is ineffective against the Indonesian, who is tiny but all muscle and double joints. Closer to the ground and more balanced too. She serves a medium-high serve that is pitched towards the baseline. The Indonesian leaps in the air. A mongoose going for the throat. She slams it back to Brinda. A low skimming shot that Brinda stretches to reach. The shuttlecock is back in the Indonesian's forecourt but she is there, tenacious and taut, coiled to strike.

The volley lasts twenty-four strokes and forty-five seconds. The Indonesian hasn't lost her focus but she is tiring. Brinda has the advantage of age. She is twenty-one, the Indonesian twenty-six. Five years older on the court stretches to almost a fifteen-year stamina deficit, or so Birdie Rao had said once. Brinda caresses the shuttlecock with the tip of her racquet, scoops it as if it were a lark's egg and sends it across the net. An attacking lob that flies over the Indonesian's shoulder – she doesn't even register it whooshing past her. Brinda holds in her smile as she clocks the point. You don't need to show the world your triumph, Birdie Rao had cautioned her. Hold it in till you have won the game. Brinda knows how to do that well enough.

It had stung the first time, when at the Diwali party at the club house, she overheard two of the aunties discuss her. Brinda had worn a lehenga choli in brilliant orange with turquoise blue and gold paisleys. The choli had a shoestring back and she had worn her hair loose. Rajesh and Sunita had been astonished to see how Brinda had blossomed. She was sixteen, but in their heads, she had ceased to grow beyond an androgynous eleven. 'Our baby has grown,' Rajesh said, unable to help himself.

Sunita had nodded mutely. Then she had brought out the jewellery. A choker and chandelier earrings set with sapphires and diamonds. Brinda had worn them with a little girl's glee. Sunita had smiled at her daughter and found matching glass bangles, which she slid onto Brinda's wrists. She watched Brinda clinking the glass bangles and holding her arms up to the light to see how they glittered and gleamed. Rajesh brought out the digicam to shoot videos of her and Brinda felt like a swan, like Princess Jasmine, like all the beautiful princesses in the fairy tales.

As she walked into the club house with her parents, the neighbours gathered to tell her how proud they were of her. Someone smiled and said, 'You look so different out of your sports clothes.'

Brinda had grinned. The music came on; the dancing began. Rajesh dragged his daughters to the floor. 'Let's show them how this team does it,' he said.

Brinda and Ankita rolled their eyes but joined in. She hadn't had such fun in years, Brinda thought. When the buffet opened, she joined the line of people. She piled her plate full of food and found a corner behind a bay of potted palms. She needed a quiet moment from all the chit-chat and music.

'Who is that in the orange and blue?' a voice said.

'Brinda Patil. The badminton girl,' another voice replied.

Brinda recognised the voice as Rinku Aunty's. Roy Uncle's wife and her mother's good friend.

'I didn't recognise her out of her short skirts. Though I often wonder why she can't wear shorts like the other players.'

'Actually, the short skirts suit her. What doesn't, is dressing up in all this finery!'

'I was thinking the same. She's like a boy dressed up. All angles and no curves. Girls need curves.'

'Do you think she's on steroids? They say most sports people take them. Male hormones and steroids. Even her face has none of the softness of a girl's.'

Brinda had walked away and tossed the plate of uneaten food into the bin. She had pleaded a headache and gone up to their apartment.

For the first time, Brinda wondered what her parents thought of her. Did they too see her as an oddity? Is that why, when they went shopping, her mother always steered her towards the jeggings and capris teamed with short tops while Ankita was found pretty skirts and dresses? Her classmates had all worn their first saris by now. She hadn't even tried wearing one yet.

The rabbit hole beckoned, inviting Brinda to lose herself in it. Instead, with a heart that felt steely cold, she tore her party clothes off, scrubbed her face, braided her hair and watched a rerun of the badminton finals at the London Olympics on YouTube: China's Lin Dan against Malaysia's Lee Chong Wei.

The earworm, who had disappeared for a while, chose that moment to announce his presence in Brinda's middle ear. *That, my girl, is what you get when you forget who you are and try to become one of them. There is no us and them. It will always be you and them! You have to have your own back. No one else is going to do that for you.*

On her seventeenth birthday, Brinda was picked to be part of the Indian contingent for the Asian Games.

All of them had seen it, from her father's partner a long time ago, to her first coach, to her opponents across the court: Brinda's killer instinct. She was a quiet girl, but her quietness was merely a façade for the intensity of purpose simmering in her. Her shot selection had always been judicious and she knew exactly how to force her opponent to make errors. But after the Diwali party, she added canniness to her tactics. Everything was combat thereafter. On the court, she was merciless. 'You need to have the mindset of a gladiator,' Brinda said at a press meet after her first international gold. 'There can only be one survivor and it had better be you,' she smiled.

They ran the picture of her grimacing as she leapt into the air and brought the racquet down on the shuttlecock in what would go on to become one of the greatest drop smashes in the recorded history of the sport. Those who had watched the match live or on TV remembered flinching at the violence of the shot; at the disbelief on the opponent's face.

The press loved her. Her dimples and slight curves made her both goddess and star. She was photogenic and, for a brief while, when she was dating a T20 cricketer, they couldn't get enough of her.

Rajesh and Sunita saw their child retreat further away from them, but they didn't think they could do anything about it. At family weddings and condo parties, Brinda wafted in almost unwillingly; they could see that she did it to please them. She didn't belong, not like Ankita. But they let it pass.

A few days after her nineteenth birthday, Brinda said she was going away for a few days to a spa retreat.

'Are you all right?' Sunita asked as she watched Brinda pack.

Brinda looked at her. Her lower lip wobbled for a fraction of a second. Then she pushed the hair from her face and said, 'I am just tired, Mum. The spa will cure me.'

Sunita opened her mouth to speak and then swallowed the words that refused to form. Her daughter was hurting, but she didn't know from what. And the truth was that she was afraid to ask.

Sunita had noticed that Brinda had missed a period. But who could find Brinda attractive, she asked herself almost secretively. For how can any mother admit, even if only to herself, that her daughter is almost sexless?

It was as if the game had leeched her of all femininity. The softness and vulnerability had been replaced by a graphite strength and the tautness of nylon string stretched to 35lb. It was as if, with her racquet, she sought to diminish her sweet spot.

In the month following the spa visit, everything was well again. The cricketer disappeared from her life and Brinda's game seemed to acquire a new aggression.

Once in a while, Sunita caught a glimpse of longing on

Brinda's face as she watched Rajesh horse around with Ankita. And she wished she hadn't sent Brinda off with him that first morning, simply because she had wanted a lie-in without the child demanding her attention.

Sunita put her arm around Brinda, suddenly overwhelmed by a sense of guilt and loss.

Brinda won't allow herself to think of anything but the moment she is in. She sips her drink. Birdie Rao tells her what to watch for. Brinda listens. She has heard it every day since she turned pro. But it cannot be said enough times, she knows.

She has wiped the court with the Indonesian in the first game, 21–11, and is poised for certain victory, at 12–5. The Indonesian looks like she is caught in a nightmare. But Brinda doesn't want to know.

There is some lacklustre cheering from the Indonesian's supporters as the two players return to their positions. Voices call out, Brinda, Brinda, Brinda...

She serves. The shuttlecock arcs and descends precisely where she knew it would fall. But the Indonesian calls for a review. Brinda waits. She watches her opponent's mouth open in silent protest as it is given in.

But the Indonesian makes a valiant effort to squeeze herself back into the game. She tries to push Brinda into the farthest corner. Brinda makes contact with the shuttlecock with an almost acrobatic movement and sends it skimming over the net. For a moment, it hovers and then drops into the Indonesian's court. She is forced to race towards the net. She makes it and scoops it just in time. 13–6. Brinda gnaws her lips. It is time to finish the game, she decides.

She takes the next five points. She can see that the Indonesian is on the verge of giving up.

It is game point. Brinda is ready to serve. Across the court, the Indonesian's face is a plastic mask. Devoid of all expression and beauty; an emptiness that speaks of the beginning of the end.

Brinda pauses. *What now?* the earworm asks.

In a few years, this will be her, Brinda thinks. Shorn of titles and power. Unable to get it right. Watching her dreams fly away on the feathers of a shuttlecock as it refuses to do her bidding.

'And every good thing generally ends with all those things which are perceived to be contrary to the good.' Who said that? She had read it in the book of quotes she dipped into on long-haul flights when she grew tired of watching movies back to back or sleeping. She hadn't understood it then. But now, the question nags at her: What for?

The hard hours and the disintegration of the ordinary, the childhood swept away like crumbs, the outbursts that ruined all her relationships with boys, the retching into the toilet just before a game, all of it will be rendered meaningless the moment she stands in the Indonesian's shoes. What for?

This is her life. What will happen to her when she no longer has this? In a few years she will be where Tasya Sinaga is now. What then?

Brinda drops the shuttlecock and her racquet.

There is a hushed silence. Then the voices rise. She hears her name being called.

'What are you doing?'

'Brinda… Brinda… what is this?'

'Miss Patil, are you all right?'

She hears it all. There is no going back now, she thinks with a tremendous sense of relief.

She walks away from the centre court.

5

# URVASHI

She woke up abruptly, wondering where she was. A slow languor filled her. She didn't need to get up if she didn't feel like it. There was no routine to adhere to. No boxes to tick. No plans to make. She closed her eyes and snuggled deeper into the mound of pillows. She had started watching a movie late in the night. Three-quarters through it, she had fallen asleep.

She picked up her phone to check the time and switched the Wi-Fi on. WhatsApp notifications pinged in frenetically. A slew of customary messages from Mahesh, her sisters, and from work. There was also a barrage of messages from him, from a new number. Her sense of well-being quickly dissipated.

She got up and stumbled to the bathroom, then put the electric kettle on. It was a little past eleven and the breakfast buffet would be closed.

She made herself a mug of coffee and carried it with her to the bed. It was too warm to sit outside in the verandah and she wasn't ready yet to find the restaurant or make conversation with anyone on the way there.

She wrote Mahesh a long message about how wonderful everything was and how the chaos in her head was beginning to sort itself out. And that she hoped all was well with him. Would he remember to collect the drycleaning before she got back? Also, her car was due for service. She added three xxxs at the end, more from sheer habit than anything else.

She tweaked the message a bit and sent it to her sisters. And sent a few emojis to colleagues at work.

Then she set about reading his messages. Most of them were messages she had sent to him, played back with captions and exclamation marks to tell her what a heartless bitch she was, what a lying slut she was, and how he would punish her if that was the last thing he did, when she least expected it. For good measure, he told her that she might think she was getting away with it but she was destined to die a painful death, with bedsores and maggots feeding on her... that is, if she survived what he had decided to do to her.

He would know she had read the messages. She wanted him to know that she had read them. If it was war he wanted, he would have it. Her diffidence would be her weapon. The supreme weapon, Sun Tzu said, was knowing how to subdue the enemy without fighting. She had read *The Art of War* just as he had.

It had been a warm summer evening when she first swiped him into her life. A gentle caress of her index finger, the right way.

He said he had looked at her profile photo on the dating app and wondered who she was. He said he had fallen in love with the mole on her chin.

Only, it wasn't a mole but a wart that she planned to excise. She called the clinic and cancelled the appointment. 'I'll speak to the doctor and re-schedule,' she told the receptionist.

She didn't want to do away with the very thing that drew him to her.

He had been working on an investment portfolio, he said,

and been struck by the contrast. One woman needing to tidy up her affairs; the other messing it up. He had looked at her profile again, wondering at how lonely she must be to look outside her marriage.

He was weary of ghost girls and fuckbabes, he said. He wanted a normal relationship but he felt as if he was an aberration. An older woman wouldn't ghost him. Or fuck with him, he added, with a wryness that surprised her.

In those first few days, when they moved their chat to WhatsApp, a statement of intent almost, the clock had ticked with the number of pings per hour. They competed with each other to see who would light the fire first thing in the day: Hello, hey, good morninggg, are you awake? You there????

Urvashi had told herself that this heat in the heart accompanied anything that was new: a new job, a new car in the porch, a new piece of jewellery she couldn't stop looking at, a new love…

What she didn't realise was that she was up against the holy trinity of neurotransmitters: serotonin, norepinephrine and dopamine. Together, they can release a sense of euphoria that knocks all sense sideways. She listened to Farida Khanum and read Neruda's poetry. She bought new lingerie and found her way to a yoga class. She was minting herself into a shiny new coin in readiness for him. She would tell herself, in retrospect, that she may as well have snorted cocaine. The consequences would have been easier to deal with.

But in those early days, Urvashi lived in the moment. And so did he. 'I wake up with crazy erections,' he said. 'Do you know what you are doing to me, baby?'

Urvashi had smiled, reading the text message. She wasn't a middle-aged woman any more. She was the sixteen-year-old who sat with a book, thinking of Rhett Butler carrying her up a white banistered staircase.

Lakshmi would choose that moment to walk in, asking, 'How do you want me to cook the brinjal?' Or there would be a call from someone at work, asking about the piece she was supposed to have sent in. The moment would be gone but the residue of the electric charge would continue to sing in her.

As the days passed, Urvashi realised that an affair, whether it translated into sex or not, was all about control. Of seeing to what extent the other would pine for you. Of knowing how far you could push the other. Of who would give in first and admit to a need that stamped down pride, caution and good sense. While, on his gold-plated tin throne some place far away, God chortled and rubbed his hands with a Gotcha glee.

Soon, it became about sex. Sex in everything and everywhere.

Sex crept into his voice on the phone and in the syllables that teased her senses long distance. Sex gazed at her over the cup of cappuccino when they first met at a coffee shop. In the lazy length of his legs that he stretched out, leaning back in his chair. Sex crawled along the line of his jaw and the curve of his lips. She crossed her legs at the knees and pretended a poise she could almost believe in herself. Sex opened the door when she went over to his flat for the first time. For a drink and no more, they had agreed.

Sex was what waited in the bottle of vodka – whisky being too solemn, beer too burpy, and everything else being what you drank with friends at a lazy afternoon lunch. Sex stirred with a long elegant finger the vodka in her glass until she felt herself open with an abandon she hadn't known in a long while. Sex clinked ice in the glass and hovered over the nest of cushions dressed in paisley fabric. Sex burnt from within the joint he rolled expertly and which they shared, their saliva mingling on the filter tip. Sex laughed with them at the silly jokes they tossed at each other. Sex twanged the strap of her bra and pulled open the buckle of his belt even as it slithered her seamless panties down her legs.

And then, as his fingers crept over her skin and her mouth sought his and his teeth nibbled the side of her neck, through all that squeezing and caressing, and all that making of love that shifted into a heated and strangely mechanical rhythm, it came to her. That beneath all that spit and polish, one orgasm was just like another.

Later, he brought her tissues to clean up, switched on the hot water for her shower, and made her a cup of coffee. And all the warmth, the sexual tension, fizzled down to a flatness verging on disappointment, a distant annoyance that made her want to walk away and slam the door behind her. A fuck is a fuck is a fuck.

She told herself that she had been overwhelmed by it all – the build-up, the secrecy, the subterfuge, the sex itself. He had, after all, made her come several times before he did.

After that, each time they met, she waited for it to become something else. An intimacy that would reveal itself to be more than just the sex. But oh, how they fucked! On the floor and the kitchen counter, the couch and in the shower… they tried all the positions he wanted to try and some she wanted to. But it refused to metamorphose into anything else. She was unable to bring back the breathless excitement of those first days, the endless possibilities the beginning of the affair held.

By the time she finished the coffee, the warrior in her was cowering. The quiet of the room, spliced only by the hum of the air conditioner, filled her with a strange sense of foreboding. As though someone was outside the door, waiting for her to emerge. She dropped the phone hastily and rose from the bed.

The Jasmine Bower restaurant overlooked the river. It was large and airy. The walkway to it was overhung with a trellis on which jasmine creepers had been trained. A flock of babblers rose from the lawns; from the trees, an Indian tree magpie made a whickering sound. Urvashi took a deep breath. She felt calmer.

It was half past twelve but there was no one else in the restaurant. She chose a table closest to the window from where she could see the river. The sky was dense with rain clouds. Thunder rumbled mutinously. It would rain again, soon. The weather forecast had said as much.

She looked at the day's specials and then asked for a fish-curry-meal. Radha had asked her to stick with the traditional Kerala dishes. 'Chef Mathew is good, but what he creates, you can find anywhere. Baby George is the real artist.'

The food, when it arrived, looked and smelt delicious. The bronze plate was lined with a piece of banana leaf, on which sat a bowl of brown rice. Arranged around it were two side dishes of vegetables, a bowl of sambar, a puffed out pappadam and a coconut chutney. There was buttermilk in a jug. On its own was the hero of the meal, the fish curry – seer fish in a thick coconut gravy. Urvashi's mouth watered. The waiter set down a plate with a piece of fried fish on it. 'Compliments from the chef,' he said. Urvashi smiled.

But she found she could only pick at the food. In her mouth, it reduced to sawdust. A longing for home and Lakshmi's indifferent cooking filled her.

'Hello, ma'am,' a voice said.

Urvashi looked up to see Brinda Patil.

'Hello,' she smiled.

'Najma asked me to give this to you,' the girl said, handing her a bit of chalk – or was it plastic?

Urvashi took it from her and placed it beside her plate, on the table. 'Oh, I meant to drop it off at the reception,' she said.

She looked up at Brinda. 'Do you want to join me?' she asked.

Brinda pulled out a chair. 'Are you here on holiday?'

Urvashi looked at her blankly and said, 'I don't know.'

The waiter came to the table holding a cordless phone. 'Madam, there is a call for you.'

Urvashi looked up, surprised. She took the phone hesitantly. Only Mahesh and Surya knew she was here. Why would they call her on the hotel line? 'Hello,' she said.

There was silence.

She said again, 'Hello.'

There was a long exhalation before he said, 'Do you remember this voice?' Then the line went dead.

The phone slipped from her hand to the table. The smile on the girl's face slipped in response. 'Ma'am, are you okay?' she asked.

'I am not so sure. Would you walk with me to my room?' Urvashi asked.

'Yes, of course,' Brinda said, rushing to help her.

The waiter watched with concern as the two women left. Then he went to find Unni to tell him. Radha madam's friend had got a call with some very bad news. Also, the river was rising.

# Sreelakshmi

Filled as I was with admiration for the composure of this young woman, and sorry as I felt for the remorse that would take hold of her when life refused to unfold the way Brinda Patil envisaged it would, I was glad to be going back to Urvashi. It was her story I wanted to know, her life I wanted to understand. I didn't know why I was so drawn to her. I just knew I was.

But even before I had a chance to discover Urvashi's secret, she left, leaving me wedged between the pepper and salt shakers. Who was that on the phone and what was said?

A potter wasp was hovering near the right-hand corner of the top frame of the window. She must have scouted other places before fixing on this as the location to build her nest. If she could hear me, I would tell her: Go away. This isn't right for you.

I knew this because I had built my dreams with the same thoughtless perseverance and reckless abandon.

Old memories pressed down on me. The irony hadn't escaped me that I was a ghost haunted by her past. What I sought was a dark place to burrow into and hide myself, where I could gain my poise. But here I was in broad daylight, a table ornament of sorts.

Through the open verandah, I heard the sound of splashing. Was it from the river? Once, I used to swim in the Nila. Once, I floated in its waters and gazed at the clouds, spinning stories about men and women.

I thought of the last time I had bathed in the river. For the dead do not forget. Like hair that continues to grow even when breath has ceased, memory stretches far beyond the grave.

Each time I stepped into my house, I felt secretly triumphant. I had a room of my own. I was the mistress of my house.

Nine years after I left home to be a lowly tutor, living with relatives and having to endure their thoughtless barging into the room I was allotted, and relentless commentary on how I ate and what I wore, I had escaped the prison with no walls. A new college opened in Ottapalam in 1962 and I decided to apply for a transfer, to fill the position of lecturer in the zoology department.

I had always written poems and stories. After being forced to return from Varanasi, I had discovered that writing helped me forget all else. So I wrote about possibilities and chance encounters. And both my father and Narendran appeared in various guises in my stories.

I had a modicum of literary success to begin with, but with the Akademi prize, I acquired a literary reputation that changed my life. Yet, I continued to teach. I continued to be the eternal paying guest.

However, once my transfer was finalised, I insisted my mother leave the tharavad at Karakkad and move in with me. I wanted a home of my own.

I found us a house to rent. A small house with an open verandah, a main hall, two bedrooms, and a kitchen with a huge back yard. As was the norm, the bathroom and toilet were separate and located a few yards away from the house.

We brought a servant woman, Karthu, from Karakkad. Her husband had left her for another woman. And so the three of us, widow, spinster, and a woman married only in name, made our home there. We brought a few sticks of furniture from the tharavad and found a carpenter who could make some more. I bought a Murphy radio and a few utensils for the kitchen. The rest we would acquire as we went along, I told my mother, who had never known any home but the one she had been born in.

I made one of the rooms mine. On the windowsill I arranged my father's small but fine selection of books. I would never know if he had actually read them or just liked to collect them. The chest of drawers he had brought from Burma was placed in one corner and it held all my possessions: a few pieces of jewellery, saris, certificates, and writing paper.

I was now the man of the house. I gave my watch to my oldest niece and took to wearing my father's Favre Leuba. It had a black dial and a gold rim with Arabic numerals. Just before my father died, he had changed the strap. Ten years later, the leather strap was as good as new.

Every morning, the first thing I did after waking up was to wind the watch. I liked the exactness it demanded. One extra spin and the spring would snap. One movement less and it would stop. I liked the weight of it on my wrist. It made me feel capable and less vulnerable. My father had always believed in my abilities, even when everyone else thought I was a bit peculiar.

Over the years, I had often wished I knew him better. I would like to have shared my thoughts with him. Offer him my stories to read and discuss the classics with him. I would like to have told him about my caterpillar heart, which gnawed at my thoughts relentlessly and yet refused to metamorphose into butterflies.

Eight days before I killed myself, I took my mother to our tharavad in Karakkad.

We made the visit every few weeks. Apart from my mother and Karthu getting to spend time with their siblings, we smuggled back rice.

When the rice we first brought back from the tharavad began diminishing, my mother had brought it to my notice. 'We can buy it from a shop here,' I said. 'There's no need to bring it all the way from there. Besides, I don't even know if it's legal,' I tried telling her.

'What do you mean?' she asked. The muscles in her neck clenched and she began rubbing her palms as if she was smoothing cream into her skin.

'There is a rice shortage and farmers are expected to sell their excess grain to the government. I think you need to get a permit to carry rice away from your fields. I am not entirely sure,' I said, trying to make her see reason.

The next day, she stopped eating. 'I eat exactly one handful of rice at lunch. For dinner, because of my sugar complaint, all I can have is that wheat loaf. I am not Karthu to be satisfied with shop-bought rice. If I can't have the rice cultivated in my paddy fields, husked and milled at the house, I might as well not eat.'

My mother was a great follower of the Mahatma when it came to hunger strikes. She would stop eating whenever my father and she quarrelled. She stopped eating when my father refused to let a pressure cooker enter the kitchen. She had fallen in love with it and its ingenious, cunning ways. She stopped eating when her sisters talked of dividing the family property. She was seldom unreasonable. Her hunger strikes were only to prove a point or exercise her will.

Getting a permit would require a lot of paperwork. My mother suggested that we bring the rice back with us. 'Who is going to check three women? Between us, we can bring enough for a few weeks. Besides, we are doing nothing wrong. It's my rice from my paddy fields,' she said with a finality that I couldn't help but admire.

My mother's elder sister lived in the village, as did her oldest daughter, with her husband and three children, one of whom would eventually perform my last rites. In time, my cousin would inherit the property, though my mother still had some claim to it. As I would, when the time came.

Next door was my mother's cousin. I was fond of her daughters. Their chatter amused me, and I sometimes took them little fripperies as gifts. Glass bangles, sweet-scented soaps, a georgette daavani or a blouse piece. I took them books once, but they barely glanced at them.

A colleague who had gone to Hyderabad had brought me a set of ornate bangles with glass pieces and beads set on them. Exactly what the girls would delight in, I thought. After they had exclaimed over the bangles and how pretty they were – and discussed the volume of my hair, which they thought was thinning – we went to the river.

I took my clothes off on the bank of the Nila and wound a mundu around me as I entered the water. I waded in and then, holding my breath, sank underwater.

A bathroom can never measure up to this. The moment when you dunk your head underwater and surface, feeling it clear with a blinding freshness. In that moment, the river becomes part of you. The fluidity, the life that lives in the waters enters you, and a sense of weightlessness takes root. The river rolls and heaves in you, it hums and throbs and sighs and cries in you. Water is the only element you can become truly part of, unlike the ground beneath your feet or the air you breathe.

When I was done with my swim, I sat on the shore and watched the girls wash their clothes. Afterwards, we would bathe with soap and scrub our backs with a loofah. They had plucked hibiscus leaves to wash my hair with. I listened to their chatter. Would I have been as carefree and happy as they were, if my life was not as shadowed by the demands of literature or professional ambition – or an unsuitable love? One of the girls looked up from wringing out a cheeti skirt and asked me, 'Chechi, how many saris do you have?'

I smiled. 'Fifteen.'

'Fifteen!' Her eyes were round as saucers. 'And is every sari green in colour?'

I flushed. 'Yes.' I didn't wear any colour but green. I didn't like making a choice.

It was her younger sister who asked, 'Chechi, why didn't you marry?'

'I didn't find the right man,' I said.

'Would you, if one came along now?' She laughed as she asked the question.

Her older sister snorted. 'Why would she marry? She has an important job; she writes stories and has so much pathras. Fifteen saris, and her name in the paper. Why would she give that up to scuttle about in a dingy kitchen like a rat?'

I smiled when she said 'pathras', the colloquial word for pomp and circumstance.

The younger girl shrugged. 'I don't want a job or pathras. I don't mind being a rat. I want to get married. I want a husband. I want babies. I want a home of my own.'

Her sister laughed as she splashed water on her. 'Isn't she stupid, Chechi?'

I waded into the river and sank into the water once again. I was afraid I would repeat what my younger cousin had said. I want to get married. I want him as a husband. I want his babies. I want a home of our own. I wanted happily ever after.

A woman came towards the table I sat on. A tall, slim woman with shoulder-length hair, immaculately dressed in white trousers and a pale blue shirt. Her fingernails had silver nail polish and diamonds sparkled at her ears and throat. She looked like she would let nothing ruffle her. Unlike poor Urvashi, who had crumpled even as I watched.

The woman went to look at the river from the window and then came to sit at the table. She stared unseeingly at me.

She took her phone and looked at it as though she was trying to make up her mind.

She touched the screen and held it to her ear. When there was no response, she placed the phone on the table. Then she looked at the menu and asked for a coconut water with vodka.

She picked up the phone and tried to call someone again.

The drink arrived. Her hand shook as she raised the glass to her mouth.

She stared at the phone screen even as her hands moved things around on the table. Eventually she found me and started rolling me between her fingers as though I was a die about to be cast in some game of chance she was playing with herself.

# The Diplomat's Wife

Rupa stretched her arms as she lay on the king-size bed and wiggled her body to revel in the luxury of space, the infinity that is a marital bed unoccupied by a spouse. Her eyelids were heavy with the somnolence that crept into her at this time of the day. She wondered what Keshav would be doing in the family home.

She could see him seated in the living room of his cousin's home, dressed in a mundu and a white full-sleeve kurta which he called a jubbah when he was with his people. The slim gold chain with a tiny pendant of Ganesha must glisten at his throat. His cousin, the unparalleled Mini with her deep bosom and breathless little-girl voice, would heap the table with all his favourite childhood dishes – unni appam and ada; ribbon pakoda and tea the colour of a slushy rainwater puddle in a glass because that's how they'd always had their four o'clock tea. Keshav would look at Mini, overwhelmed with emotion and say, 'You remind me of Mummy, you are just like her.'

Mini, at fifty-five, would gleam at him and touch the choker at her throat. Keshav had given it to her from his mother's collection of jewellery. 'No one can be like Uma Aunty but I am happy I remind you of her.'

If Rupa had been there, she would have hissed at her, 'All your life you were practising to look like her and now that you do, why this pretence?' But Rupa wasn't there. And neither did she want to be.

The first time she met Mini, she had noticed how the woman

appropriated Keshav, pushing her to the periphery and quickly making her aware of who had the first right of refusal on him. She had noticed the embers of something flare between them; a memory, or maybe several, buried by mutual consent. But how? Wasn't she his sister?

Cousins could marry each other in south India, Keshav explained as they looked through the family album; the children of a brother and sister very often did. Rupa had wondered then if they'd had sex, these two cousins who met during the summer vacations.

'What about Mini and you?' Rupa had asked, sliding her leg between his. She had wanted in those days to feel his imprint on her skin through every waking moment and even while asleep.

Intimacy was more than the filling of space. It was wanting to feel his arms around her while she curled into his side with an arm wrapped around his neck. It was feeling his breath on her forehead and knowing that in the circle of his arms was her safe haven. It was waking up and knowing he was still there and would always be there. Her love. Her companion. Hers.

'Oh, some teenage making out. Summer vacations and teenage hormones are a dangerous combination,' he said, laughing it off. It was the junior diplomat's laugh, the nothing-of-consequence-so-don't-get-your-knickers-in-a-twist sort of laugh he had been practising ever since he emerged from the Lal Bahadur Shastri National Academy of Administration in Mussorie, Rupa thought with that first glimpse of clay feet.

'And you never wanted to make more of it?' she asked, unable to help herself.

Her father, the senior bureaucrat, had told her again and again: Never show your hand unless you know where you are going with it.

That laugh again. 'I won't say I wasn't tempted, but good sense prevailed.' She felt the tensing of his chest, the pause as he held himself back from blurting out anything that would upset her.

'We were not really suited; a relationship is more than bodies calling to each other,' he said, adjusting the angle of his shoulder on which her head was pillowed.

'For a moment, I thought you had me classified under good sense,' she giggled.

'You stupid girl,' he said, absently sliding a finger up and down her thigh. 'Go to sleep...'

And she had.

In the years that followed, Rupa didn't accompany Keshav on his annual pilgrimage to the tharavad, in the little hamlet near Shoranur. Her resentment towards Mini transformed into a guarded admiration, then to a deep dislike of the woman. One day soon, it would become indifference, and she would go along with Keshav again.

But this time, on their way to their home in Coonoor, Keshav had wanted to stay a couple of days at the tharavad. Rupa had protested, but Keshav said that he wanted to be part of the puja.

'What's that?' Rupa asked, wondering which card had been flashed to lure him this time.

'The annual ancestor worship. I should go every year but haven't been able to. I'd like to go at least this year. According to Mini, the ancestors are unhappy that I have not been offering them their dues.'

'They told Mini this?' Rupa wasn't able to hide the wry tone.

Keshav's mouth thinned. 'Don't be like that, darling. Sarcasm doesn't suit you. And it will give you frown lines and indigestion.'

He didn't try to persuade her to go with him. Instead, he found a place for her to stay while he was away. Near the Nila. 'You can be my secret woman stashed away in a room by the river,' he joked as he followed her into the cottage.

Rupa looked at him, an eyebrow raised. Fence-sitter, she mouthed. He laughed. The diplomat's laugh had acquired new dimensions over the years. Now it said: Of course I'll listen to you, but I'll do just as I please.

Rupa had, over the years, acquired a laugh of her own: Of course you will, but I really don't have it in me to simper or sulk, so as the lesser nation forever seeking handouts and concessions, I will go with what you want. A lifetime of being with bureaucrats had turned the redness of her blood to a pale pink of compromise and unspoken words.

'Secret woman, huh?' she teased, crawling on the bed towards him, growling.

He stared at her as if she had just sprouted a second head. The good-sense girl didn't do such things.

Rupa chewed on her lip. What if I stand on the bed and take my clothes off in slow motion, turn into Salome doing her dance of the seven veils? Pinching my nipples, gyrating my belly and parting my thighs. What if I ask him to lick me as I stand on the bed with my quivering cunt open to his mouth? What if I throw back my head and howl, a she-wolf who can't have enough of his arcing tongue? What if, for once, I become a reckless adventuress?

What if Keshav became Herod, so overcome by desire for her that he brought her Mini's head on a plate with yellow tongues of banana fritters arranged in a circle around the dumbfuck face? What if he became her slave forever?

The slow mounting of what-ifs dissolved into a puddle of regret and a diplomatic reining in. He never would; she never would; they never would.

Rupa switched on the TV. There was something decadent about taking her clothes off one by one as the news anchors looked her in the eye and read out the headlines. She wondered if she should masturbate. Sometimes it seemed so much more satisfying and less of an emotional landmine, pleasuring herself rather than expecting Keshav to anticipate her list of desires and fulfil it. Besides, she was afraid to reveal the nakedness of her thoughts to him. It would only prompt that laugh again.

She lay on the bed and closed her eyes, allowing her mind to drift. Sometimes she wished she had a face to fix on. An image that stirred and stimulated her. Mostly she found herself fantasising about Keshav. How pathetic was she to fantasise about her own husband. Was she just limited in her thinking? A lifetime of doing the right thing had turned her into this: a woman who couldn't even conjure up suitable eye candy to ride with her to an orgasm.

Rupa rose and pulled on a caftan. The air-conditioning was way too high and she felt cold and lonely. She wondered what Keshav was doing now. She wondered what her children, her twins, were up to at their boarding school in Dehradun.

Keshav had been insistent that they move there in Class 8. 'They need to get serious, decide what they intend to do with their lives,' he said.

'At thirteen?' She laughed incredulously.

'At thirteen, I knew where I wanted to be, even if I didn't know how to get there,' Keshav said, looking at her over the papaya cubes he liked to eat every morning.

'At thirteen, I was madly in love with the school captain and all I could think of was how to make him notice me,' she said thoughtfully.

Keshav grunted and went back to his papaya. Rupa wondered if this was how he handled policy meetings when they were derailed by an unexpected development. By dwelling on the agenda at hand rather than addressing the elephant in the room. He was certainly not used to Rupa speaking her thoughts without filtering them.

A few minutes later, he wiped his mouth with a napkin and asked, 'And did he notice you?'

Rupa tried to hide her smile. Beneath that melamine veneer, he was rattled after all. 'No,' she sighed.

'And it wasn't for want of trying. I tried to bump into him in every possible way, from parking my bicycle next to his, to taking part in competitions so he would know I existed. Nothing came of it. I feel a little sad for myself, I tried so hard.' She watched Keshav's eyes narrow and his mouth tighten.

'It was a schoolgirl crush. Goodness, I had forgotten all about it, in fact. I can't even remember his name,' she said hastily. The good-sense girl had prevailed.

Keshav smiled. He folded his napkin and promised to be home soon. They were going to a reception at the Swedish Ambassador's. 'Will you wear that blue sari?' he murmured. 'You look gorgeous in it.'

Rupa had smiled at his back. He was the most attentive companion, but extracting a compliment from him was like squeezing water from a stone – or gaining a concession from the embassy for a hapless NRI in dire trouble.

Rupa glanced at the watch on her wrist. There were three hours to go for dinner. She could kill for a martini now. A dirty martini. But it was a dry day in Kerala. Apparently the first day of every month was. All liquor sales were halted for the day so men didn't drink their salaries away and women could cadge enough from their vagrant husbands to pay the rent and school fees, buy the groceries and dock in another instalment for the fridge, TV, inverter, borewell or gold loan. Fleetingly, she wished that Haris, the young man at the bar at the Hotel Imperial Gardens in Istanbul, was here at Near the Nila.

'Shall I fix you my signature cocktail?' he had asked, that first evening in Istanbul.

She had looked at the handsome young man who looked almost Middle Eastern with his fine light skin, the slight hook to his nose and the large brown almond-shaped eyes, but was most certainly from Kerala.

He had brought her a dirty martini and later, she would think of him as the olive brine who brought alive a commonplace cocktail.

Three evenings of someone anticipating her every need while Keshav sat in on banquets that accompanied the conference on the global hunger index. 'Do you see the irony of it?' she pointed out, waggling her eyebrows at him.

He pretended not to hear her.

She may as well have stayed at home, but Istanbul had been on her list of places to visit. And when she returned to the hotel, weary of feet and filled with wonder and sometimes distress, Haris fixed her his signature cocktail and brought her a bowl of salted almonds and asked about her day. When she drew out a pack of cigarettes, he lit one for her with élan, both solicitous and discreet.

'Where are you from, Haris?' she asked him, smiling.

'Kasargod, ma'am,' he smiled.

'I didn't know Kasargod had Christians,' Rupa said. 'I thought it was mostly Muslims.'

'I am not a Christian, ma'am,' Haris smiled.

'Oh, I assumed you were. Your name?'

'It's my family name and I began using it when I realised Western guests were more comfortable with a Haris than a Faesal.' He grinned.

'If I had known, I wouldn't have asked you to fix me a drink. I know it's haram for you.' Rupa leaned forward and laughed her Mrs Diplomat laugh – no offence, just a little boo-boo, I hope you understand.

Haris shook his head. 'It's part of my job, and it doesn't matter as long as I am not drinking.' He moved the ash tray closer to her.

'Have you always been in the hotel industry?'

'I was in Qatar for four years. I just moved here a year ago.'

'And you like it here?' Rupa asked cautiously.

Haris shrugged. 'There is no place like home, so then it doesn't matter where else I am.'

Rupa wondered about this failing, or was it conditioning, of the Malayali mind that couldn't conceive of any place as home except the one they could trace their roots to. Keshav, global citizen, world traveller, at home in Khartoum or Seoul or now in Madrid, was the same. The family home was the tap root they all drew their sense of identity from.

The captain of the restaurant walked by a couple of times. Haris disappeared into the shadows. Rupa took a deep drag of the cigarette and sipped her dirty martini.

The next morning, Haris was conspicuous by his absence. Keshav had left for an early meeting at the university, so Rupa set out for the Spice Bazaar alone. She wished she had asked Haris a little more about it when he had suggested that she go there.

He was sitting on the steps, on one side of the square, in front of the bazaar building. Pigeons rose and swooped around him. 'Good morning, ma'am,' he said, rising to his feet.

Rupa beamed at him. 'Oh my! Good morning indeed, Haris!'

She cocked her head at him. 'You are truly my genie! I was just thinking about you. But how did you know I would be here?'

'Ma'am, you mentioned you were coming here last night. It was my day off, so I thought I would surprise you,' Haris said, leading her to a coffee shop. 'But first, some real Turkish coffee.'

He told her of his childhood in a little village. 'My Umma was my father's second wife and I was the youngest of six children, so it wasn't easy for them or us. And it's only now that I am able to do things for them.'

'That's lovely,' Rupa said, wondering if her twins even realised the extent of their privilege.

'At the end of my first year in Qatar, I built a proper bathroom for them, with a Western commode. Both Umma and Vaapa were so pleased with it. She would show everyone the bathroom and the commode and tell them, my son got this for me.' Haris laughed. 'I never knew whether to be pleased or embarrassed. I would wonder if I should have got her gold bangles instead.'

Rupa gazed at him admiringly. 'You should be pleased. If I were your mother, I would be. A gold bangle is an object. But the toilet made her life easier. Let me tell you, after a certain age, squatting on your haunches isn't easy.'

'That's what I thought, ma'am,' Haris said, standing up and signalling for the bill. 'Umma has arthritis and she was in agony each time she used the Indian toilet. We had tied a rope from the ceiling of the toilet so she could hoist herself up to her feet and every day Umma would joke about how she was going to bring the roof down. But I could see her face was pale with the effort, and lined with pain.

'A gift should be about what the receiver needs. Not about displaying the giver's largesse. Don't you think so, ma'am?'

Rupa nodded. Such wisdom from one so young. 'You are a good boy, Haris,' she said. 'Your Umma must be proud of you. I would be.'

He smiled. 'She is, ma'am. But now let me show you Istanbul, outside of what you see in those tourism brochures in your hand.'

He took her down little streets and waited patiently as she stared at a fresco; he steered her away from the vultures waiting to pounce on wide-eyed tourists and hustlers selling trinkets as antiques. They went to a shop that sold carpets deep within the Grand Bazaar. 'It's one of the best places, ma'am,' he said.

A cat lay on a chair inside the shop. Haris sat down on the other chair while Rupa browsed through the halis and kelims. Rupa looked at the boy and the cat on adjacent chairs, surrounded by exquisite rugs. She raised her phone and shot a picture. His eyes suddenly opened and he sat up straight. 'Ma'am, please don't take my photo,' he said sharply.

'Oh, I wasn't taking your picture. Just the cat's,' she lied.

'I look horrible in photographs.' He grinned as though to make amends for his tone.

As the sun ascended the skies, he took her back to the hotel. 'Afternoon Juma prayers,' he said. 'But I will take you somewhere this evening if you would like to come along, to see real Sufi dancers. And I am sorry again, ma'am, for getting upset about the photo. I don't know what came over me.'

Rupa touched his elbow. 'It's fine. I am not offended. Thank you, Haris,' she said softly.

Keshav had a free afternoon and they lay in bed talking. 'He sounds nice but wait for the catch, my dear wife. It will come soon enough.'

That evening, she looked at Haris from the corner of her eye as he sat lost in rapture while the dervishes whirled in front of them. Later, when he saw her off in the cab he had whistled for her, she was perplexed, even a little disappointed. What had he wanted from her?

Rupa picked up the TV remote to change the channel, but stopped when she saw the red band of breaking news pop up on the screen. Bomb blast in Istanbul hotel. 40 dead and 189 injured.

She paused, unable to believe what she was seeing.

It was the hotel that Keshav and she had stayed at. Haris, she thought. Her heart seemed to have stilled. Was he all right?

If the bomb had gone off two days earlier, it would have been them.

Rupa picked up her phone to call Keshav. She didn't want to be alone any more. Keshav promised to be back soon. 'But I'll need to return later, for the puja. Also, Mini's been cooking all day long. I can't not have dinner,' he said.

Rupa continued to watch the screen as news reports came in.

When her mobile rang, she picked it up without glancing at the caller's name. 'Ma'am, this is Haris,' a distant voice said. 'I wanted to double-check that you're back in India.'

'Yes, yes, I am. Are you all right, Haris? I just saw the news of the bombing. I was so worried about you,' Rupa garbled into the phone.

'I am all right. Thank you for asking.'

'I am in Kerala, Haris,' Rupa told him. 'In a very beautiful resort. I was just thinking, if only you were here too.'

There was a pause. 'I wish I was there too, ma'am.'

With almost a sigh, he whispered, 'You are lucky, ma'am. I don't know when I will see Kerala again.'

Rupa heard voices in the background.

'I have to go, ma'am,' he said hurriedly. 'I just wanted to hear your voice and make sure you are fine. You take care.'

Keshav reached at a little past six. His face was grim. Two people he knew had died in the explosion. 'They think it's ISIS,' he said, as he sat propped up against the headboard, switching news channels to catch the latest reports.

His phone pinged. 'Apparently the bomb was set off by an Indian steward at the hotel. One of the ISIS recruits from Kasargod. Bastards! Why kill innocents? And to think an Indian was responsible.'

Rupa's mouth went dry. She took a long sip of water but her tongue stuck to the top of her mouth.

'Lie down with me, darling,' Keshav said. He switched off the TV and pulled the bedcover to his chin. 'I need to nap. It's going to be a late night. The puja will take hours.'

He tucked her head into the curve of his neck and draped his arm around her waist.

When Keshav's breathing steadied into the rhythm of sleep, she extricated herself from his grasp. She sat on a chair and stared into the twilight.

There was only one Indian steward at the hotel. Haris.

She picked up her phone and looked at the number he had called her from. She opened the photo gallery and scrolled down to the picture she had shot of the cat and him.

She stared at it mutely, not knowing what else to do.

## 6

# URVASHI

Her friends had been aghast when she confided in them about having met a man on Tinder. 'What were you thinking of, Urvashi?' Elizabeth said. 'Your marriage, are you going to risk it?'

'How could you get on Tinder?' Leela had hissed. 'What if someone you know finds you?'

'Men, all men, unless they are in diapers, are bad news,' Usha drawled. 'You should have taken up Zumba instead. At least it's for keeps!'

'But didn't all of you tell me to?' Urvashi asked, nonplussed.

'It was a joke,' Niloufer said, carefully avoiding meeting her gaze. 'If we had asked you to shave your head, would you have?'

'I am not on it any more,' Urvashi said, wondering who her friends had turned into.

Only Surya held her hand under the table and squeezed it. Go girl, go…

They had made love thirteen times. Each time they were together, Urvashi felt the attraction dwindling. And yet, because she hadn't wanted to admit to herself what a dog's dinner she had made of it, she would have gone on with the affair till it fizzled out on its own if he hadn't begun scrutinising her as if he were a monstrous patriarch. Forever finding fault with all she did, forever putting her down, questioning her every deed and thought when not stalking her every move.

'Why can't you text me in the middle of the interview? He is only a movie director…'

'Your bra strap is showing…'

'Should you be posing with a drink? You don't want people thinking you are a lush…'

'Who is this new follower of yours on Twitter? And why are you following him?'

'Why do you need other people in your life? Don't you have me?'

'Tell me, tell me, tell me…'

One day she knew she couldn't go on with it any more. She watched him as if through a sheet of glass. She felt removed from this man who was fucking her. And long after she had tipped the point, known the orgasm that felt like every other orgasm she'd had before, she watched his eyes glaze as he continued to ride her with the soul of an industrial pump. She knew then that this too had come to an end.

There was no way to tie up the loose ends for he wouldn't listen when she said that their relationship wasn't working any more. She stopped calling him and responded to him only after she had silenced a few calls. She stopped texting except when her conscience twinged at the cavalier end to what had seemed the focal point of her existence. She made excuses not to see him except in public places. She tried to show him in a thousand ways that it had ended, just as she had once sought to let him know how much she wanted him in her life.

Only, he wasn't taking a no. He was never going to, he said, when she tried to reason with him. You toyed with me. You messed with me. You can't just dump me. 'You knew it wasn't for keeps,' Urvashi said. 'You knew I was married. You knew this was all it was – an affair. And affairs end...'

He wouldn't accept it. The mouth she had kissed again and again spat expletives at her: Why does it have to end? Did your husband find out? Is that why?

For a moment, Urvashi had wondered if she should use Mahesh as an excuse to get out of this nightmare. Instead, she spoke the truth. 'I feel nothing for you any more. What part of that is so difficult for you to understand?'

'But you fucked me,' he shouted.

Urvashi glared at him, refusing to be shamed into submission. 'And so you did. We fucked each other. But that was all it was. An affair that went on too long. Don't you see we have nothing else to hold us together?'

'Are you saying I wasn't good in bed?'

'You were incredible in bed,' Urvashi sighed. 'But I feel nothing for you. How can you want to be with someone who feels nothing for you? I can't. I really can't.'

# Sreelakshmi

The ancients, the scriptures, all of them tell you that life is simple. That we complicate it with our thoughts, our desires, our hopes for ourselves, our need to immortalise ourselves even while we breathe. Sometimes all it takes is meeting another person, for everything that appeared simple to suddenly become full of complexities.

I couldn't imagine what Rupa would do. What was at stake here was her own sense of integrity. Haris was as much her friend as he was a mass murderer. Which part of him was she going to remember? Which part of him was she going to punish?

I had no such bouts of indecisiveness when I decided to take my life.

I sighed into the evening. It wasn't twilight yet and I wished I could be out by the river. While the day filled me with a sense of purpose, late evenings were my favourite time of the day. Especially once I had a home of my own. I would sit in the verandah with a book while my mother and Karthu bustled around in the garden. As the skies darkened, my mother would light a lamp and recite her prayers. She read a section from the Ramayana or the Bhagavatham every evening. I liked listening to her read, although Rama and Krishna were, I knew, no more than myths to prop up the faint-hearted.

At half past six, I would switch on the radio and tune into Vividh Bharati. There was a serenity about the evenings which I could find neither in the day nor the night.

Two of the waiters came and picked up the table I was on. They took it, along with another table, to a gazebo outside. From there I could see the railway bridge across the river, the old, collapsed bridge, and the new one. The Nila seemed to be rising. Maybe it would rise and rise, till it swept me away to salvation.

When I returned to Kerala from Varanasi, my entire life seemed to stretch ahead of me. But like the broken bridge over the Nila, it soon fell apart. An anguished cry rose up in me. Why is it that some of us seek to destroy what sustains us? Why is it that we cannot help ourselves from doing so?

My grandmother often said that the soul lingers in the body for a whole day and night even after we stop breathing. It gathers half-formed thoughts, sorrows and unfulfilled desires, collects the balance sheet of karma and finally escapes, baggage attached, into the next birth. As long as the soul still lives in the body, there is life deep within.

If there was even a shred of it left in me, it died when I saw him there. For Markose finally came to see me on the day after I killed myself.

After the post-mortem at the Government Hospital in Ottapalam, I was brought back to the tharavad in Karakkad by late afternoon. Though I had lived in a house near the college in Palapuram, it was decided that I should be taken to the family home and cremated on the banks of the river Nila.

I remained shrouded in silence while strangers took over. Once you are dead, there is even less control over what happens to you and what is done to you.

They laid me out in the hallway. A lamp with a single wick was lit and placed near my head. A handful of incense sticks were placed in the corner of the room so the fragrant smoke would add to the significance of the moment. An old relative sat at my head, reading aloud from the Ramayana, though everyone in the family knew that I didn't believe in gods or rituals. I did not know the import of the page he had opened. That was the belief, you see. The said page would decree if I was going to heaven or hell. I had chosen to take my own life but they were going to ensure that my passage to the hereafter was theirs to dictate.

My head to the south, my feet facing north, all of me covered with a white sheet, and my jaw bound as well. That was the norm for the dead.

My mother lay curled in a corner, weeping quietly, while Karthu, our maid, alternated between whimpering and screeching her sorrow. My sisters wept copiously while their husbands maintained a taciturn silence, except to discuss the arrangements for my cremation or greet visitors. Relatives I had tried to avoid and neighbours I had merely exchanged a smile and an occasional nicety with wept for me with an expansive grief that made me wonder who they were grieving for.

Only the children were free of pretence. They played their games, running this way and that, till someone asked them to pipe down. 'Stop this noise. This is a house of death. Show some respect, you unruly scoundrels,' I heard one of my cousins hector them.

Children do not understand death and so they don't fear it. They are not hypocrites either. In a little while, they resumed their games again, accompanied by high-pitched shrieks and laughter.

The students whom I'd had to implore to keep decorum in class trooped in with downcast eyes and in studied silence. Among them was the paper plane pilot, I was sure. My colleagues, the men who had undressed me with their eyes, the women who had impaled me with their scorn, all those who had treated me with a diffidence bordering on disdain, were here to offer their respects. Writers rushed from Thrissur and Kozhikode, Kochi and Kottayam, Alappuzha and Kollam. The members of the Sahitya Akademi arrived with a wreath. Local politicians and several people I didn't know, including the mahout I walked past every morning on my way to the college, showed up. It was only then that Markose walked in.

Markose didn't join the line that walked past me with folded hands and bent heads. He stood with a group of men, his arms crossed. Once in a while, he would groom his beard with his fingers. His eyes didn't stray even once from my big toes, which had been bound together with a scrap of white cloth. He didn't cry for me. He just stood as if he had turned into stone. What was he thinking? Even when I was alive, I could not fathom his thoughts. So how could I in death? Besides, what would it accomplish? Death nullifies everything. Death takes away all power. Death and love.

They took me away to the Nila. It felt like I was going home. The north-east monsoon had set in on time, but was erratic. The rain had stayed away on the day I killed myself. But as they carried me over the path down the side of the bridge, a slow drizzle began.

The mango tree my mother had marked for her funeral the day my father died had been chopped down and the logs cut to size. It wasn't customary to cremate the body of someone whose older siblings or parents were still alive. But they had decided that I was better cremated than laid to rest in the ground.

Green logs interspersed with a few well-dried out ones were heaped on me to ensure the flames were steady and strong. The heat of a funeral pyre has to be constant and intense. I felt a sense of relief. Soon it would be over. Soon I would be ashes, to be taken away by the river for the sea to swallow.

All of me, my words and mortal remains, would cease to exist. There would be no more of Sreelakshmi, a spinster of some thirty-five years, teacher of zoology, writer of stories, peddler of female angst, winner of a few prizes, and a failure on all other counts.

'She can't even make a decent cup of tea,' my mother liked to tell everyone with a mortified laugh.

My cousin's son lit the pyre. I lay in the middle of the blaze and felt nothing except the heat singeing my spirit. Love and death have this in common: they consume you so that everything else ceases to matter.

As the dusk turned to night, they left, the mourners and fixers of funerals. Sreelakshmi was dead. On the third day, they would come to collect what was left of me. Bones and ashes. On the fifth day, all of me would dissolve into nothingness.

Except that Markose didn't let me have that either.

I looked away from the river, unable to bear the sadness weighing me down. The gazebo was set with two tables laid out. Candles had been lit and stewards were bringing in plates and cutlery, arranging napkins. Mosquito coils with gleaming red eyes were scattered around. A group of foreigners walked across the lawn towards the gazebo. I heard a strange language being spoken and some English.

A young foreigner seemed to be in charge. She turned to the waiter, made a mudra to suggest excellent, and said in heavily accented Malayalam. '*Unni sir nodu parayanam nannayitindu.*'

One of the women asked her something. The young woman smiled and translated, 'I was just thanking the manager for the setting.'

They sat at the two tables which had been pulled together and soon the clink of cutlery, their voices and the sound of cicadas filled me with calm, erasing all feelings of remorse. Perhaps I would even find a brief reprieve this evening, in a story that wasn't mine.

I was on a table that already had two elderly couples. One of the men leaned sideways and spoke to the young woman at the next table. 'You look very familiar. Why do I know you?'

The young woman paused mid-sentence. Her hand on the table trembled. She reached for the salt and pepper basket in front of him. Of its own volition, her hand found me and her fingers clung to me, seeking some form of sustenance, or was it merely something to hold on to, as she tried to compose herself.

'Oh honey, stop it…' his wife butted in. 'He is always doing that. Last year, on an aerobridge, he saw a busty woman with black hair, dressed in a pink velour track suit, and thought it was Kim Kardashian.'

The young woman's mouth twisted into a smile. Then she took a deep breath, like she'd made up her mind, and asked, 'Are you thinking of Pussy-Mouth?'

# Pussy-Mouth

Even after a year, Liliana woke up wondering where she was. She waited for the church bells to start ringing, for the street-cleaning trucks to park at the entrance of the road and for the giant motorised brushes and men's voices to come alive. For Alessandro's bike to go hurtling down the street with a rev and a vroom. No one knew where he went so early. She would never know now.

The sky outside the open window was streaked with thin lines of light. It was only four, she saw in the little alarm clock she kept on the bedside table. She groped for her phone, then remembered it was in her bag. She didn't use a smart phone any more. Or a laptop. Or an iPad. She had severed ties with technology. The worldwide web was a nightmare she had extricated herself from.

Liliana turned on her side and pulled her knees towards her chest. She tucked her hands between her thighs. An image came involuntarily to mind, of a millipede curled into a ball to protect itself from marauding paws and the mouths of predators. The skies grew lighter but Liliana lay there unable to move, unable to weep, unable to go back to sleep.

When the alarm clock trilled to life at five, she jumped out of bed. Her day had begun and she could lose herself in the rigour that it demanded of her.

Liliana let the bed air as she brushed her teeth. It was twenty past five when she emerged from the bathroom. She made the bed with great care; plumping the pillows and folding the sheet she covered herself with at night, into a neat rectangle she left at the foot of the bed.

Until she got here, she hadn't known there was another way of making a bed. She pulled a thin tie-and-dye bed sheet in place of a top cover over the bed. The vestiges of a routine from another life were the hardest to shed. Her eyes darted to the clock: half past five.

The almonds had soaked into a mush that was in no way almond-like, but it was all she could stomach this early. Once, Liliana had woken up at eight, to lie in bed checking her emails and messages, browsing Instagram and Twitter…

Liliana changed into the pyjamas and kurta she wore for the morning regimen. The skies were beginning to brighten but there was a cool breeze and she could, for a moment, forget she was at Near the Nila, far from what was once home.

She closed her eyes, folded her hands and made a salutation to the earth, the gods, her guru, in gratitude for the fact that she was here and not lying dead in a basement with her wrists slit.

As she stretched her body, she tried to focus on all that she had been taught in the previous lesson.

But the music wouldn't stop playing in her head. *Aliveni, njanyenducheyvu?*

Liliana had asked the teacher, 'What does it mean?'

The teacher had tried to explain the meaning of the lyrics. '*Njanyenducheyvu* – What do I do? Beautiful lady with long hair – that is Aliveni.' She smiled at Liliana. 'Like you…' She gestured to the braid that Liliana had tamed her hip-length hair into. They humoured her at the dance institute, the teachers and most of the Indian girls. Sometimes she saw herself as a baby chimpanzee in a white diaper – a lovable oddity.

She hummed the tune under her breath. The rest of the words refused to form. She wasn't ready to start on a padam yet. That was for someone who had studied Mohiniattam for at least a dozen years and not a novice like her. But the performance she had watched at the institute had filled her with a deep yearning to be that woman, the dancer, pleading *njanyenducheyvu*.

Liliana continued to practise. Soon the alarm was trilling. It was a quarter to seven. There were chores to be done before she left for class.

It was a little past eight when she wheeled the bicycle onto the path that ran along the compound wall of Near the Nila. A couple of years ago, she had stumbled on the website of the hotel and the name had lodged in her head. In the days after the scandal broke, when she was looking for a place she could run away to, she had gone back to it and found that it now had an additional entry – Applications Open for Dance Residency.

She had filled in the application. Strangely, it asked for no prior exposure to dance or experience as a dancer.

She danced like most of her people did, at raves and parties. Sometimes on a beach and, once in a while, when she tried on a new dress, she pirouetted on her toes. But at that point, she would have applied for a balancing-a-teacup-on-the-tip-of-the-nose residency if there had been one.

The mail, when it came, took her by surprise. A Skype call had been set up with Shyam, the director of the Koman Memorial Trust. She was nervous. Would he recognise her? Know her as Pussy-Mouth, whose video had gone viral and gained two million YouTube hits officially, and who knew how many millions as downloaded Messenger and WhatsApp forwards? But Shyam either lived under a rock with no internet, only to emerge for Skype calls, or was a fine actor.

She had been prepared to answer any questions he had. She wasn't going to lie. All she had left was her honesty. A willingness to accept the consequences of her actions, and survive. But he had been gentle and affable. His queries touched no nerve ends.

The residency was for six months and they would extend it by a year if the visa worked out. But it wasn't going to be enough, Shyam said. Dance needed a lifelong commitment.

Liliana had smiled. 'I know,' she said.

'So is this what you want to do?' His voice seemed a long way away but the intensity of his gaze travelled distance and time.

'I don't know,' she said. 'I need a refuge for now. Some place and some activity that will take me away from myself.'

There was a moment of silence. She realised that she had blown it. This innate lack of discretion was what had turned her into Pussy-Mouth, she thought with loathing.

She hadn't felt so vulnerable when she saw the video the first time, of her crawling on her knees towards F as he stood lighting a cigarette. At that point, it had just seemed like good fun.

The party was at an acquaintance's home in Milan. An artist she had met a few times. She had been glad to come home to Italy after a tough year at Cambridge. Giddy with relief and the sheer pleasure of being back again, she had dropped acid with two others. Later, in the bathroom, she had found a bag of cosmetics, probably left behind by the artist's girlfriend. She had drawn whiskers on either side of her mouth with the eye pencil and emphasised her mouth with fuschia lipstick. She had dropped to the floor on her knees and hands and gone looking for F. Cat-like, she had pawed and tugged at the zip of his jeans. Pulling it down with her teeth. A wave of silence filled the room. Someone in the room had pulled his phone out. Or was it a she? Liliana didn't care. She was a furry feline; a huntress seeking her quarry that nestled within boxer shorts.

Someone laughed out loud. She had looked up sideways as a cat would, blinked and meowed at the camera.

That was it. A playful act. She hadn't given anyone a blowjob, swallowed semen, or been fucked in the arse. She hadn't parted her legs or mounted a man, gone down on a girl or let a dog fuck her. She hadn't been in an orgy or been a mistress with a whip. She hadn't done anything but pretend to be a cat. But someone in the group there sent it to her ex in Sheffield, who had with grim relish forwarded it to his school, university and work groups, with a caption. She had a new name: Pussy-Mouth, and a new classification: Deviant.

Liliana discovered the power of the male imagination. The person who had streamed it live may have meant no harm. In this time and age, how could invasion of privacy be termed a crime? All of us do it all the time, she told the blogger who tracked her down. We Instagram our food and friends, our bodies and beds, our lovers, she said, laughing.

Later, someone told her that those words, that laugh, damned her. Her playful attitude to sex crucified her. Sex had to be sacred, or dirty, or sanctified by the four-letter word: love. Playful=Deviant.

Her mouth became her. No one looked at her breasts any more. No one watched the sway of her hips. Her hair, her legs, the curve of her waist, the upward tilt of her nose, her thoughts, her feelings, everything ceased to matter. The men, they looked at her mouth as if they would at a ripe cherry, a doughnut; it was an orifice of deviant delight. Everywhere, the eyes followed her mouth.

Someone created a fan page on Facebook, someone else a Twitter ID. Pussy-Mouth posts and memes made an appearance. The Instagram eye caught up with her: eating an ice cream, smoking a cigarette, trying on a lipstick… they spared her no moment. She was the girl attached to a pussy mouth.

What broke Pussy-Mouth's feigned nonchalance? Was it that one evening at the dining table, her father's husky voice with its whiplash: Basta!

Enough? Enough of what, she had wondered and turned to look at him, her mouth parted, fork arrested mid-air, a strand of spaghetti still caught in it. All she had been doing was twisting spaghetti into her mouth from a fork to amuse her little niece.

Her father glared at her mouth and hissed: 'Don't you have any shame? Haven't you put us through enough?'

There had been a stunned silence. Until then, no one in her family had mentioned her new-found notoriety. Her mother had clattered the dishes, her sister had turned to her daughter with a frown, her niece had burst into tears, and Liliana twirled her pasta round and round the fork, unable to eat, unable to leave.

Earlier in the day, she had gone to church. She was attending Sunday Mass after a long time. She didn't believe in religion, or God, but the old church with its stained-glass windows and high ceilings seemed like a sanctuary that offered respite from all the eyes that were fixed on her mouth. When she kneeled, nobody turned to looked at her or whisper. She did everything everyone else did.

For the first time in many weeks, Liliana felt light; the heaviness inside her seemed to dissolve. Except, when it was time to receive communion, she saw the men look at her and look away. She heard the snort of contempt from the woman standing behind her. As she raised her face to receive the wafer, she felt the priest's eyes swoop on her mouth, the brush of his fingertips on her parted lips as he slid it into her mouth instead of placing it as he would have otherwise.

She had thrust his hand away and run out of the church, her clattering heels echoing with shame and undisguised fury at the unfairness of it all.

Someone must have told her father about the kerfuffle in the church, Liliana thought as the twirl of pasta around her fork grew bigger. She felt as if her heart was going to burst. The fork slipped from her fingers and her head dropped into the plate. She pressed her mouth into the sauce-speckled pasta, trying to contain the pain that threatened to erupt.

Liliana cycled towards the institute. She stayed as close to the edge of the road as possible. Indian men were not to be trusted, she had decided. Every day, at least one of them would swerve towards her for no reason. Clearly, a woman on a bicycle or a bike, or even in a car, needed to be taught her place. They annoyed Liliana but she wasn't angry with them, not like she was with the invisible men who had derailed her life. She would merely shake her head and cycle on.

In the long interval between classes, some of the other girls came up to speak to her. With gestures and a few words – she trying out her Malayalam and they English – they conducted a conversation of sorts. Their questions were about her everyday life in Italy – banal but relentless. Once again, the image of Koko the chimpanzee came into her mind.

Dhanya sidled up to her. 'I have internet on my phone. You can check the meaning of the song.'

Liliana shook her head. 'No, no, you tell me the meaning. I don't want the internet,' she said, trying to keep the vehemence out of her voice.

'Why?' Dhanya asked.

'I don't like it,' Liliana replied, not knowing what else to say.

'You sound like my mother,' Dhanya giggled.

Liliana smiled. The truth was, she felt like her Nona, her grandmother who had disappeared into herself as she grew older and weary of living.

Liliana felt someone's gaze on her and looked up to catch Tara glaring at the two of them. She said something to Dhanya. Liliana didn't understand the words but she heard something that stayed in her head: koothichi. She saw Dhanya flush.

'What was that?'she asked Dhanya.

Dhanya frowned. 'A bad word. The next time she uses it, I am going to complain to the teacher.'

When the class resumed, Liliana went back to it gratefully. As long as she was trying to understand footwork and gestures, there was no time for introspection, no room for Pussy-Mouth to emerge and treat her cortex as a scratching post.

Liliana cycled back slowly to her room. It was almost noon. She would bathe and take a nap.

It was a quarter past one when she woke up. She pulled on a long skirt and blouse and tied her hair up in a high knot, then used an eye pencil to line her eyes. She was ready to eat at the restaurant.

That was part of the residency programme. She was given set vegetarian meals at the restaurant twice a day. She had to pay extra if she wanted fish or meat. Liliana had grown to like the Keralan food – though, each time she said it, both Shyam and Radha corrected her and said, 'It's not Keralan, it's Malayali.'

The steward greeted her and led her to the table closest to the plate-glass window that overlooked the river.

Some of the tables were occupied by guests – a family of four, a couple and their two young children, another family with two grown-up daughters. A very good-looking couple sat in an alcove while Radha's aunt Maya and her son sat at their usual table.

Unni, the resort manager, came towards her with a smile. 'Hello, Liliana,' he said. She smiled at him. 'How are you?'

Unni was a prince, she had heard. She had wondered if that was one of the yarns they fed tourists along with appam, stew, meen pollichathu and classical dance performances. But apparently Unni was really a prince; all five feet eight inches, bald pate, thick shaving-brush moustache and curving fullness of belly. Liliana liked him and his ready smile.

'All good,' Unni said, pulling out a chair. At first Liliana had been thrown by the easy familiarity that most Indians adopted in their everyday dealings. Now she was used to it and found it a relief from the pretentions that had once been part of her life. Signorita to the face and Pussy-Mouth behind her back.

'I have a request, a request from Shyam sir,' Unni said.

Liliana murmured, 'Yes.' What now, she wondered.

'We have a group of ten checking in, two days from now. Mostly Italians and some English people. We need someone who can handle both languages. He was wondering if you could make some time to show them around.'

Liliana shook her head. 'I don't think I can.'

Unni's face fell. Then he roused himself and said, 'Will you think about it?'

Liliana held his gaze. 'I will. But my answer will still be no.'

As Unni rose to go, Liliana asked, 'Unni, what is the meaning of koothichi?'

'What?'Unni yelped in consternation. 'It's a bad word. Please don't use it!'

Liliana opened the book she was reading and propped it against the salt and pepper cellars. When the food arrived, she ate slowly. The afternoon stretched ahead of her, empty till her 3.30 p.m. Malayalam tutorial.

She had begun putting together the letters of the Malayalam alphabet. Fifty-six of them. It demanded more from her than she had expected but it was precisely what she needed.

'Sir, I have a question,' she said as she walked in.

'Sit down.' Poduval said, gesturing to the chair.

Liliana flushed. Poduval was an old-fashioned man, a retired schoolteacher and a well-known poet. He treated her like she was five years old and probably would continue to do so until she could read an entire sentence in Malayalam.

Liliana sat on the chair assigned to her. He opened the book and asked her to read.

'What is your question?' he asked, once he had closed the Class 1 primer.

'I heard a word today, sir. Koothichi. I know it is a bad word. But what does it mean?'

Poduval glared at her for a long moment, his mouth stretched in distaste. 'Che che,' he muttered under his breath.

'What?' Liliana asked in a whisper. Pussy-Mouth had struck again.

'It is a bad word; it means prostitute,' Poduval said tersely.

Liliana was confused. 'But doesn't koothu mean dance? At the institute, we have the koothambalam, which is the dance temple. So how can it be a word for prostitute?'

Poduval pulled at the bridge of his nose. 'Koothichi comes from koothu – dance – and aachi – the one who performs it. There was a time when dancers couldn't become wives. They ended up as kept women. It's easy to see how the word came to mean what it does now.'

Liliana nodded and changed the subject to the words of the padam. She wanted to surprise the girls in class. 'See, you don't need the internet,' she would tell them.

There was a performance at the koothamblam in the evening. Liliana rode her bicycle to the institute. She would watch the performance and go home. Heads turned as she weaved her way through the seated audience to a vantage point.

She gathered her skirt and sat down in a single eloquent movement and tucked her legs beneath her.

From behind her, she heard a whisper: Koothichi. A giggle followed.

Dhanya, who sat beside her, stiffened at the slur. Liliana felt a voice scream in her head. Would she never escape this? What had she done now?

Dhanya murmured, 'Liliana, they did an internet search on you this afternoon. It's Tara. Until you arrived, she was the teachers' pet. She was the girl who had moved from Calcutta to study here. But you moved countries. She is jealous. Don't let it bother you.'

Liliana said nothing. The performance was a blur. When it was over, she walked out of the koothambalam quietly. Tara was standing with her coterie.

'Pussy-Mouth,' Tara called out. The girls with her tittered.

'So that's why you came here? You thought no one would find out,' Tara said when Liliana kept walking. 'Listen, Pussy-Mouth, what we learn here is dance. It's not for sluts like you. Why don't you go and find a dance-bar somewhere?'

The other girls looked at Tara, trying to comprehend the English words. 'What did you say?' one of them asked.

'I just told her that Mohiniattam isn't for koothichis,' Tara snorted.

Liliana went up to her. Dhanya followed her, as though aware that something ugly was about to transpire and there was nothing she could do to stop it.

'Tara,' Liliana said. 'If I am a koothichi, you are one too.'

Tara reared her head and hissed. 'You bitch…'

'No, not bitch. Koothichi. Like you. Like each one of us.' A small crowd was beginning to form around them.

Dhanya tugged at her elbow. 'Hush, it's a bad word.'

'No, it's not. We made it a bad one. Do you know what koothichi means? Someone who performs koothu, dance – a dancer. If we ourselves don't respect dance and dancers, who else will? If you don't believe me,' she said turning to Tara, 'look it up on the net. Isn't that where you went to look up dirt on me?'

Tara walked away without speaking a word. Someone sniggered. The crowd dispersed, knowing nothing more salacious was coming their way.

Liliana rode back to the resort, lost in thought. By tomorrow, everyone at the institute would know all about her. Where would she go now? What had she been trying to flee from? The spider's web stretched to the far ends of the world. There was no place to hide. And she didn't want to any more.

She was tired of running, of trying to erase the person she was.

She leaned her bicycle against a tree and went into the reception. Unni was there, working on the desktop.

'Hi Unni,' she said.

He looked up and smiled. 'Have you thought about it?'

She smiled. 'Yes. I'll do it! But…'

Unni leaned forward. 'Shyam sir said that your fee will be 20 euro for each guest for two hours. So it would be 200 euro for each group.'

Liliana smiled. 'Excellent!' She walked to the restaurant and ordered a beer.

It was a little past nine when she entered her room. She opened the wardrobe and pulled out her iPad. She found the charger and plugged it in. Unni had given her a piece of paper with the Wi-Fi code.

Liliana stepped into the shower and came out naked. In the long mirror, she examined herself. She was at her toned best. But it didn't matter, did it? Whether she was fat or thin, flat-chested or with perky breasts, with orange-peel skin or a high curvy butt, no one was looking at any part of her except her mouth. Had she thought of it as dirty too?

She wrapped a mundu around herself, tying it above her breasts so that a hint of the gold border was visible. Then she painted her lips carefully with a deep carmine lipstick she found in her make-up kit.

She curled on the bed and logged into her FB, Twitter and Instagram accounts. She took a selfie of herself: bare shoulders on which her braid lay, pouting face and deep red lips.

She smiled as she keyed in, *Hello darlings, I'm back!*

A moment's pause, and she added: *Meow*.

Every soldier knows that the only way to keep the enemy from following is to burn the bridge behind. She had burnt her bridges too. There was only the way ahead.

# 7

# SREELAKSHMI

I didn't know what to think. How had the world changed so much in five decades? Or hadn't it? Gossip, scandal, and the casual destruction of lives had always been with us. Now they used gadgets to propagate these.

Liliana had introduced me to three things that seemed to rule the world: Facebook, Twitter and Instagram. From where I saw it, Facebook was no more than a village well where daily updates were shared and Instagram was the bathing spot in the river where either you looked or were looked at. As for Twitter, it was no more than an extension of the tea shop where men gathered more for news and debate rather than for the tea and parippu vada. The only difference between then and now was that men and women bathed together, and men fetched water from the well while women sat on the narrow benches in the tea shop with their knees crossed and discussed politics and world affairs.

While there was nothing in Liliana's story that resonated with mine, I knew what it felt like to be the object of sexual speculation. I knew the overriding desire to escape it all.

On the third day after I was cremated, they gathered the rest of my bones from the cremation site. These were wrapped in a red cloth and put into an earthern pot and strung on a frangipani tree beyond the little wall that separated the front yard and the garden. The bones of the dead are always strung on trees that ooze sap when cut. Perhaps because the remains of a life need the affirmation that life will go on, no matter what. I was glad they chose the frangipani, not a ficus or a jackfruit tree. I had always thought of it as my totemic tree. For I knew the anguish of being that tree.

They give you a beautiful setting, a context even, placed in a sacred grove on a hilltop. Birds sing sitting on its branches, but they don't nest there. Bees drink the nectar of the white waxy flowers, but they go to the mango or the jackfruit, the tamarind or an alcove somewhere, to build their hive and store their honey. Flowers are picked to adorn a deity but seldom worn in the hair. This is the story of the frangipani. It was also mine.

Every day, countless people die. In their homes and hospital beds; on the street or in their back yard. Each death is tragic in its own way. So why did my death turn into this circus of heartbreak, I wondered, as a black pall settled over everything.

In the days after I killed myself, they turned me into a person I didn't recognise. She always had a smile and a fact to share with us, a student said. She was so fond of my children, a neighbour claimed. Everyone had a Sreelakshmi story and most of it was untrue. It was their stories, and not mine, that gave me a mythical status.

Since I did not have children or a husband to do the annual srardham, it was decided that my nephew and nieces would take my bones to Thirunelli in Wayanad. There, it was believed, I would be set free of all earthly ties and my nephew would be free of his responsibility to pay annual homage to his aunt. Otherwise, what if she came back to him in his dreams, demanding her dues?

Only I knew I was never going to be set free. Damaged goods in life. Damaged goods in death.

Markose had ensured that by smuggling me away and burying me in his heart and his almirah. I would lie in limbo forever.

# Urvashi

It was almost midnight. The restaurant and the river were bathed in darkness.

The sky lit up with a giant slash of lightning. Thunder rolled and rumbled. A cold breeze blew. The rolled-up blinds on the outer edge of the verandah slapped against the pillar. The bamboo copse at the edge of the lawns creaked and groaned.

The storm had kept her up for a while. She had turned the air conditioner off and opened the windows to let the cool breeze in. Rain drops had stung her face as she stood at the window, watching the sky light up. Urvashi remembered getting into bed and propping the pillows up so as to watch the storm as she lay there.

She woke up at daybreak to silence and calm.

She woke up remembering what Surya had told her when they last met.

She had turned to Surya in sheer desperation. 'What do I do? I can't go on like this.' Urvashi had tried to keep the quiver out of her voice. 'It's destroying me.'

He turned up everywhere. Including Facebook and Instagram, with new names and identities. But he always left a footprint so she would recognise him. A cryptic clue from the language of love they had once shared.

He emailed her pictures with a threat: Don't push me. I will send them to your husband. I will send them to your sisters. I will send them to your colleagues.

He called her home number and said nothing.

He would come to the apartment block and register his name in the visitors' book. The security guard would call her on the intercom to announce his arrival but there would no knock on the door, no bell ringing, not even steps approaching her door or going away from it.

She began seeing him everywhere: at the gym and beauty salon, the supermarket, and in the cafe across from the newspaper office where she worked. But only a fleeting glimpse, so she was never sure if he was there or if she had imagined it.

'I am losing my mind,' she said again, looking over Surya's shoulder at the back of a head that seemed to be his. Did he have a shirt like that? The angle of the right shoulder was familiar. 'I think he is here.'

Surya pushed the chair back abruptly and got up. She went to the man with his back to them. She said something to him. Urvashi watched him turn, her mouth dry and her heart hammering against her chest.

It wasn't him.

Urvashi smiled, not knowing what else to do.

Surya came back to their table. 'So what is frightening you? Exposure?

'Look at the kind of world we live in, Urvashi. Do you think all the men accused in the #Metoo campaign or that lecturer in a college in Tamil Nadu, who lured girls into sex work, or the army man in Kashmir who used a human shield, won't survive, despite their lives being exposed and plastered all over social media?

'Our lives are not ours any more. Everything is out there. If

I went looking for it, I could even find out when you last had a yeast infection or if you wear thongs or granny panties.

'A woman looking outside her marriage isn't even news in this world where everyone is talking of polyamory.

'So you need to get over this fear. What is the worst he can do? Tell your husband or family? As for your colleagues, do you think they really care? And if it does happen, you will know how to deal with it. We always do. Nothing is as bad as we imagine it to be.

'But he is feeding off your fear. And you are letting him.'

Urvashi had nodded. But within her rose a tide of resentment for this woman who had it all laid out in her head in neat little columns and tables.

She knew she couldn't organise her feelings with such sangfroid. She had told herself that they needed each other. But the truth was that she had used the young man. Chewed and masticated his need and spat it out to prop up her own self-worth.

Urvashi sat up. She would go for a walk. That would clear her head of the putrefying thoughts that filled her with the vile, sweetish stench of an overflowing septic tank.

The resort grounds were awash with the beauty of a rained-in dawn. The leaves were washed clean and glistening, the grass burgeoning with moisture, and the soil a deep shade of coffee. The air was cool and fresh. She kicked off her sandals and walked barefoot on the grass for a bit. She raised her chin to the skies and let the cool breeze caress her face.

A long time ago, one of her schoolteachers had told her to stand barefoot on the grass and gaze at the stars. You will find that nothing in between is of any consequence, she had told her, when she caught Urvashi crying silently into a book in the darkest corner of the school library. No one particularly cared for the teacher with her ill-fitting blouses, dull saris and pebble-like eyes behind soda-bottle glasses. Besides, she taught maths.

She hadn't asked Urvashi what she was crying about. Everyone had known that she hadn't been picked to be school captain when she was the most obvious choice. Urvashi didn't know what caused her to weep – the humiliation or the hurt. She remembered raising her tear-smudged face and looking at the teacher: was the woman stark raving mad?

Thirty-seven years later, she finally discovered the wisdom of that counsel. This moment would always be hers and no one could take it away from her.

As she walked towards the restaurant, she shuddered, thinking of how she had left it the afternoon before. Brinda had seen her to her room and sat talking to her for a while. They didn't talk about anything of consequence but it was as if a tentative friendship had sprung up between them. Urvashi decided then that there would be no exclusive on why the girl had left her career mid-stride. Brinda was entitled to choose how to live her life. Besides, you don't abuse trust.

She remembered the piece of plastic that Brinda had given her. She had meant to return it to Megha. She wondered if it was part of some toy.

When she walked into the restaurant, she found Maya and Naveen at the table she had occupied earlier in the day.

Urvashi had been introduced to Maya the second time she had come to Near the Nila, a year ago. 'Meet Maya, my Uncle Koman's wife,' Radha said.

'Actually, I was not his legal wife. I just lived in sin with him,' Maya said softly.

'Didn't you get married in a temple?' Radha asked, surprised.

'We did. But Koman thought I was committing bigamy, so we never registered it. At our age, we didn't think it mattered.'

Urvashi had looked at Radha, nonplussed.

'Good morning,' she said now, walking towards them.

Maya looked tired, she thought, as she watched her ladle egg curry carefully into a little bowl which she placed on a plate, with two appams arranged on one side so they wouldn't touch the bowl. She pushed the plate towards Naveen. 'Have your breakfast, darling. It's just the way you like it, see?'

'Early breakfast?' Urvashi asked.

'It's our birthday and we thought we would come in before the other guests do,' Maya said. 'It's a treat we give ourselves every year.'

'Happy birthday, Maya. Happy birthday, Naveen.'

Maya smiled. 'Thank you.'

Naveen stared into the distance.

'He isn't having a good day,' Maya said quietly, tucking a grey strand of hair behind her ear.

'I had left something here. I'll just pick it up and leave,' Urvashi said, reaching for the pepper and salt shaker tray.

'Oh, is it a chalk piece like thing?' Maya asked.

Urvashi nodded.

Maya leaned forward. 'Naveen has it with him. I'll get it from him in a bit and bring it around. If I take it from him now, he might make a scene.'

Urvashi walked out of the restaurant slowly. Her teacher had said something else that day. Look around you to get a perspective on your life. Sometimes that's all you need to do.

# How to shape happily-ever-afters

Maya tapped the cigarette on the granite countertop. She felt the tobacco flakes shift beneath her fingertips. She held it to her nose and took a deep draw of the sunshine-brown fragrance. She placed it between her lips and lit a match, cupping the flame as she tilted her head to light the cigarette. That first draw and she felt the year-long abstinence, the knots in the nerves, the loneliness, the unshed tears, dissipate in a curl of smoke. She closed her eyes as the earth spun around her. She held on to the counter top for support. From where she stood, she could see Malini in her cage.

'Ganda, ganda!' she thought she heard Malini say. The parrot had added ganda to her list of words. She had learnt it from Naveen.

Koman had had the parrot for several years. She was a cantankerous old bird but she had taken to Naveen and often rubbed her head against his cheek. Sometimes she would sit on his shoulder and whisper in his ear and Naveen would lean his head ever so gently towards the parrot. It was about the only time he displayed a human need to connect with another living being.

Maya looked into the darkness outside the window. Koman was gone five years now but it was like he had never left. She took another drag of the cigarette. Neither of them had been smokers but in the eight years of their life together, this had become a ritual of sorts. The smoke at night, sitting on the verandah facing the Nila. Everything about the day, her day, ashed with a minute-long indulgence that corroded the lungs and stained the teeth. Then they would eat a fruit he would feed her; segments of orange, or slices of apple or watermelon, flavoured with the aroma of tobacco from his fingertips. Maya swallowed down the tears, stubbed out the spent cigarette and washed her hands carefully.

They had planned the kitchen together. From the handle to the hinge, the height of the counter and the depth of the overhead cabinets. 'We are playing house,' she smiled at him.

'Neither of us ever did, wife,' he had laughed.

'You knew, didn't you?'she had asked suddenly. 'You knew I was a divorcee.'

Koman had taken her in his arms and murmured against her hair, 'I knew that it wasn't what you made it out to be. I knew you were keeping secrets from me. But I didn't want to probe. You would tell me when you were ready, I knew.'

'Does it bother you that I didn't commit bigamy?' She laughed against his neck.

'It does, it hurts deeply.' Koman held her away and crumpled his features into the face of grief. Eyebrows slanting down at the ends, eyes crinkling, mouth drooping.

Maya touched the corners of his mouth with her fingertips and pulled them up. 'Are you happy, Koman? Do you miss Kathakali? Being a dancer?'

He put on another expression. Or was it the wiping clean of all traces of emotion? Shantam. A coming to terms with life, as he had described it for her. 'I have you and I don't miss being a performer. That part of my life is over. But my art lives with me. Now, enough of chit-chat, the kitchen people will come from Thrissur and we need to be ready for them,' he said with mock haste. Or was he just changing the subject?

A little later, she saw him amuse Naveen with the navarasas.

Stop second-guessing me, his eyes said as they met hers over Naveen's head. Don't think beyond the here and now.

For a moment, she stared at the ingredients unseeingly. What was she doing? Then she shook herself out of her reverie and whisked the oil, curd, baking soda and sugar in a mixing bowl. Briefly, she lifted her eyes from the bowl and let her gaze stray to the living room where Naveen sat engrossed in nothing. She had left the television on, tuned to a cartoon channel. The truth was, it didn't matter which channel or show it was, as long as it was on.

'Is the cartoon nice?' she asked.

He turned towards her and blinked. He would have done the same if she had asked him: Does God exist?

God doesn't exist, she thought viciously as she added flour to the bowl and began mixing it with her fingers. God doesn't exist, or her Naveen wouldn't be sitting in front of a television, dressed in pyjamas with a print of blue bunny rabbits gambolling on it, waiting for her to lead him to bed and tuck him in as if he were six and not thirty-eight years old.

God doesn't exist, or Koman wouldn't have died a few years after they finally found the well of content that had evaded them all their lives.

That evening, Maya had waited for Koman to come back to the cottage. He had decided to bathe in the river, which was unlike him. They had a beautiful open-air bathroom with a rain shower and a stone bench to sit on and dry themselves. It had been Koman's idea that, in the new bathroom, they would bathe in the moonlight.

He had explained every detail to Shyam, who had it built for them but wouldn't let them pay for it. 'It's my gift to you. Besides, I've decided to incorporate the design into the honeymoon cottages so you pretty much paid for it yourself,' he had insisted.

Every day, in a thousand ways, Koman had wanted to evoke a forgotten youth, the slumbering senses. And Maya had opened like a bud blooming; which woman wouldn't if she was caressed and stroked, loved and loved again, like she had never known it was possible for anyone to be loved.

'You spoil me,' she said to him one night.

'I have a huge reservoir of love in me. Who am I saving it for? I want to empty it out before I die,' he had laughed.

What if one day you discover the reservoir has run dry, she thought to herself, still unable to believe that she was here with him. Between that call thirteen years ago, and her making the decision, two years had gone past. Koman had no doubts about them living together. She had been the one to dither till he demanded that she make the move.

'What's holding you back?' he had said as they sat across from each other in the house. 'I used to think it was your husband… so then?'

'He and I are divorced.' Maya had stirred another spoon of sugar into her coffee.

'That's the fifth spoon of sugar you have added to your coffee. What is it? I knew you weren't living together despite all the elaborate stories of his weekly card games you fed me for years.'

Her gaze dropped. She felt sheepish, and guilty. A child caught with her fingers in the jam jar. Maya cleared her throat.

'I have a son,' she began.

'I know you have a child. I saw the stretch marks.'

'And you never asked?' Maya's hand flew to her mouth.

'I waited for you to tell me.' Koman reached across and took her hand in his. He weaved her fingers through his. 'What is it?'

'He is autistic. I am supposed to say he is on the autism spectrum, but that doesn't change the fact that he has the mental age of a five-year-old at the most. A querulous and sometimes very difficult five-year-old.'

'How old is he?' Koman asked gently.

'Twenty-six,' Maya said. She pulled out a photograph to show him.

'And you think I may not want him with us?' Koman stood up and went to sit by her side.

'It's not a walk in the park.' Maya feigned a diffidence that she had practised hard to perfect, ever since the day Naveen's condition was diagnosed.

'Parenting never is,' Koman laughed. 'Radha is not my biological daughter but I am her father in every other way. You think I don't know what it is to be a parent?'

And that was it. Once in a while, when she saw Koman with Naveen, Maya was filled with a sense of loss and a million synapses of regret. A lifetime frittered away, keeping him away from Koman. Of maintaining her life as a cemented walkway when it could have been a garden of wilderness resplendent with trees, birds and the neon-green arc of fireflies at night.

Naveen's fever had come down. He had kicked off his blanket and refused the kanji she tried to feed him. They sat in the verandah, waiting for Koman to return.

'Koman,' Naveen chirped every few minutes. 'Ganda, ganda,' Malini squawked from her cage.

'He will be home soon,' she said mechanically. But the dread spiralled within her.

Twilight turned into night and Koman still hadn't come home.

She took a flashlight and went towards the steps. He wasn't there. She called Radha and Shyam. The resort staff went looking. They found him slumped beneath the pala tree with a serene smile on his face. Around him, a handful of flowers were strewn. He had been gathering them for her.

She sat with him all night, asking herself what she was going to do. Once again, her life had emptied itself out.

Fine breadcrumbs. That was what the mixed ingredients ought to resemble. Her fingers pulled and rubbed at the flour mixture gently despite the savagery of her thoughts. God doesn't exist, she said aloud, or would she be here at seventy, fashioning treats for a child lost in a man's body? What kind of God would rob someone of a full night's sleep for all of thirty-eight years?

At first, the fretful baby kept her awake. And then, as Naveen wouldn't cross his milestones, as the paediatrician called them, she couldn't sleep for the night terrors. Why me? Why us? She railed at the gods in the puja room and the temples her husband dragged her to. How was she going to cope? But she may as well have prostrated before the No Parking sign. God didn't respond because God didn't exist. And why the hell was she thinking of God with a capital G?

She added a little water to the flour mixture. A little at a time, to form a soft dough. That's how you need to deal with Naveen, the paediatrician had said. The fretful baby had turned into a child she couldn't understand. He stared at her unseeingly or made faces. Any loud noise would set him off, and he would begin to hurt himself. It was hard to watch the mindless brutishness with which he inflicted pain on himself.

'What's going on at home?' Dr Padmini, who had become a friend of sorts – a crutch mostly – asked as she watched Naveen slap his own face viciously. 'Tell me, Maya. What's going on?'

'Vipin loses his temper when Naveen doesn't do what he is asked to do. I do too. Sometimes Vipin slaps him,' she said, unable to meet the doctor's eyes. She looked up and added, 'Sometimes I do too, because I don't know what else to do. When Vipin slaps him, it's more like a punch; mine is just a slap, but it stops Vipin from hurting him.'

Does shame bear a stench, she wondered. What kind of mother would hurt her own child?

'You have to make Vipin stop. Slapping or screaming at Naveen isn't going to help. Do you see what has happened? Naveen associates anger with beatings. Anger to him is any loud noise. That sets him off. And he deals with it by hurting himself. In a strangely convoluted way, he is trying to save you from what he thinks you are forced to do. Somewhere in his mind he sees a connection between Vipin's anger and you hurting him. Instead, talk to him. Tell him again and again what you want him to do. One thing at a time.'

It was a moment of epiphany for her. That Naveen may actually be sensitive to her feelings. She kneaded the dough gently with her knuckles. Like she had worked with Naveen, to braid the unravelled skeins of his mind as best as she could.

Vipin had turned to alcohol to numb the pain. It became easier to talk about divorce then. Naveen wasn't the reason why the marriage fell apart, it was Vipin's drunkenness and the loud angry words afterwards. When he moved out, she was more relieved than devastated.

Vipin found someone new. He stopped drinking. Once every week, he came to spend a few hours with Naveen. Maya could see that these visits distressed both him and Naveen.

She moved back to Chennai where she had grown up. The flat her parents owned became hers again. She had a few relationships that went nowhere. The presence of Naveen killed passion in most men. One of them didn't mind Naveen; what he minded, he said, was not being her top priority. He had even quoted what seemed like a line from a self-help book: Never get involved with someone for whom you are not a priority but an option.

She also learnt in those years the particular gift of the X chromosome. Men don't delve into what-ifs. At least, most men don't. Leave that to the women. Look at Pandora. If it had been a man, he would have kicked the third box beneath the bed and shared a post on Facebook: out of sight, out of mind. Not Pandora. Not her descendent, Maya. They would open the box and carry the guilt all their meagre lives, of having brought grief into the world.

After a while, Maya had no use for passion in her life. It was best, she decided, to become a shadow. She was Naveen's shadow. Once she had put her hopes and her mind to rest, she thought she found a sense of contentment.

Then she met Koman. And discovered a love so vital, so necessary for her to survive each day that she learnt the delicate art of lying by omission. All it needed was a deft change of subject, an unfinished thought, an opportune pause. Maya often ruminated on the epitaph that would perfectly describe her life:

Here lies Maya

A liar by omission

But the fatigue caught up with her. Delicate arts wear you out, for the machinations are subtle and demand nimbleness. When Koman laid out his life to her, and his expectations of her, Maya knew that the time had come to tell him the truth. She was prepared to live with the consequences, she decided.

Koman had surpassed her expectations with his easy acceptance of Naveen and all that it entailed. Yet, she couldn't stop worrying that one day it would all end.

'Sit down, Maya,' Koman said one evening, a few months after they began living together. 'I want to talk to you.'

Maya sat on the cane chair in the verandah. Naveen was in front of the TV. Koman and he had walked along the perimeter of the resort for over an hour, and now it was time for Koman's evening ritual: his drink.

Maya watched him pour brandy into a glass and top it with warm water. 'Shall I pour you one?' he asked.

She nodded. He went inside and brought her a glass of gin and lime juice.

'What is it?' she asked, wondering how he was going to phrase it. She had heard so many versions of this-is-not-working by now that nothing surprised her any more.

Koman began, 'In the eighties, I was part of a Kathakali troupe that went to Canada. The venue in Toronto was a giant auditorium. The stage was enormous. I was told that it was usually used for ballet performances.

'It was a wooden stage polished to a fine smoothness. Vasu was playing Ravana and I was Jatayu. It was a battle scene, and you know how demanding that is, both emotionally and physically. As the scene was drawing to its end, I was sweating with the exertion.'

Maya took a sip of her drink and wondered where this was going. His opening sentence had made her less afraid. He wasn't telling her that it was over.

'The sweat was dripping from me on to the polished floor. It was an accident waiting to happen.' Koman gazed into his glass as if he could see the memory unfold.

'I fell, and with it my crown too. Fortunately, Vasu had the presence of mind to speed up the scene, to chop my wings off.'

'So it ended all right?' Maya asked, still wondering what had triggered the anecdote.

'Not really. The man who was to pull the curtains down sat on a high perch. He had been instructed to act when I fell on a particular spot on the stage. A white cross had been marked there. But I fell a few feet away. The man waited for me to fall on the marked spot. I waited. Vasu waited. For the curtains to fall. The next three minutes – they were the longest three minutes in my life.'

'Why are you telling me this story now?' Maya asked. Her voice had sunk to a whisper.

'The story is not about me but the man on the high perch. I feel like him sometimes, sitting in my place, watching something I have no clue about. All I know is, I have to pull the lever when the dancer falls on the marked spot. There is a certain helplessness one feels in that position, Maya. It is out of one's control.

'And you are me. The helpless Jatayu, the king of birds, with his chopped wings. Waiting for the curtain to fall. Waiting for it all to end. It fills me with anguish to see you do this to yourself.' Koman's voice in the night was strident. Angry even.

'I am not a perfect man. Not even a good man. But you are the woman I love and Naveen is our son. I am not going to tire of you or him. How feckless do you think I am?'

Maya flinched at the pain in his voice. She stood up and went to him. She wrapped her arms around him. 'Forgive me,' she said.

The next day, she set about making the cottage their home.

It was the only home she had been happy in. When Koman died, she asked Shyam if she could buy the cottage. He shrugged and said, 'I am not the one you should be talking to. It's Radha's.'

But Radha wouldn't agree to sell it. 'It is yours for as long as you want it,' she said. 'Do you think I'll ever turn you out?'

Maya had offered to pay rent. But Radha wouldn't accept that either. 'You are family,' she said.

Shyam had taken to dropping in at the cottage most evenings. In a seamless transition, he had taken Koman's place in Naveen's life. She wondered if the ease with which he did it was because Naveen wasn't truly his responsibility.

Other people's burdens are easily shouldered because you know that one day they will be lifted off your back. Not your own – the weight cuts into the flesh even as you hoist it onto your back. You know the burden and you will never be parted until you die. You know there is no escaping the constant ache along the shoulder blades, so it becomes your first thought before you wake up and the last thought before you slip into a troubled sleep.

One evening, Shyam turned up with swimming trunks and flippers for Naveen. 'I am going to teach him how to swim,' he said, dragging an inner tube to the poolside.

Naveen had stared at the pool without a trace of expression. There was neither anticipation not fear. Just an utter indifference that would throw most people, but not Shyam, Maya thought. Shyam did what he wanted and everyone had to surrender to his force-field. There was no option.

Maya had watched Naveen flap in the water. He couldn't stop giggling. She smiled at the naked joy in his eyes and on his lips; his exaggerated splashes and the high-pitched shrieks of delight.

Why didn't Shyam and Radha have a child of their own? He would have made a good father. Any man can father a child, but to be a father requires commitment, it means giving some bit of yourself every day, without tiring. Shyam would have done that with the same jauntiness with which he strode through the resort when he took Naveen for a walk before the swim.

She looked at the ball of dough in the bowl. She would have to wait for the ingredients to work their magic in their own time.

She went to sit beside Naveen. As always, she hoped he would turn and speak an unprompted word. A phrase that was not governed by hunger, cold, or some basic animal urge. A hello would suffice. 'Boost!' he said.

He hated plain milk. 'Ganda,' he would say. A Bihari servant she had once hired to assist her as Naveen grew older and bigger had taught him the word. Ganda. Bad. Plain milk was ganda. Chota Bheem was ganda. Mama was ganda when she refused him what he wanted. Strangers were ganda. Autorickshaws were ganda, ganda, ganda. And to deal with ganda, he needed to slam his forehead hard against the wall. Again and again, again and again, again and again.

She looked at the clock. It was 9.30. She fed him dinner and got up to fetch him a glass of warm milk. Any later would mean needing to pee at night, and then there would be accidents.

'Give me two minutes.' She smiled and rubbed his arm. A slow smile appeared on his face. Does he smile at me or at the thought of the warm milk? she thought. A sob escaped her lips.

She watched him as he sipped his milk, into which two spoons of Boost had been added to disguise the taste of the crushed sleeping pill – .25 mg Restyl. It was a decision she had made without consulting a medical practitioner. She needed to snatch a few hours of uninterrupted sleep to face the next day. And she could get that only if he did.

She had forgotten most of what she had learnt as a young bride. But tonight was a special occasion. Naveen would turn thirty-nine at midnight and he loved badushah more than any other sweet. So she had dug out an old recipe book. It seemed some forgotten corner of her brain had begun ticking again, for her fingers seemed to remember how to shape the badushah.

She took a ball of dough and patted it into a circle. With the edge of her nail, she shaped the swirls. It was imperative to avoid cracks in the moon-shaped dough, lest they widen and break the surface.

The rule was the same, whether it was to do with cooking or childcare. On most days, Maya reined in all that she felt. Naveen did most of what she asked him to. She had taught him to eat from a plate. She stood outside the shower cubicle and poured shower gel into his hand. If she gave him a bar of soap and left him alone, he would rub at the same spot on his arm again and again till the soap dwindled into nothing. Every few seconds, she would murmur instructions. 'Now wash your left arm. Now your right leg!' She taught him to shave. But she had to stand at his side so he didn't shave the skin off his face. She also taught him to be as inconspicuous as possible.

But she felt a crack appear each time a stranger eyed her 95-kg son as if he were an ungainly animal, a baby hippo perhaps. Mostly they turned the other way when she spotted them staring at him. But if it was an acquaintance, the voice would ring with a 'Hello Naveen!' Unnatural, syrupy sweet and laden with fake emotion: 'Let's show Maya that we are blessed with a benevolence of heart, and how much we feel for her.' Sometimes she felt as though she couldn't bear to go on any longer.

Maya watched the oil heat up and thought of how she used to want to fling hot oil and scathing words at their faces. But as she grew older, and so did Naveen, she knew that it was necessary that she endure every blow to her soul and the dignity of her child without the cracks showing. Keeping a smooth, unruffled façade facilitated many things: a seat in the bulkhead row of a plane, a corner table at a restaurant, a quick passage through the hospital when Naveen's kidneys were acting up.

She pinched a bit of the dough and dropped it into the oil. It rose perfectly. She added three pieces of the moon-shaped swirl-edged dough and switched off the stove. The dough would cook in the preheated oil. When the pastry turned brown, she would switch on the heat again and turn it over. That was the trick to get a perfectly layered badushah.

She drained the discs of fried dough on a tissue. For a moment, she gazed at the sugar syrup she had prepared, single-string consistency, exactly as it was supposed to be. She hummed under her breath as she added saffron strands and cardamom powder. She didn't want Naveen tossing it aside after a bite, saying 'Ganda!'

How many drops of rat poison would one need to fell a man? How many pieces of badushah would it take to kill an adult? Maya shook her head. Does it matter, she asked herself as she emptied the contents of the bottle into the sugar syrup.

Shyam had bought the rat poison for her. She had told him about the garden rats. He had frowned. 'I wonder how you have rats.'

She had pointed to the river. 'We are closest to the river and since there is hardly any water round the year, they come looking for food, I suppose.'

'We don't want rats nibbling your toes,' he had said, tickling Naveen's feet. Naveen kicked him and Shyam flinched.

Naveen was having a bad day. He was lost in some realm of his mind that no one could penetrate. His jaw was slack and his lower lip drooped, a welt of pink rubbery flesh. Maya tried to see Naveen through Shyam's eyes. He looked the idiot he was. She looked away. Enough, she decided then. It was time.

At midnight, she would turn seventy-one and Naveen would turn thirty-nine. It was time she settled the fear in her: What would happen to Naveen when she was gone? She dipped the pastry in the sugar syrup and laid it on a tray spread with silver foil. Silver for her tin baby. By the time she turned the stove off and cleaned the kitchen, the sugar coating had set and there were just a few minutes left for it to be midnight.

She picked up the tray and went towards Naveen. His eyelids were drooping. The sleeping pill had begun to kick in.

'Happy birthday, Naveen,' she sang softly. 'Happy birthday, my golden boy.'

She held out the tray to him. There were nine badushahs on it. When he had eaten them all, she would hold his hand to see him through to the other side. And then she would lie down on the twin bed in his bedroom and close her eyes.

His eyes gleamed at the sight of the sweets. Then he looked at Maya and said, '...appybdaama!'

Maya felt her breath snag in her throat. They shared a birthday, Maya and he. But not once had he let her know that he knew. It was too much to expect that he would, she had told herself year after year.

'Appybdaama,' he said again. Their eyes met and it seemed that he was looking at her. She wasn't just his shadow. She was herself and he knew her.

She seized the tray and walked back into the kitchen. She tossed the sweets into the bin and offered him a giant chocolate bar instead. Together, they sat eating it. One bite at a time. In the morning, they would find something new to do.

# 8

# URVASHI

The doorbell rang. Urvashi opened the door to find Maya standing outside. The verandah light caught the silver glints in her hair.

'I brought this back,' she said, holding out the piece of plastic.

Urvashi took it and invited Maya in.

'I'll come by tomorrow. Shyam and Radha will be back and Shyam usually spends time with Naveen in the evening. That's when I get out,' Maya said.

'In which case, I'll walk with you. I need to go to the reception,' Urvashi said.

They walked quietly, side by side, without speaking.

At the reception desk, the clerk told her Colonel Naidu and his family had checked out that afternoon.

Urvashi looked at the narrow white stick, wondering what to do with it. Slowly, and with mounting horror, she realised that it wasn't a piece of plastic as she had supposed it to be. It was the skeletal remains of a finger. Bleached and brittle, and looking more like an ivory relic from some bygone time. She shuddered. The child must have picked it up in the cupboard without knowing what it was.

She walked swiftly into the passage where the cupboard loomed, silent and secretive. She tugged at the doors until they opened with a plaintive creak. Urvashi placed the bone in a pigeonhole with infinite care. 'Whoever you are, rest in peace,' she muttered aloud as she shut the doors firmly.

She glanced at her phone. It was a little past eight. She walked slowly back to the cottage.

As she walked past Maya's cottage, she could hear music playing from within. Urvashi wondered what it must be like to be Maya. Of the resilience she needed to conjure up every day to open her eyes at daybreak and get a move on. Of the self-recrimination that must shadow her even in her sleep. Of having to put on a brave face even when she was quaking within.

Her own troubles seemed insignificant, silly even.

'Are you all sorted in your head?' Mahesh would ask her when she returned.

'I am,' she would admit truthfully.

He would pour them both a drink and sit with his laptop and she would do the same. Once, they had watched TV together. Now they both lurked on their social media accounts, looking at other people's lives and avoiding asking each other anything of consequence. This had become their definition of togetherness, Urvashi realised. Only, she wanted more. What it was, she didn't know. But she couldn't live the rest of her life like this.

She would wait for a few weeks, then broach the subject of their marriage and how they had come to the end of that road. She felt nothing for him. Did he want to be with someone who didn't particularly want to be with him? She didn't know how the conversation would go. But she didn't want to think about it now.

She picked an apple from the fruit bowl and took it to bed with her. She ran her finger along the stalk and touched the tip of the fruit knife to her lips. Then she called him. It was her way of throwing the gauntlet at him. *I am not hiding from you any more.*

He picked up on the second ring. 'I knew you would come back to me,' he said, unable to hide the triumph in his voice.

A thin line of steel inserted itself into her spine and entered her voice. 'I was never your prisoner, to escape. You are just a silly boy throwing a childish tantrum. But I am not your mother to indulge you. So listen to me: it's over. You and I are finished, no matter what you think. Nothing you say or do is going to change that.'

She put the phone down.

Then she pared the apple and ate it slowly, piece by piece. Life would continue to surprise her, one way or another. But there was no running away from it.

# Eating Wasps

## [i]

The door shut firmly. All was dark. All was quiet.

I was in my bat cave once again. Here I would probably stay till chance or circumstance released me from an eternity of inexactitude.

When I was shut away in the almirah the first time, my anger and sorrow had kept me company. This time around, I was flooded with secrets. Like the bats who fly into each other, not knowing which way to go inside the cave, all these lives, all these stories had flung themselves at me. There was no escaping them.

I had always believed that we must evaluate our lives by gauging how close we come to perfection. For the first time, I looked back on my life against the firmament of other people's stories. For the first time, I wasn't entirely certain about my choices.

In hindsight, we are all philosophers who know how to separate the chaff from the grain. But while you are in it, the truth of the moment overrides everything else. I wished there was some way to flee all that haunted me.

## [ii]

Two months before it all began, a well-known writer had come to the Arts & Science College I taught at, to deliver a lecture. He was the sort of man who could mesmerise you with his diction as much as by his expanse of thought. As for his words, they were like dagger thrusts in close combat. The Malayalam department saw it as a major coup that they were able to bring him in.

I had long admired this writer, so I ensured that I was in one of the middle seats in the second row. I was determined to absorb every word he spoke with the fervour of a sponge. I had hoped that it would dispell the constellation of anxieties that circled around me.

He stood as he usually did, holding the edge of the rostrum with his hands. On the rostrum were three glasses of water. I remembered someone saying that the duration of Professor Varier's talk could be calculated by the number of glasses of water on the rostrum.

He began speaking and I leaned forward.

'You look like an eager schoolgirl gazing at her favourite filmstar,' Sarah Kuruvilla, who taught chemistry, murmured.

I straightened and leaned back.

By the time he finished his first glass of water, I felt the distress push up against my throat. We didn't exist for him. Every woman and I on this planet. Where were we in his reckoning?

By the second glass of water, I could bear it no more. My mouth was acrid with the taste of wasp. I stood up. The professor paused. We had been told he didn't like interruptions. 'Is there a problem?' he asked.

I took a deep breath and tried to form the words. 'Why won't you use "she"?' I asked in a low voice.

'Speak up,' he said. His eyes through the heavy spectacle frames pinned me to the spot. I felt the weight of everyone's curious gaze, like a specimen the class had gathered around to look at before it was dissected.

'She – why do you hate the pronoun? Why do you only say he and his? You even use an it. But you avoid the she. Why?'

The silence slammed against my eardrums.

The professor took his hands off the edge of the rostrum in an exaggerated gesture of bewilderment. 'It is the customary manner in which a man, I apologise, a speaker phrases his, I apologise, strike that out, a speaker phrases thoughts.'

A titter spread. I had been firmly put in my place. I sat down and endured the rest of the talk while humiliation spread like a blotch of red ink that wouldn't wash away even if I tried.

When the talk was over, I pushed back my chair and walked quickly to the lab. I didn't want to go to the staffroom. I was afraid of the mockery and pity that awaited me there.

I would make a few slides. That always calmed me down.

They didn't see me, nor did I see who they were.

'She made an ass of herself,' one of the boys said.

'She did have a point,' one of the girls offered tentatively.

What were these zoology students doing at a Malayalam seminar, I wondered.

'Really? And what was the point?' the first boy asked.

'I did tell you about her. Haven't you read her stories? It has damaged goods written all over it. If you don't believe me, read that novel of hers that won the prize!' someone else said.

I turned on my heel and walked away. I would go home. But the whispers wouldn't leave me alone. I heard them in the keening of the bamboo that grew alongside the fence of the rented house I lived in, in the cawing of crows in the mango tree near the window of my room; I saw it in my mother's eyes, and when I looked at myself in the mirror.

I went from the window to the bookshelf. I touched my books, sliding my fingers along their spines. You are my only friends, my real companions, I told them.

On a lower shelf, all on its own, stood my novel, *A Fistful of Shadows*. It had not been an easy book to write, for I had based it on Narendran, Subhasini and me. It was called bold and thought-provoking. It was exactly what a girl who had eaten a wasp would write, I had told myself when I sent the manuscript to the publishers. Until you open your mouth, how will you know what a wasp tastes like?

I was resigned to my book being dwarfed by the literary greats of Malayalam writing and gathering dust in a corner of the few bookshops that stocked it.

So, when I received the telegram informing me about the prize, I thought of it as a salute to my talent. I was just thirty years old and the youngest person in the history of the Akademi to have won the prize. I saw it as the beginning of a life of literary triumphs and much happiness. I saw myself being embraced by my peers and welcomed into their fold. The loneliness I wore like a crown of thorns would snap and my life would bloom with stories.

I discovered adulation. I discovered what it was to be lionised. I discovered spite. Fierce competitiveness, mockery even. But I didn't find the companions I sought – the conversations on literary matters, the artistic process and the self-doubts, the deconstruction of a novel or a poem – all of it remained a figment of my imagination. Nothing much had changed from the time I ate a wasp thinking it was a bee full of honey.

I went back to my books and slides. I went to the college each day and taught my students. I toyed with the idea of working on a doctorate. I dusted my books and wrote ideas down for stories.

That night, I read each one of my stories again. What did they reveal that made them think of me as damaged goods? It wasn't the first time I had heard that expression. Narendran had said it too.

I wrote about women whose lives didn't go the way they would have wanted. I wrote about heartbreak and loss; of temptation and giving in. I wrote about what it was to be a woman. Did that make me damaged goods?

Later, I would wonder if this was what Markose had meant when he said, you are like no one I know.

Did he see me as damaged goods too?

## [iii]

That we met at all had as much probability as one human sperm surviving the journey to fuse with a waiting egg. A one in a forty-eight million chance. When I told him that, he held me tight. 'In which case, aren't you lucky that I made it despite the forty-seven million nine hundred and ninety-nine thousand nine hundred and ninety-nine other sperm warriors jostling to be there?'

I laughed. I loved that about him. His quick wit that turned a biological fact into a poetic whimsy.

I was thirty-five years old. I wanted for nothing. But I didn't know what to do with my life any more. I had a master's in zoology and a job that could be mine until I retired. I had written several short stories and a novel. Until the novel was published, it was all I thought of when I came home from my students and slides. Now that I had won the prize, I was overwhelmed by what I could only refer to as performance anxiety.

The editor of the most prestigious literary weekly in Kerala suggested that I write a novel for serialisation. 'No need to look down upon it. Dickens, Thomas Hardy, Henry James, Mark Twain, all did it.'

I said I would, but it was one thing to agree to write a novel that could be serialised and another to actually write it. I would have to wait until the story stirred in me. Those fallow times were the hardest, for I felt like a failure: I remembered that I had never fallen in love or learnt to sing a song.

I needed something to fill my life that wouldn't make me feel irrelevant. Ever since the wasp story became a fixture in my life, I had veered towards entomology, but not with any true intent or purpose. Now, however, it seemed full of possibilities; locating myself in a field of insects would still the talking heads that jostled within the insides of my skull. I decided to start on that long set-aside dream: a Ph.D.

Outside the window, a wasp hummed as it darted back and forth along the window frame, building its nest with mud pellets.

It was a sign, I thought. My leitmotif would now become the subject of my study.

My mother called the potter wasp 'vetalan'.

'Why?' I had asked her as a child.

'Haven't you noticed how it chases you if you go anywhere close to its house?' Amma said. 'Break up the word and see. "Veta" means hunt. "Aalu" means man. So vetalan means one who hunts a man.' She added, frowning and smiling at the same time, 'Now don't go eating it!'

Later, when I was old enough to understand, I realised that she had probably concocted an explanation to shut me up. I was a persistent, pesky child. I also realised then, who I owed my literary gene to.

I had always been drawn to the potter wasp. I saw it everywhere, but there was little I knew about this solitary creature beyond the basic information. Scientific name: *Eumeninae*. Higher classification: Vespidae. Order: Hymenopterans. Rank: Subfamily. Kingdom: Animalia.

I was going to have to do some ground work first.

As always, I needed to begin with the written word. I booked my ticket to Trivandrum. And thus we met at the Kerala University library.

I was in the zoology section, looking for any studies on wasps. There were a few volumes of research by foreigners and a few journals. There was no Ph.D thesis to be found. I was both daunted and excited by what I was setting out to do. I had broken new ground with my fiction. Perhaps I would with my wasps as well.

I took down all the volumes I could find and carried them to a table near the shelves. I noticed a man sitting at the adjacent table but didn't give it a second thought. This was the best library in all of Kerala and scholars came here from everywhere.

I felt him dart a glance at me, then look again. I felt the weight of his gaze as though he had placed his hand on my arm. I stiffened. I wasn't used to male attention.

He cleared his throat. 'Miss Sreelakshmi,' he murmured. 'Miss Sreelakshmi?'

I looked at him, startled.

'You don't know me but I know you. Rather, I know of you.' His smile was friendly, no more. 'My cousin Paul Verghese was your student.'

I dropped my gaze. What had Paul told him? His departure from college had been my doing. He had become wildly infatuated with me, and let me know it too. A teacher cannot be waylaid by such inappropriateness. He threatened to be my undoing. So I had to do what was required of me: complain to the head of department.

Before Paul went, he left a copy of Pushkin's poetry for me. A cheap Moscow edition, and in it a cryptic note: When I came to kneel at your feet, you closed the door on my face.

'How is he?' I asked. I saw an emaciated Paul wearing the countenance of Jesus on a cross. I saw in my mind a boy I had reduced to a shadow.

The man smiled. 'He is well enough. The best thing that happened to him was the suspension from college. It shook him up. He is now in Madras studying biochemistry. He has also applied to colleges in the US. We have family there.'

All these years, I had been burdened by the guilt of having single-handedly destroyed Paul. But I seemed to have turned into his saviour instead.

'I have read your novel,' he said.

I flushed. I still hadn't learnt how to respond when I met a reader face-to-face.

He continued to look at me.

'My name is Markose Mapila Karrukattil. He stood up. 'I have a meeting to attend. Will you be here for another hour?'

I nodded. 'Why?'

'I would like to talk to you some more. I didn't ever think my path would cross yours,' he replied.

I watched him walk away, this dusky slender man with a slight hook to his nose and a long bushy beard. Who was he? What did he want from me? He looked a little like Narendran had in the last few months as a PSM member; a militant poet.

At twenty minutes to the hour, I gathered my notes into a file and left the library. He was standing by the steps. I saw the lazy but amused widening of his lips. A cat that knew the shrew would eventually emerge from the hole in the wall.

I felt foolish. I felt elated. Within me, a bird beat its wings in fear and exhilaration. What did he want from me? What did I want from him?

We walked down the road towards the university hostel. We talked about books and poetry. When we drew closer to the hostel, he pointed to the India Coffee House there. We went in and found a table. We ordered coffee. We continued to talk. By the second sip of coffee, I felt as if I had found Narendran again.

We discussed Russian literature and the English poets. We moved to Darwin and God. We argued about evolution and creation.

He was emphatic in his arguments. 'You say the cell is the building block but tell me, where did that first cell come from?' He cocked an eyebrow at me as he asked, 'How did mitosis and meiosis happen?'

I smiled, struck by the fact that it wasn't often I met someone who used words like mitosis or meiosis and knew the difference between them.

'Tell me when you have an explanation and I will worship you,' he joked, his eyes raking my face while his fingers ran through his beard.

I burst into laughter, amused and aghast at how easily he jumped over any fences I put up between us.

Those three days were a hymn to love. An incantation of careful syllables to appease the hunger in me and him. He examined my life and thoughts as if he had me on a slide. I had never known anything like it before. I revelled in the feeling of significance. Perhaps I wasn't the solitary wasp I had thought myself to be. I could be a woman like every other woman. I could desire and dream. My stories would no longer be about women on the fringes of life. I would write about women replete with loving; of women who leaned into men, knowing they were there to stay.

Give me a wasp or an elephant and I will tell you about its mating rituals. But when it comes to a man and a woman, I don't know the dance of power play. Can we tell when an attraction turns into something more luminescent, almost as if it were ordained? Or how the love that soared with the lightness of a kite is snagged by the branch of a tree? Are we to blame the tree for its hunger to possess? Would the tree do so if it knew that with possession comes the end of the glorious flight?

## [iv]

I was staying with my father's cousin, Devi Mema, not too far from the university library. Her husband worked in the secretariat and it was most convenient for me to make the daily visits to the library. Besides, Mema was happy to reminiscence about my father. 'He was like Sinbad the Sailor,' she said. 'Handsome, daring, smart. There isn't a place in India he missed going to.'

I imagined my stern-looking father, tufts of hair sticking out of his ears, in harem trousers and a sleeveless vest, as depicted in children's books. I saw him hide under a piece of meat so he could be picked up by the giant rocs and escape the island with his diamonds. I shook my head. I couldn't reconcile the image of the taciturn man I knew, a permanent frown on his narrow forehead, with the adventurer she made him out to be.

My father had died when I was twenty-two and with that my life had changed. My brothers-in-law, who had no say when he was alive, were now firm in their decision. 'Enough of this nonsense, no more living away from home and studying!'

I thought a great deal about my father during those three days. What would he have thought of the woman I had transformed into, almost overnight?

I went to the library every morning and, each afternoon, he would arrive as though we had arranged to meet. It was assumed that he would come and I would wait for him until he did. We would walk a little, talk a lot, and eventually seat ourselves in the India Coffee House for coffee and cutlets – vegetable for me and mutton for him. And then I would return by bus to Devi Mema's home and her stories of Sinbad the railway man, which grew more fantastic with each telling.

On the fourth evening, he tapped the strap of my wrist watch. 'You wear a man's watch.'

'It was my father's.'

'It is not usual to see a lady wearing a gent's watch,' he smiled.

'I am not the usual kind of lady,' I smiled back.

'That's true,' he said. 'You are not like anyone I know.'

I flushed, wondering if he found me lacking as a woman.

As if to change the subject, he asked, 'When are you going back?'

I dropped my gaze. 'Tonight. The night train.'

'And when were you planning to tell me this?'

'This evening, before going home,' I said. I gestured to take in our surroundings, and us. 'I couldn't deny myself this one last time.'

A sound escaped his lips. I didn't know if it was a sigh or a snort.

'The coffee or the cutlets?' His voice sounded as if he was being strangled.

'The coffee, cutlets and you,' I said, dredging up the courage to do so.

He smiled then. 'I am not going to let you disappear from my life.'

He placed his hand fleetingly on mine: the feel of his skin, the pressure of his fingers, the flash of gold on his ring finger.

'What about your wife?' I asked.

He looked at me for a moment. 'And you know I have a wife – how?'

I gestured to his ring. 'It's a wedding ring,' I said. 'A zoologist is nothing minus observation.'

'Should I tell my wife about you?' he asked, placing his hand on mine again. He was asking me to define the timbre of our association.

'You should do what you think is right,' I said eventually.

He looked at a point above my head but didn't take his hand from mine. Neither did I remove my hand from under his. We sat there in silence while our coffee cooled and the cutlets wilted at the edges. I felt tears rise in my eyes.

'She has a master's in physics. She is very sharp. Nothing escapes her. She measures pauses with vernier calipers and checks my tone with a tuning fork.' He was a doctor of philosophy and his understanding of physics didn't extend beyond high school lab work. He was trying to insert a joke into a dire explanation for why we couldn't meet as often as we wanted to. Why I couldn't write letters to his home address. But I didn't smile. Love, when it is uncertain and furtive, eats away the smiles first.

I tried not to show my hurt either.

'I should go,' I said, standing. 'I have a train to catch.'

He stood with me and we walked to the bus stop. He followed me into the bus and sat alongside so our shoulders touched and our sides brushed. The words had dried up. I wished he would say something. Later, he would tell me that he had wished the same.

When my stop arrived, he took my hand in his again. 'I will be in touch,' he said. I nodded.

Maybe he would. Maybe he wouldn't. I wasn't going to think about it. I had a doctorate to work on. And perhaps a new story to write. That had sufficed once, and it would have to now.

My mother welcomed me home with questions about what I planned to do with the rest of my life. A cousin and his wife had been staying with her while I was away. They had most diligently pointed out to her that I couldn't be allowed to live my life out like this. 'I am not going to live forever,' she said.

'Neither am I,' I retorted.

'There is a proposal. The boy is an assistant professor at Presidency College, in Madras.'

'How old is he?' I asked curiously.

'Thirty-eight.' Her eyes lit up.

'Hardly a boy,' I said. 'And no.'

'Why won't you agree to this, Sreekutty?' she sighed. That was her name for me. I was the eternal child. She looked at me and asked again, 'Shall I ask the broker to bring a photograph?'

'What part of no don't you understand?' I snapped.

'Every person needs a mate. A companion. Someone who can fetch them a glass of warm water when they are laid up in bed,' my mother continued, brushing aside my surliness as if it was a child's temper tantrum.

'That sounds like a servant rather than a companion.' I smiled at my mother to blunt the sting.

'A servant will fetch the hot water but isn't going to check to make sure it doesn't scald your tongue.'

I let it be. My mother and I had had various versions of this conversation. We were never going to be able to convince each other about the veracity of our respective points of view.

And yet, I knew a strange pang that day.

I remembered him asking for an empty cup when I complained that the coffee was too hot to drink. He had poured the scalding coffee from one cup to another a couple of times to cool it and then placed it in front of me. 'This should be all right!'

I went to my room and unpacked. When the trunk was empty, I sighed into it – all the unsaid words and nerve-end longings, all the secret desires and the weight of unshed tears that had gathered in me through the train journey – all of it went into that little brown trunk which I then stowed away beneath my bed. I would sleep atop my Pandora's box, knowing that to open it would signal my fall from grace.

## [v]

A week after the college reopened after the Onam vacation, the department peon told me that I had a visitor. Looks like someone important, he added, as if to hasten me. I stared at him nonplussed. I seldom had visitors. To most of my literary peers, I was still the upstart writer teaching in a nondescript college in a provincial town. They thought my fame had more to do with fluke than talent, I had been told with almost malicious glee by a journalist who had come to interview me after the award was announced.

A priest, he added, when he realised that I wasn't jumping out of my chair to go meet my visitor.

I went to the lobby at the entrance, wondering why a priest had come to meet me. I had been invited to a college or two to address the students there. I presumed this must be someone who had come to invite me to a function.

The visitors' lobby was an open hall. One of the inner walls had the college noticeboard and to its left was a corridor that led to the principal's room and the admin department. He stood leaning against a pillar. He was dressed in a black cassock and wore a tiny cap on his head. On his chest was a wooden cross. I stared.

He was a priest. He was a married man. He had come looking for me. My Pandora's box had opened on its own. I wanted to turn and flee. But my foolish heart pushed aside all caution and good sense and propelled me towards him.

He straightened when he saw me.

'You are a priest,' I said, stating the obvious.

He stood there looking at me and there was a deep sadness in his eyes. 'I didn't mean to deceive you,' he said.

'But you did anyway,' I heard myself say from very far away.

'I didn't know how to tell you. So I thought I would let you see for yourself.'

'I know now,' I said carefully. Why wasn't I turning on my heel and walking away?

'How are you married then?' I asked, wondering what else he had lied to me about.

'My denomination has married priests,' he said quietly. 'Does it matter that I am a priest?'

'How will you make peace with your God?'

'I don't know, but I will have to find a way.'

How will you make peace with your wife? I thought but did not ask.

## [vi]

I decided to go ahead with my illicit love affair and my doctoral thesis on the same day. It was with a scientific rigour that I planned how to go about each one. Science and the heart cannot fear the sting, the consequences of stirring up passion and breaking rules.

The first law of any scientific work is to understand the subject of study. That evening, I looked at myself in the mirror, trying to see what he saw – the high forehead and heavy brows, the straight nose and full lips.

'Your gaze is like that of a microscope – you see through everything, leave nothing unexamined, and yet you claim you did not see me or how I felt about you,' Paul Verghese had once hurled at me.

I turned the microscope on myself. Was I a woman in love? But what was I to do with this love? There were enough irrefutable reasons why it was wrong.

I should have turned my back on him the moment that thought occurred to me.

I shouldn't have gazed at the hollows in my throat or the slight curve of my breasts and imagined his lips there. I shouldn't have placed the flat of my palm on the washboard of my abdomen and seen him drawing me towards him. I shouldn't have caressed the curve of my narrow hips and felt the rasp of his skin against mine. I shouldn't have stared at the mirror and smiled. But I did, even though I knew I was doing wrong. I justified it to myself with the thought that I wasn't taking anything that he was unwilling to give. You know that you will be walking into a hornet's nest, don't you? I asked myself. But I let that strange smile persuade me: After all, I was the girl who had eaten a wasp.

I decided I would make an attempt to understand a man in love. What would the physical manifestations be? What about his thought process? What changes in behaviour could be perceived?

I went to the English department library and from its scanty shelves brought out all the love stories I could find. Romance, whether written by Tolstoy or Changampuzha, was something I had scorned. It bored me. But not any more. I gathered a pile of books with a greed that surprised me as much as the library clerk. *Anna Karenina*. *Madame Bovary*. *Wuthering Heights*. And because it seemed strangely appropriate, a slim volume on Heloise and Abelard. Somewhere within these stories lay the secrets of the heart.

The library clerk meticulously noted the details of the books and their library index numbers in his register. When he had finished, he threw me a curious glance. 'I suppose this is for your new book.'

I smiled.

I knew what he would tell everyone. That I had borrowed a whole pile of books and in all probability my next work would be derived from them. He wouldn't accuse me of plagiarism outright. That would be construed as malicious envy. An off-the-cuff remark would suffice: 'Once you have a literary reputation, you can cobble together any nonsense and people will read it and go ooh and aaah,' he would say.

Even now, although several years had passed, I did not understand why I was so intensely disliked. Why did they think of me as stern and aloof? Why did they think I was incapable of having an imagination of my own?

Late that afternoon, when I returned home, I put the pile of books alongside Sinbad the railway man's collection. So what do you think? I asked him.

I opened my file of notes from the library. The first discovery I had made was the lack of information on the anatomy of a love affair, and the nature of wasps.

The Danish zoologist Johan Christian Fabricius had recorded, in 1804, thirty species of the sphecid wasp from the Oriental region, among which were three species from the Malabar region of Kerala. I presumed Fabricus had never come to India. What did he base his documentation on? Specimens collected by travellers?

In 1903, the Irish military officer Charles Thomas Bingham had recorded six species of Sphecidae from the Western Ghats in Kerala. His specimens were sent to him by Major E. Stokes-Roberts, R.E. But how could they know anything about wasps without seeing them for real in their natural habitat? How could anything beyond the taxonomy be accurate? Why wasn't more work done on wasps?

I looked through the books I had borrowed from the library. Why weren't there studies on how to conduct an affair with a married man? Surely there must be others like me who needed to know?

## [vii]

I changed into a pale green salwar kameez with three-quarter sleeves that I had brought back from Varanasi. I still fitted into it, I realised with a hint of satisfaction.

My mother glared as she placed a glass of tea on the dining table. 'What is this?'

'I need to do some field research,' I said as I took a sip of the tea.

In a plate was a single ela–ada. Every day, for the last three years since my mother and I set up home, she had served me this as a teatime snack.

At first my mother had wanted to try other snacks but I had insisted that this was all I wanted. She complained it gave her heartburn and in time it would give me heartburn too. My mother was seldom wrong but I wasn't yet ready to give up the childish pleasure of imagining I was eating a book as I devoured it.

I opened the folded banana leaf and tore a piece of the ada. I let the aroma of the steamed leaf, the bite of the coconut and jaggery and the smoothness of the rice dough flood my mouth.

'Are you going out wearing that?' My mother's eyes lingered on my clothes. To her, the salwar was about as vulgar as a piece of clothing could be. It hinted that a woman had legs. And between those legs was the seat of sin.

Was this why the temples in Kerala insisted on women wearing a mundu or a sari? No temple in Varanasi or Madras did. Mothers in north India would only question their daughters if they left home without a dupatta covering their chest. My mother didn't care whether I covered my chest or not. She was used to seeing bare-breasted women, women who wore a blouse and a mundu, and others who draped a towel over their upper half only when they were out in a public place. But a salwar wasn't respectable.

'Yes,' I said, and crossed my legs at the ankles. 'I cannot go chasing wasps in a sari. Or a mundu and blouse,' I added.

My mother's mouth tightened but she didn't say anything. I did hold the purse strings after all.

That first day, I had none of the equipment required to trap a wasp but I was determined to make a start.

Among my father's things was a badminton racquet. Its strings were loose and I had often wondered why he kept it and wouldn't allow any of us to even touch it. I wondered about Sinbad the railway man and who he had played badminton with. Did he have a woman friend? Did he play more than badminton with her? What about her? What did she think of being the other woman?

I found a thin mulmul mundu in the stack of old clothes my mother kept aside. I snipped out the mesh of the racquet and sewed the cloth onto the rim with large ungainly stitches. My wasp net was ready.

I stepped out into the wilderness surrounding the house. The land was densely wooded with several trees and shrubs. Silk cotton and teak, mango and jackfruit, laburnum and rosewood, hibiscus and red pagoda, ixora and white orchids. Flowers that attracted butterflies, which laid eggs that would become caterpillars. Food for wasp babies. That's where I would find my wasps, I figured.

All through the day and the year I heard them, the wasps, their hum that blew in with the breeze or magnified in the stillness. As I walked through the trees, I was undecided on my exact area of study. I would be able to decide only after I had trapped a few wasps and scrutinised them. Perhaps I would discover something that had eluded Fabricus and Bingham, Ayyar, Usman and Puttarudriah. However, the solitary wasps eluded me too, that day. Instead, I stirred up a hornets' nest.

The hornet belongs to the Vespidae family and is bigger and more aggressive than a wasp. I knew this when I approached the globular leaf nest on the silk cotton tree that probably contained a few hundred workers. A couple of specimens were all I needed. It was not too high, so I give the nest a gentle tap.

I had a long bamboo stick with which I touched the nest. It moved a little, and the humming grew louder and angrier. I touched it again, hoping a few would fly out, allowing me to trap one or two. Any kind of wasp is a danger and I hoped that I could trap a couple with minimal damage to their habitat and my person.

A swarm emerged. I turned and fled, but a few of them followed me. I laughed as I ran, in fear and wild exultation. One stung me on my arm through the kameez. Another descended on my face with the fury with which Markose's wife would if she found out about me.

The hornet has a sting like a curved dagger. A sting that it sinks into the perceived threat till it has emptied the venom sac.

The hornet dived at my face and bored into my cheek again and again. I would never know the pain of the pelvic girdle opening to squeeze a child out. But it couldn't be worse than this. The hornet venom rushed up into my brain and froze my mind. All I could think of was flight.

I stumbled and fell hard on the ground. My lip split and began to bleed.

Later, as my mother rubbed a shallot vigorously on the spots where I had been stung, she muttered under her breath that I must be mad. 'Who in their right senses would go poke a hornets' nest? What is wrong with you, Sreekutty? You were four years old when you ate a wasp. But you are thirty-five now. How can you be so rash?'

She gave me the piece of shallot to continue rubbing the spot where I had been stung on the cheek. The pain had reduced considerably and the Lacto Calamine which we always had at home would settle the inflammation and redness.

'People can die of a hornet's sting, especially if it's one of those giant jungle kinds. You teach others about animals. Don't you know this much? There is a way to approach these things.' My mother took over the rubbing with a freshly cut shallot.

I was grateful that she knew what to do. I also knew that tomorrow, as soon as I left for the college, she would go to the temple to offer thanks to her deity. After that, she would head for the astrologer's, to check if my planets had tilted at an improbable angle or colluded to form dangerous cliques, for what else could explain this madness of mine? Her next stop would be the ayurveda vaidyan for a lehyam or kashayam to steady my eccentricities.

I looked at my mother's head fondly. Her love held me together. But it couldn't hold me back from what I had set out to do: court the wasps and rush headlong into love with a married priest.

## [viii]

Madness is beautiful. As it crawls through your bloodstream, it devours reason, logic, and allows you to do what your innermost desire propels you towards. I wanted to be completely and irrevocably mad.

But not for me the howling at the moon, lunacy that waxes and wanes with the moon. Not for me the crouching under the bed, smeared with the brown of neglect and the red of faeces and menstrual blood. Not for me the holding up of the sky or conversations with gods. Not for me the catatonia of one in whom the words had forever run dry. My madness was a beautiful thing. My madness was a noumenon; it existed independently of all that happened around me and to me.

In the cave, I sat chained with my back to the fire. The shadows that leapt and gambolled on the wall in front of me were the only people I knew and gave names to. My madness was such that I wanted no more than that allegory of the cave and the solace of the chains that kept me fettered to the shadowscapes and their reality.

The madness told me what to do. I wouldn't go to the wasps. I would make them come to me. But to him, I would go again and again. My desire was insatiable. My sex thrummed like it never had before. My madness was such.

I would write him love notes in public. I would reveal myself to him in the stories I wrote. Now that I had found him, I wasn't going to play coy or hard to get. I had no feminine wiles, nor did I know how to play cat and mouse, or whatever was required to draw him to me. My love was such. It had no pride or shame. It had no fear of consequences, nor would it be haunted by the question that usually accompanies love's trajectory: what next? My love didn't need to possess or be possessed. It was enough that we loved.

There were days when I woke with the taste of spider's eggs in my mouth and my fingers and toes looked like ancient talons. Then I would go to St Elijah's Church in Kunnamkulam where he was a priest and stand by a shop across from it, to catch a glimpse of him. There would be days when shadows weren't enough to fill the hollow spaces in me, and I would go to the post office and make a call to the church office, hoping that he would be there. Mostly the phone would just ring and I would imagine him sitting across from me and running his fingers through his beard while his eyes ate me up. There would be days when I stayed in bed and drew a pillow close to me as if it were him I was holding. I would drape my leg over him and curl into the curve of his neck. I would hear his heart beat. And I would tell myself, this is my circle of heaven: my stories and him. There would be days when I heard just the hum of the wasps.

I scraped out the insides of a coconut shell and asked Karthu to rub it clean with a koovalam leaf. I made a thick paste of turmeric and egg white and smeared the insides with it, then left it to dry. When the sun had sucked the moisture out, I tapped the shell and the loose flakes fell off so the insides of the coconut shell glistened yellow. I made twenty such pan traps and placed them around the house and deep in the wilderness behind. One by one, I filled them with water and added a drop of liquid soap I had created by dissolving soap flakes.

They would come now. The aphids and sphecids. Tiny insects, bees, and my parasitic wasps. They would be lured to the yellow. They would light upon it, secure in their knowledge of the language of water. Besides, they had their sting. Straight and curved. And who dared stand in the way of such speed and venom?

But soap is a wily foe. It breaks the surface tension of water. My wasps would be pulled down by the undertow and sink to the bottom of the shell. They would be forever lost in their watery graves with their stings and stories intact. My wasps would come to me and when they did, I would go to him.

I received a telegram addressed to me at the college.

I lied when I said I would go to him. Instead, I had laid a yellow pan trap in the form of a story to be published in the *Weekly*. They had announced it: From the unflinching pen of Sreelakshmi, 'Letters to a Man Never Met', a new novel to be serialised fortnightly, about love, life and chances.

He asked in the telegram how I could write letters to a man never met when I had already met him. Had coffee and cutlets with him.

I smiled. I didn't know that smile lived within me. A smile that grew from words unspoken, a longing that had never found expression.

Later that day, I heard one of my students tell her friends, 'What on earth just happened? Sreelakshmi Teacher actually smiled at me!'

Had I? I must have walked past her just when my secret smile split my face.

I touched the paper and let my finger glide along the printed letters that made up his name. I let the smile seep into my guiding finger as I picked up my pen.

How do you know these letters are about the man with whom cutlets and coffee were shared? How do you know?

Who was this Sreelakshmi? Gatherer of wasps and wantonness.

After college, I went to the post office and sent the telegram to his place of work. I don't even know where he lives, I thought with a pang.

The following afternoon, he came to the college.

'Namaskaram,' he said, smiling as if he wouldn't ever stop.

The smile stayed with me as I went back to the lab. But once I was among my slides and specimens, I felt it slip. I clutched the edge of the table, asking myself, what am I going to do?

I told myself, this isn't like standing with your mouth open for a wasp to fly in. This is life. There is no going back.

Later that evening, I brought my pan traps in, one by one. Those that had been placed near flowering shrubs and trees were dense with specimens.

My mother and Karthu watched with horrified fascination as I drained the contents of the pans into a sieve. 'The Puranas say that if you kill even an ant for no good reason, you are condemned to a thousand years in hell,' my mother said to Karthu, as a reproof to me.

'Which Purana is that?' I asked, not taking my eyes off the specimens. There were wasps, bees, leafhoppers, mosquitoes, and even a few beetles.

'I don't know which one. But it's in there somewhere.' My mother snorted and walked away.

Karthu followed, muttering about mosquitoes that would breed in the pan and give us all malaria.

The scientist, the writer and the lover have one thing in common: they will be thwarted at every step. That is the reality of their choice.

I washed the specimens in clean water. There were four kinds of wasps I knew by sight, and one I didn't recognise. I would take them to the lab in the college and preserve them in ethanol.

And then I sat down and began to write. The scientist knows. The writer imagines. The lover tries to read between the lines. What would he make of my story?

The first instalment appeared on Friday. I didn't know what to expect, but I waited. There would be the usual letters of appreciation or downright recrimination. But it was his response I needed to know.

On Saturday morning, he came to the college. He looked at me for a long moment. My eyes dropped first.

'I am your Murad,' he said.

I gasped.

'I am your Murad,' he laughed. I heard the triumph in his voice. There was desire too, and a tenderness that made me want to cross the distance between us and lay my head against his chest.

I had them both now – my wasps and him.

But what was I going to do with them?

## [ix]

I sent him the second instalment of my story before I sent it to the *Weekly*. He came to see me the day after he received the envelope.

'Have you been in love before?' he demanded.

My eyes widened.

'I mean, have you been with a man before?'

'I am a student of biology, a teacher of zoology. I know the human body in great detail,' I said. I knew which part of the story had churned him up.

He leaned against the wall and folded his arms. 'You are driving me mad,' he said, sounding angry with himself.

'Would it make you feel better if I told you that you have driven me to the brink of insanity as well?' I asked softly, dropping my gaze to his hands. His small childlike hands. I wanted to feel them on me.

The college corridors were bustling. A group of students walked by, pretending not to see us. One of them turned and darted a glance our way. Soon someone would start whispering about Sreelakshmi teacher and her bearded visitor, if they weren't already. He was dressed in black trousers and a black shirt, so they wouldn't know he was a priest.

A few boys stood around a motorcycle, admiring it. There weren't many like it in Ottapalam.

He saw me looking at them. 'That's my motorcycle. It's a Jawa, come all the way from Czechoslovakia,' he said with pride. 'Come, let me show it to you.'

The students moved away as we walked towards the motorcycle. 'See this,' he said, pointing towards the teardrop-shaped petrol tank. 'No other motorcycle has this beautiful shape or these two exhaust pipes. One of these days, I will take you for a ride on it.'

I had realised by now that he came from an affluent family. Had they chosen his path in life, I wondered. Had they chosen his wife too? Perhaps all that he had ever chosen for himself was his motorcycle and me. Was that what I represented? An act of rebellion?

'Let's go for a walk. Show me your campus,' he said. And so we walked through the college grounds, our hands occasionally brushing.

The following Tuesday, he came again. I had told my mother I was going to Victoria College in Palakkad.

I eyed his motorcycle apprehensively.

'What are you frightened of?' he laughed, inserting the key into the slot and pushing it in. 'A Jawa key can open any Jawa bike but how do I open your heart to my Jawa?' he asked.

'You are an idiot,' I said, perching side-saddle on the bike. I felt the wind tease my hair into tangles. I couldn't hear what he was saying but I didn't care. It was enough being with him.

It was late evening when he dropped me back. I watched as he left, sparks flying from the centre-stand when he took a sharp turn from the campus road to the highway. And I thought again that he was drawn to danger, almost as if he couldn't help himself.

'Letters to a Man Never Met' had already raised many brows in literary circles and in my college. I knew that men who had read the story were appraising me to figure out how I knew what I had written about. They probably had half a dozen sayings about me. The alley cat is a quiet cat. The stealthy cat breaks the pot. From a moth on the wall, I had become a seductress. Once, I would have cringed and sought the shadows. Not any more. If other men found me desirable, so would he.

'We cannot keep meeting like this,' I said. We were sitting in a tea shop in Palakkad town.

He nodded. 'I realise that. Someone in my position…' The words hung between us.

What about me, I wanted to ask. A woman in my position cannot afford to do this either.

He continued to speak. 'If we could have a day together, just you and I, without worrying about who can see us or speculate about us. Just for us to share what's consuming us. Is that too much to ask, Sree?'

I shook my head. The frustration in his voice echoed my own feelings. He would never ask it of me. So I did. 'Let's go away for a day or two where no one will know us.'

'Are you sure?' His eyes shone with a million stars.

It had come to this: I wanted to be with him and he with me.

I smiled.

**[x]**

While we laid our plans, I began studying my wasps. I had taken the specimens to the laboratory and sorted them, pinning them to boards with appropriate insect pins. I had stretched the antennae, legs and wings and labelled them. Date of collection. Locality. Habitat. The specimens had been air-dried at room temperature and kept in insect cabinet boxes. I brought them out and based on the general morphological characters of the sphecid wasps, I grouped them into morpho species. I examined each one under a microscope and classified them into families of Spheciformes using the available keys. I had very little to go by for identification to subfamilies and genera. But I used the keys provided by Albert and Charles, and Bingham, as extensively as I could.

Prema, one of my third-year students, came in. She was a studious girl who was interested in her subject and devoted to me. She lived not too far from my house and when I had to call in sick, I usually sent a message through her to my HOD.

'Can I help, Miss?' she asked.

'Not really. But watch me and learn,' I said, showing her how to separate the head and abdomen of a wasp using a pair of micro-scissors. 'Now we'll place it in a test tube containing ten per cent KOH solution and leave it overnight.'

I pulled out a specimen I had prepared the day before. We washed it repeatedly to cleanse it of excess potassium hydroxide. I then placed it in glycerin on a slide for further dissection.

'Why are you doing this, Miss?' she asked when I had finished washing my hands.

'It's for my thesis,' I said. 'But first I need to find a chink in the existing knowledge base about wasps. I need to do an empirical survey. I need to find a senior professor to be my guide.'

I wrote my findings down and posted it to Professor Mary Ipe in Trivandrum, who had expressed interest in my choice of thesis and tentatively agreed to be my Ph.D guide.

## [xi]

He booked us a room at Hotel Dasaprakash in Madras. 'It's a quiet, discreet place. No one will know us there,' he said when he came to see me on Friday afternoon. It was the day the second instalment was published. We would leave on Monday night and spend all of Tuesday and Wednesday there and take the train back on Wednesday night.

That evening, I told my mother that I needed to go for a seminar in Madras. 'There will be others going with me from the college,' I told her, even though she didn't ask. She served me dinner without speaking a word.

'I'll be back in two days,' I said.

My mother picked at her wheat loaf, pulling it apart into soggy crumbs. I knew something was bothering her. She was a simple woman who thought the best form of aggression was to affect a sulk. And I had learnt over the years that the best way to handle it was to ignore it. Eventually she would accost me with her complaint and the air would clear.

I knew that I wouldn't have the time to write the next instalment of my novel. I went to my room and took out Sinbad's fountain pen and sheets of paper.

I sat at my table and stared at the blank sheet. A moth hovered by the light bulb. Happiness lit me up from within. The words flew from my pen with a magical flourish. When I raised my head, three hours had passed and the story was written. I would edit it in the morning, I told myself.

Thunder rumbled. Soon the thulavarsham would begin. I imagined watching the rain in his arms.

Did I mention that I hadn't slept a wink for more than twelve years now? I usually lay on the bed and stared at the ceiling. Or I closed my eyes and stared at the insides of my eyelids.

I lost my sleep on the train journey back from Varanasi after my father died. I didn't reach in time for his cremation but all through those three and a half days, I lived it in my mind. I was there to drizzle the drops of water into his already stiffened lips.

I stroked his brow like I had never done when he was alive. I did not remember hugging my father ever, or even holding him, since the time I turned eleven. Fathers and grown-up daughters had very little to do with each other. That was the norm. But he had watched out for me like a demon guarding treasure. Because he was feared by everyone, I had been left alone. I realised then that without his protection, if I were to so much as close my eyes, my family would take my life away from me.

The next day, I rose at dawn.

I switched on the light and looked at the neatly stacked papers on the table. I heard my mother stirring in the next room,the screech of the heavy double doors that led into the kitchen as they were opened, the flat sound of the hatch door of the well being flung open, the creak of the pulley as Karthu drew water. An inexplicable sense of well-being filled me and I almost skipped into the kitchen.

'I need coffee,' I told Karthu.

'The milkman won't arrive till six,' she said, flustered to see me up so early.

'Black will do,' I said, walking towards the bathroom.

When I returned, the coffee was in a glass on the table. I took it with me to my room. I wound my watch. I read through what I had written. I didn't need to change a word. I wished I had made a carbon copy but it didn't matter. The uncrossed lines were a testament to our love.

I went to college as usual. On the way, I posted the story. It was a day of classes followed by a staff meeting, then a debate which I had to attend. I was one of the judges. I was exhausted when I reached home.

My mother placed the ada and tea on the table, and sat down without speaking a word. I could bear it no longer.

'What's on your mind, Amma?'

She looked at her clasped hands.

'Why aren't you speaking to me?'

My mother sniffed.

'Tell me,' I said, touching her hand.

She moved it away.

'What's wrong, Amma?' I persisted.

'My cousin came to see me yesterday afternoon.'

'Oh, what did he want,' I asked, tearing a strip of the ada.

'He read your story in the *Weekly*.'

'So?' I asked.

'It's vulgar,' she said.

'What is vulgar about a love story?' I smiled.

'You are an unmarried woman. How would you know what men and women do together? How can you write such things? That, too, when you are a teacher!' The words burst forth like a swarm of hornets, each seeking to sting and cripple.

I had been stung enough times to know that you can flee a wasp but not an entire swarm. There is no point in flailing your arms and running; neither is hiding under the table an option. The only recourse is to hold your breath and stand still. Play dead till the swarm decides there is no further threat and leaves you alone.

My mother spoke of how society's approval made the world turn on its axis and a spinster had to be twice as careful, for all she would leave behind as a legacy was her reputation and it was certainly better to be dead than live with dishonour. 'If you must write and publish your stories, why can't you write children's stories? No one will fault you for that. Look how much everyone loves Mali's stories!'

'There is no disputing Mali is a great writer. But how can I write what I am not inclined to write?' I asked quietly.

'Then it's best you stop writing,' she said with a firmness that surprised me.

'Amma, do you even realise what you are saying?' My voice rose.

My mother walked away as if she hadn't heard me.

I went to my room and opened my chest of drawers. I pulled out all the clothes and rearranged them. It always soothed me, this mechanical folding of clothes. I thought about what I would take with me. Any doubts about what I was going to do had been overturned by my mother's words.

On Sunday, I took my mother to Karakkad. She had been asking to go for a while now. It seemed to me that each time she spent time at the tharavad, she came back happier.

He was going to meet me at Olavakkode station. It was better we didn't board together at Shoranur or Ottapalam, he had said. As the train drew into the station, my mouth went dry and wasps hummed in the pit of my belly. What if he had changed his mind? The platform was filled with passengers and people who had come to see them off, as well as porters and vendors. I finally saw him near the water faucet. He was looking for the compartment I was in. He was looking for me. I thrust my hand out of the window and waved to him.

The moon burst through a mass of rain clouds.

He came into the compartment. He smiled at me. I smiled back. There was nobody else in the seats near us. We sat alongside, our shoulders brushing, and for a long while we didn't speak. It was enough, this closeness, this togetherness by osmosis.

He had brought his dinner with him; so had I. Curd rice and pickle. I glanced at his food packet. Chappati and potato fry.

'Will you have some?' he asked. 'She didn't make it.'

She. His wife. The she we didn't refer to. But she was always on my mind, probably more than in his. I wondered what she looked like; about the timbre of her voice and how she laughed. I wondered a great deal about how they were when they were together.

I shook my head. I could barely swallow a morsel. She sat in my throat, not letting anything pass.

When the lights were turned off and the blue night lamp switched on, we continued to sit leaning into each other. He took my hand in his and it felt as solemn a gesture as an oath of troth. A little later, I could see his eyes shutting. His head lolled onto my shoulder. I felt a great tenderness. I wanted to trace the lines of his face with my lips. I don't want fame or a doctorate, I want him, I would have said, if someone had asked me what I wanted from life just then.

He slept. I listened to him breathe and watched the night turn into day through the window. Not once did he let go of my hand.

'Why didn't you wake me up?' he asked when he finally stirred and realised where he was.

'I was watching you sleep,' I murmured.

He sat up and let go of my hand. I felt as if I had been cut loose. I was drowning. Tears beat their tiny fists at the back of my eyes.

'Why are you crying?' he asked.

'Just the grit from the engine,' I said, rubbing my eyes.

'You have charcoal smears on your face,' he smiled. He took his handkerchief and wiped my face clean.

In silence we took the taxi to the hotel he had booked us into. In silence we checked in and went to the restaurant for breakfast while the room boy took our bags up. In silence we went up. In silence we sat on the bed.

I opened my bag and took out a mustard-yellow velvet case. 'This is for you,' I said, holding it out to him.

He opened it and looked at the pen. It was my father's. I wanted him to have it.

'I didn't bring you anything,' he said quietly. 'She packs my bag when I am going away.'

We sat in silence for a while longer. The words seemed to have dried up.

'Why don't you bathe? You must be tired from the journey,' he said eventually.

I nodded and opened the suitcase to take out a change of clothes, a towel, a toothpaste and toothbrush, and a bar of soap.

I saw him watch me as if he was committing to memory every movement I made. 'What?' I asked.

'You seem to know exactly what to do,' he said.

'For five years I lived outside Kerala. First, when I was in college in Madras, and then in Varanasi. Madras was a night's journey away but Varanasi was three and a half days of travel with two change of trains in between. I learnt a thing or two about travelling then,' I said with a smile.

'I wish I had met you then,' he said.

'I wish we had.' I didn't remind him that he was six years younger than me.

## [xii]

I walked into the bathroom and turned on the tap. There was hot water, but I needed it cold to swill the uncertainties away. I watched the water fill the bucket. I hesitated as I took my clothes off. We were separated by only a wall. The thought made me feel dizzy. In the mirror, I didn't recognise the woman I saw.

I heard a knock on the door. I opened it a fraction of an inch. He was bare bodied. I dropped my gaze. It wasn't as if I hadn't seen men before, with just a towel slung around their hips. 'You look like a frightened rabbit,' he said.

I looked up. He smiled and put his hand on the door. 'I want to see you bathe,' he said.

'What?' I stared at him.

He smiled. 'Just watch you. I won't touch you. I promise.'

I looked at him for a long moment. We had always known where this was going and who was I fooling by being coy?

I let go of the door and it swung open. He came in.

Can a man make love to you with just his eyes? He did. He didn't touch me, merely stood and watched me pour mugs of cold water on my naked body. I felt his eyes tuck away the strands that had slipped out of the coil of hair piled on top of my head. His gaze ran with the bar of soap along my body. Over my nipples, across my pubis, and between my thighs. The fragrance of Chandrika soap filled the room.

When I shut my eyes to pour water over my head and wash my hair, I felt his fingers undo the coil and slide through my hair. I opened my eyes abruptly but he hadn't moved. All of me was open to him. I was enveloped in the wetness of water and desire. 'Come,' I said.

He laughed. A rich ripe laugh. He reached for me, shedding his towel. I turned into his arms as they went around my waist. I stretched my neck backwards and rested it against the crook of his shoulder. His clasp tightened around me. My love, I whispered in my head.

And so we came together. Our love melded in a welter of arms and legs, tongues and touch; my sex was his, his moans mine. Our bodies teased and withdrew. Our words came to rest and blossom in the bed we created for them.

I lay there in his arms, spent and fulfilled. I trailed my fingers through his beard while he ran his fingers up and down my spine.

'You know that I am completely and irrevocably in love with you,' I murmured as I felt my eyelids droop. I felt butterfly kisses rain down on my closed eyes.

I slept.

I woke up as abruptly as I had fallen asleep. I reached for him but he had placed a pillow so I wouldn't stir when he got up. I looked at my wrist watch on the bedside table. It was a quarter to two. I had slept for almost three hours.

I put on my clothes. My fingers were all thumbs as I draped the sari. I touched my lips. They felt swollen, as if a bee had stung them. I smiled to myself. I was sore between my legs but I wore the soreness like a badge of completion.

I wondered where he was. I hoped he wouldn't be too annoyed with me for having slept so long. He must have gone out, tired of waiting for me to wake up. I went downstairs, wondering if he was in the lobby. He wasn't. I left word with them that I would be in the restaurant.

He wasn't there either. He had probably stepped out for a smoke. I ordered a butter masala dosa and filter coffee. He had said it was the speciality of the place. 'You'll never find anything like it in Ottapalam,' he had said with a smile.

I was indifferent to his suggestions at breakfast but now I was ravenous. I wanted to savour every mouthful. I wanted to sing and dance. I wanted to rush back to our room where he would be waiting for me and fling myself on him.

As I took my first sip of coffee, I realised that I had forgotten the blood- and semen-stained towel on the bed. I was aghast at the thought that the room boy would see it.

I put the coffee down and rushed back. But someone had been in already and smoothened the creases and wrinkles. The pillows had been fluffed up and the top cover that had been kicked to the floor was back on, and the bins emptied. Everything was as it had been when we first entered the room. And then I saw that his bag and things were gone.

It was as if he had never been here.

I stood there hesitant, unsure, afraid even. What just happened?

I would have been glad to spot the semen-stained towel, evidence of what had transpired. I was willing to clutch at any straw, anything to suggest that our love was real and that I hadn't imagined it all.

The thought that I had been removed, replaced even, crippled me. The aftertaste of humiliation and the bitterness in my mouth told me that I had merely served a need. I wiped the little beads of salt on my forehead and upper lip with the back of my hand. I knew that there would be no going back from here, nor a way ahead.

I was cursed to be in the limbo of not knowing.

I sat on the bed, arms wrapped around myself, feeling alone and defenceless. What did I do wrong? Or did I say something?

I went to stand by the window. The room overlooked the front of the hotel. I would see him enter the gate if I stood there long enough.

My hands were clammy. I tried not to think of his face. Of the wild abandon as it loomed over mine. The dilated pupils, the slackening mouth, the arched neck, the short bursts of breath, his sweat on my breasts, a drop landing on my lips. The salt of his sex, I had thought, licking his lips.

I swallowed. I swallowed again to stifle the scream of rage and despair growing in my throat. Then I went to sit on the bed.

I played countless scenes in my head: he had run into someone he knew at the hotel and gone with them to save himself from explaining what he was doing here; a family emergency had come up and he had to leave. Had I heard the phone ring as I slept? Why didn't he wake me up? Perhaps he was afraid I would be furious. Why didn't he leave me a note then?

I didn't want to admit that he'd had a change of mind. That

he left because I no longer held any appeal for him. I had been a conquest; a trophy; a way of redeeming his self-esteem.

I didn't want to accept that he may have been swamped by guilt and fear. That he had fled because he couldn't deal with the deceit. I was the heady danger that had lured him at first and then frightened him. I didn't want to believe that of him, or that he had put himself first.

I continued to sit on the bed, waiting for him. I waited through the night and the following day until the evening came and then I packed my bag and left the hotel after paying for the stay. I wondered if he would be on the same train. But I bought a new ticket for myself.

I stood by the compartment we should have travelled back on. But he didn't appear. The train wasn't full and I found a seat in the ladies' compartment easily enough. I clasped my hands and weaved my fingers together as we had when we took the train the night before.

They were all the same. The revolutionary and the priest. Perhaps the fault lay with me. No man wanted me enough to put me above everything else.

When the train pulled into Ottapalam station, I stepped out knowing that I had nothing to look forward to.

## [xiii]

Literature teaches you that you can make peace with anything. Time will heal every cut, every blow, every dripping wound. The mind will find within it the strength to say: This too shall pass.

But some of us just don't have it in us to go on. To invest in the chimera that our tomorrows will somehow be better than the here and now. Some of us sew stones into our hemlines and step into the river, some of us choose to put our heads into an oven and breathe in death, but each must find her own way to sail to stillness, to that quiet place where there are no crippling upheavals.

I scraped my face together into the semblance of a smile as I walked through the gate. My mother was in the front yard, looking at the bitter-gourd creeper and telling Karthu to add wood ash to the roots. Everything that had happened to me seemed like it had happened to someone else. I had no more agency or standing than that of a voyeur.

My mother said I looked exhausted. Karthu said I looked like I had been pulled out of a drainpipe.

'It was very hectic,' I replied in explanation.

I went into my room and unpacked quietly. I held the sari I had worn in the train on my way to Madras. I could smell him on it: saffron and sandalwood. I ran my fingers through the ends of my hair, imagining it was his beard. But still the tears wouldn't come.

I went to the college and the day went past in a flurry of classes, lab work and meetings. In the evening, I had my ada and tea and told myself that yes, I would be able to get past the hurt and humiliation. If I could get through the weekend, I would be able to make a fresh start. To give myself enough work to fill the hours, I had already announced a test for the next day for the first- and second-years and asked the third-years to submit their lab records by Friday.

In the evening, I sat with my pen and paper. The fourth instalment of 'Letters to a Man Never Met' had to be written. But I was weary and the words couldn't be coaxed to appear. I paced outside the house, trying to marry thoughts to phrases. When it began raining, I stepped back in and joined my mother on the verandah. She told me a long convoluted story about a property dispute in the family which I pretended to hear. I wanted to lay my head in her lap and weep. To tell her how defeated I felt. After dinner, I went to bed early with a book. In the morning, everything would be better, I told myself.

I went to work the next day as usual. I had a plan. I went to see Sarah Kuruvilla. 'Are you going to Kunnamkulam this weekend?' I asked. She had invited me a few times to visit her family, who lived there. 'May I come along?'

'Yes. My husband will come on Saturday morning to pick me up,' she said. Sarah lived with two other lecturers in a house very close to the college. 'We will return on Sunday evening. I am so happy that you are able to come. My family will be pleased to meet a writer in the flesh. And someone as famous as you are.'

I smiled my thanks. I would walk into his church. Once he saw me, all his doubts about us would be erased. He would be mine again.

'What is happening in Kunnamkulam? Any literary event?' she asked.

'I wanted to visit a church there. Attend a service. For a story I want to write,' I said, hoping it sounded plausible.

'Which one?'

'St Elijah's.'

'That's an Orthodox church. We are Marthomites. We worship elsewhere, or you could have gone with us.'

I sighed in relief. What would have happened if she belonged to his church and had spotted him visiting me? Someone was watching out for us. His God for sure. I took that as a sign.

By afternoon, I sensed knowing glances coming my way. Some were arch and sneering.

My male colleagues gave me the once-over without even bothering to be circumspect about it. My older male students were like a pack of hyenas circling around me. As for the women, both colleagues and students, they hummed like needled wasps. Giant wasps who sought to paralyse me forever.

They had read the third part of 'Letters to a Man Never Met'.

I would have requested the afternoon off and gone home, but I was afraid that if I left, I would miss him. I was quite certain that he would seek me out in the afternoon as he had done before. How could he not? I had given all of myself to him in this instalment as I had in real life. Would he toss away so carelessly the truth of what we had shared; that we belonged together, he and I?

I went to the lab where I would be safe from the whispers and pointed looks. The skies were pewter-like, dense and steely grey, and an irate old man grumbled within, finding fault with everything and everyone.

A little later, a paper plane came flying through the window and landed on the table. When I unfolded it, I saw a drawing of a woman on all fours. Her hair was parted sideways like mine. Her hands rested on two books, which said 'zoology'. She had a penis in her mouth. A giant penis that stretched beyond the margins of the page. Along the length of the penis was a line: Murad, should I spit or swallow?

On the train to Madras, I had thought about placing a trunk call to the editor of the *Weekly* and asking him not to run the third instalment. MTV was a fine editor; a celebrated writer himself, who had changed the literary landscape of Kerala with his novels. He would have understood my reasons for not wanting to run the story. And he wouldn't have run it anyway if it was of a questionable nature. But I remembered how the story had emerged in one single uninterrupted stream of ideas. And of how I had surprised myself by what I had written.

I thought, too, of how much it would please him to see such

a naked admission of my feelings for him. He had said he liked to see me vulnerable. So I hadn't made the call.

I tore the paper plane into strips. It had begun raining and each drop bore an eye that glared at me. Everywhere I turned, the beady eyes followed me. The whispers grew louder and the eyes more fierce, more lascivious.

I gathered my sari tightly around me, picked up the test papers, opened my umbrella and hurried home through the thunderstorm.

## [xiv]

The main door was latched. I wondered where my mother was. I could hear Karthu pounding rice in the covered part of the back yard. As I went past her, I saw my mother sitting beside her. She pretended not to see me.

I placed my bag and papers on my table. I took my lunch box with the food still in it and walked to the front yard, where I emptied it under the bitter-gourd creeper. Here, feed your bitterness, I said to it. Take it all. Tomorrow I'll bring you some more. And the day after that.

I left the box in the back yard where the dirty vessels were kept and went into the dining room. The dining table held the usual assortment of objects: a vessel of water and a steel glass, a bottle of pickle and a cream-and-chrome porcelain jar of salt. For the first time in many years, it didn't hold the covered dish with my ada and glass of tea. Had my mother also read the third instalment?

I sat on the bench and put my elbows on the table. My head drooped into my arms. I heard a sound and looked up. My mother stood in the doorway.

'The landlord came by a little while ago,' she said.

There was a meaningful pause.

'What's wrong?'

'He wants us to leave,' she said.

'What do you mean he wants us to leave?' I stared at her.

She hissed, 'You should have thought about that when you published your obscenities.'

'We'll find another house,' I whispered, suddenly afraid.

'Really?' she asked. She could no longer hide her anger. 'And they will ask us to vacate too, when you publish the next instalment of that thing you call a story. But do you care? Do you really care what I or anyone else thinks? You are no better than a bitch in heat, a whore, a brazen whore. I am glad your father is dead. You would have killed him with your writing.'

I looked away, shutting out her anger. Instead, I thought of him. There was a perfectly logical explanation for why he had left. He would tell me all about it when he came to see me. He would take me away to a place where no one else existed, just the two of us. No censure, no anger, no disapproval. Only love.

I went to my room and lay on the bed. My mother came in and dropped a letter on the table. 'This came for you.'

I felt the blackness lift. He had written to me.

But no. The letter was from Professor Mary Ipe, whom I had written to about my thesis.

When I had gone to meet her in Trivandrum, she had been warm and welcoming. She had said she admired the way in which I had brought art and science into my life without one overshadowing the other. But her tone had changed now. My area of study, she said, was too speculative. Imagination is all very well in literature but science is built on data, analysis and the distillation of these into inviolable facts. Besides, she had some personal commitments which didn't allow her to become my guide.

The brusqueness of her note told me that she had been reading the *Weekly*. Even if she hadn't read the third instalment while writing the note, she would have turned me away for good once she did.

I latched the door of my room and lay on the bed. It had started raining again and the breeze blew in drops of rain.

Saturday dawned. I rose and wound my watch. On my way back from the bathroom, Karthu gave me coffee. 'Your mother hasn't slept a wink all night,' she said.

I took the coffee and went back to my room and told the beady eyes that watched me from the shadows: You can take away everything else but you can't take away my writing.

I filled my pen with ink and took a fresh sheet of paper from the chest of drawers where I kept a full sheaf. I sipped my coffee and sat at the table. Once I began writing, I would put away everything else – his abandonment of me, Professor Mary Ipe's refusal to be my guide.

A car pulled up outside the house. I peered through the window. It was Sarah. She opened the gate and came in. I had forgotten all about going away.

I opened the door and rushed out. 'Good morning, Sarah. Just give me five minutes. And do call your husband in,' I said, gesturing to the man seated in the black Herald parked outside. He was a PWD engineer and quite high up in the pecking order.

'Wait, Sreelakshmi,' she said. 'There is a problem. My husband has some guests coming over. So we won't be able to host you.' I saw her gaze drop.

'That's fine,' I said.

When she left, I went back to my room.

The words refused to come. They stayed away as if to make a point, like angry relatives refusing to attend a wedding. An adjective or two danced in front of me. A few verbs did cartwheels and a group of nouns turned somersaults. But the opening sentence sat with its back to me. I cajoled and pleaded but she wouldn't listen. As long as she did that, the rest wouldn't emerge either.

I put down my pen, defeated, and took out another pen with red ink. I would correct the test papers.

I waited for the creak of the gate. I waited for him to announce himself. It was a holiday and if he did go to the college, someone there would tell him where to find me, I told myself.

It rained through the day. The leak in my room had worsened. That night, I lay in bed, listening to the rain drip into a vessel.

It was around mid-morning on Sunday when I heard the gate open. I waited in my room, trying to still the feverish beating of my heart. I smoothed down the pleats of my sari. I checked my face in the mirror. I waited for my mother to come and tell me, 'There is someone here to see you.'

I heard loud voices. Familiar voices seething with rage and reproach. I went into the main hall where they were.

'Here she comes,' my brother-in-law said.

'Sreekutty,' my mother began.

The eldest one, the ticket examiner, interrupted her. 'Don't you have any shame? Do you think you can write any rubbish and no one is going to mention it?' He was shouting.

'Our reputations are mud,' the second one, the man of means, said.

My mother stood wringing her hands and weeping.

'Look at your mother. Have you thought of how your stories will affect your sisters?'

Not to be outdone, the younger one added, 'My girls are still young but his daughter is of marriageable age. What sort of an alliance is going to come her way with you as an aunt?'

I walked away into my room and latched the door. They left soon.

The house was sunk in a pall of silence. It was like someone had died.

I waited for him till twilight turned into night. It continued to rain. The drip into the vessel continued through the night. The humming in my ears drowned out everything.

I rose at dawn. The skies were clear and a beautiful blue. I sat at my table and wrote a note to Prema. I gave it to Karthu to pass on to the milkman. He would drop it off at Prema's house.

'Aren't you going to college?' Karthu asked.

I walked past her.

I went back to my room and opened the cupboard. The fragrance of Chandrika soap filled my nostrils. I took out the sari I had worn on the train. Bottle-green, with a tiny floral print in white. It was all I had to tell me that I hadn't conjured up the events of that day. I took the soap with me. I would relive the time we were together and all would be well again.

Once, a long time ago, a powerful king asked the wise men in his court to make him a ring that would help him overcome any sort of tragedy. They brought him a slender band of copper on which was inscribed, 'This too shall pass'.

The king wore it on his thumb and turned it each time a sorrow came to perch on his shoulder. And then came a day when the king fell in love. The skies were striated with rainbows by day and at night, the stars, as big as oranges, were just as luminescent.

A hoopoe sat on his shoulder and his love at his side. The breeze blew with the scent of frankincense and, occasionally, saffron and sandalwood. She fed him pomegranate seeds from her mouth and he ate them thinking there couldn't be anyone happier than him.

Then his gaze fell on the ring. This too shall pass, it said.

I bathed, letting the cold water sluice my uncertainties away, like it once had. The fragrance of the soap filled the bathroom and I felt comforted. Every journey has a beginning and an end. I wasn't going to let anyone else decide how my travels would end.

I changed into fresh underclothes and wore the sari. How beautifully it draped around my body, I thought.

My mind went back to the little girl who stood with her mouth open, ready to eat a wasp. I thought of how brave and hopeful she was. I felt tears sting my eyes.

Carefully, I unwound the sari I wore. I slung it through a wooden beam in the bathroom and made a noose. I upturned the bronze cauldron that stood on the ledge and stood on it.

I was weary of the cycle of life. Yes, this too would pass. There was nothing left inside me to dredge hope from. I was done. All I wanted to do was leave.

How simple it was, I thought. All I had to do was place my head in the noose and kick the cauldron.

The cauldron clattered to the floor.

On the day I killed myself, it was clear and bright. It was a Monday. A working day.

# EPILOGUE

Shyam strode down the corridor. The building contractor and Unni tried to keep up with him.

'If we open one end of this corridor, we can create an extension. An annexe of rooms here,' Shyam was saying.

He stopped abruptly. At the end of the corridor, with its back to the wall, stood the cupboard with its doors half open. He had bought from an acquaintance. 'Why is this here?'

'I didn't know where else to place it,' Unni said, flushing. 'You would decide when you got back, I thought. And it wouldn't be in anyone's way or spoil the reception area.'

'It wasn't meant to be delivered here,' Shyam said, pulling the doors wide open. 'It has a bit of history apparently.'

'What history is that?' Radha asked.

Shyam turned and smiled at his wife.

'There was this writer, Sreelakshmi. She killed herself in the mid-sixties, before we were born I guess.'

'So this was her almirah?' Radha asked, going closer.

'No, no. Many years ago, her nephew went to buy an old Jawa bike from a priest's family who were immigrating to Canada. When he discovered who the nephew was, the priest gave him the almirah for free, saying he was Sreelakshmi's most ardent admirer.

'The nephew took it happily enough. It is a magnificent piece of furniture, you'll agree. He gave it pride of place in the old house in Karakkad. But they are selling the property now and I had gone there to look at some of the old furniture.'

'Why did she kill herself?' Radha asked, looking at the cavernous old cupboard.

'No one knows, madam,' Unni said. 'I have read her stories. She wrote sad stories. No one knows why she did it. There were rumours. A love affair gone bad. An incurable disease. That she had plagiarised her prize-winning novel and been found out. There wasn't even a suicide note. Instead, she sent a note to a student to collect the test papers she had corrected and left on the table. It was both a big scandal and a tragedy.'

'Get rid of it, Shyam,' Radha said, her hand on her husband's arm. 'It may have had nothing to do with her death, but we don't want remnants of other people's lives here.'

Shyam nodded. He hadn't meant to keep it anyway. He had a potential buyer already – an antique dealer in Kochi. 'I'll send it off right away,' he said.

Radha turned to look at the cupboard one last time. It was dark and decrepit-looking, with a broken handle. Had the weight of some secret sadness cracked the wood? It seemed lost in the poorly lit end of the corridor. A wasp hummed and hovered by it, its drone filling the silence and the shadows.

For a fleeting moment, Radha thought she saw a woman standing there. A slight woman with thick eyebrows, her hair parted on the side and hanging loose to her waist. She was dressed in a bottle-green sari with tiny white flowers. A distinct fragrance of Chandrika soap filled her nostrils. She thought she had never seen anyone as lonely or as bereft as this woman.

She shook her head to dispel the image. Then she ran out into the sunshine.

In the far distance, gunmetal grey clouds were building, laden with rain and fury, swallowing the sun and light. The river crept up to the topmost step of the landing adjoining the gazebo. A few inches more and it would gather the resort in its arms.

Rain fell. The river waited. So did I.

# ACKNOWLEDGEMENTS

Arvind Bhat, for insights into the game of badminton and answering my questions with patience and enthusiasm.

Dr P. Girish Kumar, for sharing his published paper titled 'Observations on some behavioural aspects of the Potter Wasp'.

Jayanth Kodkani, my first reader as always, who cast out the uncertainties and gave me the fortitude of spirit to take the novel forward. V.S. Rajesh, for recreating the Trivandrum of 1965 in word pictures. Sunil Koliyot, for romancing the Jawa. Gentlemen, a writer is nothing without friends like the three of you.

Aarushi Chandel, for being there as part-time amanuensis and forever beacon.

As for Karthika V.K., friend, editor and publisher, what would I do without you?

An abbreviated version of 'Najma' was first published in Italian in *La Repubblica*.

An abbreviated version of 'Half a Sin' was first published in Malayalam in *Kerala Kaumudi*.

An abbreviated version of 'How to shape happily-ever-afters' was first published in *Femina*.